THE RUINS

SOUL CURSED

BOOK ONE

JONATHAN PONGRATZ

Copyright Page

The Ruins (Soul Cursed #1) by Jonathan Pongratz

Cover by Mario Lampic.

❀ Created with Vellum

For Jessica.

CHAPTER ONE

Tyler smoothed his clothes one last time before focusing on the video drone hovering several feet in front of him. "I'm good. Ready?"

Gabe gave a thumbs up behind the drone, then counted down with his fingers. *Three. Two. One.*

"Hey spirit seekers. Welcome back to Jaunts and Haunts. We're here in Altalona, Peru on our quest to find the fabled ruins of Ayar Kachi."

Tyler gestured to the village behind him, a sad little cluster of beaten down clay buildings in mismatched, faded colors. Beyond the hamlet, emerald forests stretched across the horizon in every direction.

"Rumor has it that its location is a well-guarded secret known by the townspeople, but to this day no one has ever explored its depths and lived to tell the tale. Join me as we explore the mystery of these haunted ruins and the unknown horror of what lies inside."

Gabe pressed several commands into his phone and the video drone descended to the ground.

"How was that?" Tyler asked.

Gabe ran a hand through his long brown hair, avoiding eye contact. "Great, just great."

"What's wrong?"

Gabe sighed before meeting Tyler's gaze. "Are you sure this is a good idea? You don't speak a lick of Spanish and we hardly know anything about this place."

Tyler walked up to Gabe and took his hand in his. "Baby, *baby*. You were worried when we got this assignment, worried on the plane, and you're worried now. I get it. We're in a strange place and sure, we could be a lot more prepared than we are, but you know how long I've been working for this. I know things aren't great right now, but we've gotta muscle through. Alex says if we hit a million views on our YouTube channel, I'll have my own network show in no time. Can you imagine that? We'll be one of the first gay paranormal investigation shows!"

Gabe scoffed and threw his hands up in frustration. "Oh, well if Alex said so, he must be right. Tyler, you know all I want is to support you, but these places have been getting more and more dangerous. I mean, you nearly fell through the floor of that abandoned sanitorium just last week. Alex should've had it checked for safety before we even got there. What if I'm not around the next time something happens?"

"What is *that* supposed to mean?"

"Nothing. I'm just tired from the plane ride."

Tyler wrapped his arms around Gabe's neck and gave him a kiss. "Lighten up, babe. Why don't we go find our room? I'm sure I can think of something that'll relieve that stress you're carrying."

Tyler winked, and after a moment of hesitation Gabe grinned back. Gabe gathered the drone and they walked hand in hand down the dried-out hillside through tall grass and withering shrubs to their rental car.

The panoramic view of Altalona and the rainforest

beyond put a twinkle in Tyler's eye. Somewhere in that sea of green were the ruins of Ayar Kachi and his meal ticket to success.

GABE MOANED IN ECSTASY, his body giving a sharp throb as he climaxed.

Tyler savored the moment before moving from his perch atop Gabe and rolling onto the bed with a smile. "How ya feeling now, sexy?"

Gabe nodded with a huff as his chest heaved up and down.

Thank god he finally came. Tyler wanted to get a head start on scouting out ideal filming spots around town and the sun would be setting soon. Despite his urge, he hesitated. Dragging Gabe out of bed now would just make things worse, and he didn't want to worry him more than he already was.

Tyler hopped out of bed and walked to the bathroom, closing the door behind him. He washed his hands, then took a look in the mirror. His icy blue eyes reflected back at him as he admired his slim physique and lightly tanned skin. *Damn, I look good. I hope I get a nice tan from all this sun.* He moved on to adjust his short and spiky blonde hair. As he nitpicked, the reflection of the freestanding tub in the corner of the room caught his attention. He smiled to himself as an idea bloomed in his mind. Several minutes later, with a hot bubble bath ready and candles lighting the small area, he called for Gabe.

Gabe entered, the candles bathing his pecs, sculpted buttocks, and ample manhood in a rich golden light. He glanced at the bath and smiled. "What's all this?"

"It's my official 'sorry for being an asshole' apology. I got the bubbles and everything."

Gabe cocked a brow, then looked down to his groin. "But uh …"

"I know, I know. You just came. I'm not trying to fuck again. I just wanted to do something to help you relax. While you're doing that I thought I'd walk around a bit and see if I can find some good filming spots."

"Wait, shouldn't we go together? It could be dangerous."

Tyler flicked a wrist at Gabe. "Oh, don't be such a worry-wart. I'll bring my knife and mace with me, and I'll only be gone for thirty minutes, an hour tops. Promise."

"You sure?"

"Absolutely. Just rest, then maybe we can have round two when I get back." Tyler waggled his eyebrows.

"Alright."

Gabe leaned in for a kiss and Tyler accepted it greedily, tugging on his lower lip and groping him before breaking contact.

"Tease," Gabe said.

"You won't be saying that later. See ya in a bit."

Tyler got dressed and slipped out, hoping he'd pick up some clues on the ruin's whereabouts. His career depended on it.

Exotic plants and flowers hung from baskets overhead as Tyler walked down the hall toward the shabby inn's lobby. Near the end of the passage, a bizarre wooden sculpture caught his attention and made him stop in his tracks. The figurine was a horned little man with crazy bulging eyes and sharp teeth. Its cheshire grin spread from ear to ear.

Tyler rolled his eyes. This place seriously needed a reno-vation, or maybe they should just gut the whole thing and start from scratch. He and Gabe had to splurge for a 'suite' just to get a decent room, and even then he had to take down all the tacky art from the walls. Passing the carving, he ambled through the bare reception area and stepped outside into the stifling summer heat.

The egg yolk yellow sun hung high in the sky, hitting the inn from behind and casting Tyler in blue shadow. Down the street worn clay buildings lined the road, many with mismatched or patched tin roofs. In front of the dwellings were crates filled with fruits and vegetables, covered tables, or blankets spread out with colorful clothes, fabrics, and other miscellaneous items sprawled across them.

The market area had a relaxed ambience as villagers browsed over items and bartered with their vendors in friendly tones. At least until Tyler came by. Once he was in sight, the villagers eyed him suspiciously, their eyes narrowing and noses crinkling. Tyler's stomach churned as he realized he'd put on his tight rainbow shirt and skimpy shorts out of habit. *No wonder why they're staring. I'm a one-man pride parade. Damn it, what was I thinking?* He considered going back to the inn, but there wasn't much time before sunset. Staring firmly down at the ground Tyler hightailed it through the market, breathing a sigh of relief once he was out of the crowd's sight.

Continuing down the road, he searched Altalona's streets for scenic points of interest and anyone that might be willing to talk to him. Locals that were out and about scurried away from him the moment he locked eyes with them like he had some kind of disease. After noting several spots worthy of film coverage, Tyler looked to the sky. The sun had deepened to a golden orange and dipped a noticeable degree towards the horizon. *Better get back.*

He headed back towards the inn, nervously reentering the market area. To his surprise, a panicked energy had replaced the village's comfortable hustle and bustle just thirty minutes prior. Those still present hastily finished their purchases, hurried to their homes, or packed up their displays as if they were stepping on hot coals.

Huh, that's weird. Who knew Peruvians were so crazy about early bedtimes? Tyler chalked up their strange behavior to superstition and continued on his way. As he neared the nondescript inn, the woman who checked them in earlier exited the building. She closed the front door and an iron screen door before fumbling with a heavy padlock.

Is she locking up? What the hell? Tyler jogged up. "Hey, don't lock me out!"

The short woman jumped and dropped her keys. *"Dios mio!"*

"Sorry if I scared you. I just didn't want to get locked out. I checked in earlier, remember?"

The woman smoothed her shoulder-length black hair, then took a deep breath. "It is alright, *señor. Por favor*, get inside."

The woman jolted Tyler as she grabbed him by the arm and pushed him inside before locking the screen door with a heavy click. She turned to leave.

"Wait!" Tyler called. "What about dinner? That's part of staying here, right?"

"Si, I just finished cooking. Look in the kitchen. You and your … *friend* can have that. I must go." With that, the woman skittered out of sight.

Tyler stood at the door, perplexed. *Jesus, what is everyone's deal with running home at sunset?* He shook his head before closing the door and walking to the kitchen. Inside, there were two covered plates on the main counter. He uncovered one of them and a cloud of steam lifted with it, revealing stuffed green peppers over a bed of spanish rice and some black beans.

Tyler picked a morsel from inside the pepper and gave it

a quick taste, nodding to himself. *Mmm, nice and spicy.* Grabbing both plates, Tyler headed to his and Gabe's room.

When he entered the suite Gabe was sitting on the bed shirtless, wiggling his toes with his laptop on his lap. His long brown hair was swept back and pulled into a bun, and he wore browline glasses that made him look like a sexy professor.

"Hey babe," Gabe said without looking up from his screen.

Tyler grimaced. Would it kill him to give him his undivided attention for just a second? "Hey. I brought dinner."

Gabe waved a hand at him. "Oh, you can set mine on the dresser. I'm not hungry yet. How'd it go?"

"It looks like we have our work cut out for us. I found some okay spots to film at, but I have no idea how we're supposed to find these ruins. Everyone pretty much ran at the sight of me."

Gabe looked his way, giving him a once over. "Well look at what you're wearing. We're not exactly in Palm Springs."

"I know, okay? I made a mistake."

Gabe frowned and focused back on his laptop, a tense silence filling the room.

Tyler cleared his throat. "Anyways, I noticed something weird on the way back. Once the sun started setting, everyone cleared the streets like a plague of locusts was gonna come any minute. And before you say anything, it wasn't because I showed up. They were already scrambling away."

"Hmm, that is strange. Maybe it's some kind of local superstition?"

"I don't know, but by the time I got back the lady that checked us in was locking the front door."

Gabe continued to stare at his computer screen.

"Gabe, did you hear me? She was going to lock me out!"

"Sorry, sorry. I'll have a talk with her tomorrow, see if we can't come up with a compromise."

"Okay, thank you." Tyler walked over to the bed. "What are you looking at?"

"I decided to do a little more research on these ruins we're looking for. Babe, you should hear some of these accounts. Apparently a lot of people believed there was a legendary underground city called Akakor, but it's never been found. Percy Fawcett and his party went missing in the 1920s, so did some explorers from the 80s who were led by a guide named Tatunca Nara, and there's dozens of accounts of people coming to this area of Peru only to never be seen again. What if this place is what they were looking for? Are you sure we should seek it out?"

Tyler scoffed. "Oh, come on. You don't really believe those urban legends, do you? Did you ever summon Bloody Mary in the bathroom? Do you believe all the creepypastas you've read? I didn't see any chupacabras on the way here."

Gabe closed the laptop. "Alright, alright. Point taken. What do we do now?"

"Relax. We can figure everything out tomorrow. As for right now, I'm a little hungry."

Gabe looked over to the dinner plates and Tyler shook his head with an impish grin.

Tyler slinked into bed and straddled Gabe's ripped body. He kissed Gabe's hairy chest, working his way down slowly until he reached his gym shorts. Tyler maintained eye contact as he pulled them off with his teeth, exposing Gabe's aroused member. Gabe gave a low moan as Tyler went down on him, beginning a long night of unforgettable sex.

CHAPTER TWO

Tyler woke to a gentle kiss from Gabe.

"Morning, babe. It's time to get up."

Tyler groaned. "What time is it?"

"Nine. We'd better leave soon."

"Ugh, I'm tired. I hardly slept at all."

Gabe smirked. "What, did you hear a ghost or something? Don't tell me you're starting to believe all those *urban legends*."

Tyler grabbed a pillow and smacked Gabe with it. "Oh, shut up." He stumbled out of bed naked and dragged himself to the bathroom doorway before turning around. "You gonna join me or what?"

❧

Tyler stood before the hovering drone recording him, holding the concerned expression he'd practiced earlier in the mirror. Behind him was a ramshackle wooden structure, covered in missing persons posters, some of them so old they'd yellowed and curled under the stress of the elements.

"Welcome back, spirit seekers. Our journey to find the ruins of Ayar Kachi has led to some troubling discoveries. Behind me is a wall filled with missing persons' posters. The number of missing is concerning for a village this small. Is this what they consider normal here? We also found reports that well known explorers who have sought out a rumored underground city called Akakor went missing in this area of Peru. Is there more to these disappearances than meets the eye? Is the city of Akakor actually the ruins of Ayar Kachi? Stay tuned as we continue to investigate this perplexing mystery."

Tyler held the gaze of the drone's lens several seconds before saying, "Alright, that's a wrap."

The video drone lowered to the ground as Gabe frowned at his phone.

"What's wrong? I thought that one was good," Tyler said.

"Sure, if we were filming a ghost town. Look around, Tyler."

Tyler sighed, knowing all too well what he was referring to. The dirt road they were on had been heavy with foot traffic when they arrived, but once they'd shown up it had been devoid of any almost all activity. The few individuals brave enough to pass by scurried away when they addressed them as if they couldn't get away fast enough. "What do you want me to do? Everyone that sees us runs off. It's not my fault."

"Tyler, calm down. I'm not blaming you. I'm just saying we've got to find someone willing to talk to us if we're ever going to find those ruins."

"And how are we supposed to do that? Run after people, ambush them in an alley? If they're avoiding us they clearly don't want to talk."

"Look, I'm just trying to be helpful. If you don't want my

help I'll gladly go back to the inn and watch some shitty telenovelas."

Heat flushed through Tyler's veins at Gabe's sharp words, but before he could snap back at him an idea sparked in his mind, turning his anger into excitement. Tyler ran up to Gabe and kissed him. "Oh my gosh. Babe, that's it!"

Gabe grimaced. "What are you talking about?"

"The inn! Maybe the lady that checked us in knows something. She's the one person that hasn't avoided us since we got here. Come on!"

Gabe snatched his drone and they rushed back to the inn. When they entered the small reception area the woman who checked them in stood behind the counter, twirling a strand of shoulder-length black hair as she stared at her computer. They approached, and she gave them a cavalier nod of acknowledgment.

"*Hola.* I'm Tyler, and this is Gabe. We checked in the other day?"

"*Si, si. Soy* Rosalinda. How can I help you?"

"Uh, right. We're here doing a travel video on this area and local points of interest. I was wondering, do you happen to know where the ruins of Ayar Kachi are?"

Rosalinda shook her head emphatically. "No. No ruins."

Despite her knee-jerk reaction, a knowing, steely glint in her brown eyes contradicted it. Tyler pressed further. "Listen, I'm not asking you to take me there yourself. Just point me in the right direction. Maybe someone in town knows where it is? Please, it's very important."

Rosalinda turned away from him and returned her gaze to the computer screen.

Tyler looked to Gabe. "What do I do?" he whispered.

Gabe rolled his eyes, then rubbed his thumb over his index and middle finger.

Ohhh. Tyler pulled out a crisp fifty-dollar bill from his

pocket and displayed it with a flourish so Rosalinda couldn't miss it.

She glanced at the money, ignored it for a moment, then reached over and snatched it out of his hands before stuffing it down her shirt. "Esperanza. Esperanza Jacinto."

"Where's that?"

Rosalinda's brow furrowed. "Not a place. A person."

Heat rushed to Tyler's cheeks. "Oh, sorry. Where can we find them?"

"Three streets down, take a left. Her house has a sign in front. Be back by sundown. I lock up then, *no exceptions.*"

Gabe leaned against the counter. "Um, why is that exactly?"

Rosalinda held her chin high. "It is how we do things here. *Familia* and tradition are very important to us. We are not like the US here. We care about our parents and children."

"*Si, gracias.* We'll be back by then."

"You better be."

Tyler opened his mouth to protest, but Gabe looped an arm through his and quickly led him away. Once they were outside beyond earshot, Tyler wrenched himself free. "Why did you do that? Do you seriously believe that bullshit lie she told us?"

"No, but if she's the only one willing to talk to us, we can't afford to alienate her. We got the info we wanted, didn't we? Let's go see this Esperanza lady and see what she knows about the ruins. The sooner we do that, the sooner we can get out of here."

Tyler bowed his head. "You're right. Thanks, Gabe."

Tyler and Gabe followed Rosalinda's directions and passed through the small market area. They didn't make much commotion in their less colorful garb, but the villagers still leered at them like lepers. At the third intersecting street they came upon, they turned left.

Blood rushed to Tyler's cheeks when he observed the street. Many of the worn clay buildings had distinctive signs displayed on their facades, all of them in Spanish. "What the hell? They all have signs. Do you think Rosalinda lied to us about this too? Is Esperanza even real?"

Gabe shrugged. "I don't know. It seems pretty dumb of her to do that when we're staying at her inn. Maybe she just left out some details? Let's give her the benefit of the doubt."

With no other option Tyler and Gabe started knocking on doors, slowly making their way down the street. Those who answered crinkled their noses, slammed the door in their faces, or spat at them when they mentioned the ruins of Ayar Kachi.

By the time they reached the last building on the block, Tyler was ready to give up. This house had a rusted red tin roof and a small wooden plaque mounted near the entrance with a carved image of a plant with the words *Medicina holistica* on it. The front door was open with a beaded curtain blocking his view inside.

Tyler looked to Gabe. "What do you think?"

"Let's give it a shot. It can't get much worse than being spit at. What are they gonna do, chase us with torches and pitchforks?"

A grisly image of the villagers chasing them through the streets with cries of outrage flashed in Tyler's mind.

"It was a joke, lighten up."

"Okay fine, then *you* go first." Tyler gestured towards the open door.

Gabe rolled his eyes and entered with a loud clack of beads.

Tyler followed after him, a thick woody scent of incense filling his nostrils. Past a tiny foyer was a large room lined with cabinets that were filled with jars of herbs, crystals, and stones of every shape and size. Dried plants hung from the ceiling in rows, and the walls were covered with misshapen decor made of wood and bone with indecipherable carvings on them. To their right, a young woman sat at a small table crushing herbs with a mortar and pestle, an old woman with braided gray hair across from her watching attentively.

A young man with shaggy black hair hanging over his eyebrows and a pockmarked face walked into the room. He stopped in his tracks when he saw Tyler and Gabe. "Esper-anza, *tenemos visitantes.*"

The old woman looked over, and her pleasant smile was quickly replaced by a grimace. "*Quiénes son estos gringos?*"

"*No sé.*" The young man shot them an awkward half smile. "*Hola.* Can we help you with something?"

Gabe looked to Tyler, and he cursed under his breath before taking a step forward. "Um, yes. My name is Tyler Collins. I'm looking for Esperanza? Rosalinda sent me."

"*Pregúntales que quieren,*" the old woman said to the young man in an unenthusiastic tone.

"*Hola,*" the man said in a light accent. "I am Diego, this is my cousin Maya, and this is my grandmother Esperanza. She doesn't speak English. She asked what herbs you were looking for."

"*Herbs?* I'm looking for the ruins of Ayar Kachi."

The three strangers stared at them incredulously.

Tyler shifted his gaze downward and scratched at his forearm. "Um, Rosalinda told me you may know where to find them."

Esperanza grimaced, then nudged Diego to get his atten-tion. "*Traduce para mi. No se les puede permitir encontrar las ruinas.*"

"Esperanza would like to have a few words with you. I'll

translate for her. Please, come sit." Diego gestured towards two empty chairs at the table Maya and Esperanza sat at.

Tyler and Gabe took a seat, and Diego perched on a nearby stool. Esperanza continued speaking, this time much too quickly to follow.

"Why are you looking for the ruins of Ayar Kachi?" Diego asked.

"We're making a travel video about your, um, delightful town, and heard that the ruins haven't ever been filmed."

Diego translated back to Esperanza, and her nose crinkled as if she'd smelled bad cheese. She responded to him in harsh, clipped words.

"The ruins are not for tourists," Diego said. "It is *maldita*, cursed. That is why no one has ever filmed there."

"I understand, but we came all the way from the United States. We have to see them for ourselves."

Diego relayed the information to Esperanza, and she shook her head vehemently.

"She doesn't want to tell you where the ruins are."

"Why not?"

Esperanza spoke slowly in her deep alto to Diego. Her tone was severe and ominous, making Tyler's hairs stand on end.

"The history of the ruins goes back hundreds of years. Ayar Kachi and his seven siblings were the beginning of the Incan empire. He was different from his brothers and sisters. It was said he could throw stones that reached the sky and created rain and thunder. His brothers and sisters were jealous of his gifts and betrayed him, but he escaped. He wanted revenge, so he built an empire of his own in the rainforest where he wouldn't be found. He gained followers and wanted to make his brothers and sisters pay when he was powerful enough. But his pride got the better of him and he upset the gods. They cursed him and he and his followers were never seen again. It is said that the spirit of Ayar Kachi still haunts the ruins to this day, killing anyone brave enough to enter his territory. That is why it is forbidden to go there."

Tyler's breath hitched, and a heaviness settled on his shoulders. They'd traveled thousands of miles to get here. Was there really nothing he could do? Without the ruins his growing audience would fade away, Alex would withdraw his support, and his dreams of hosting his own paranormal reality show would go up in flames. All because this old lady was too uptight to tell him where some stupid ruins were.

Tyler clenched his fists tight, his fingernails biting into his palms. "I have to see the ruins. I'll do anything. What do you want, money?"

Diego conveyed Tyler's message to Esperanza, and she spat out a string of words dripping with venom. Diego tried to speak soothingly to her but she snapped back, pointing a wrinkled finger at Tyler and Gabe. They continued their tense conversation for several more moments before Esperanza rose from her seat and stormed out of the room.

Diego frowned. "I'm sorry, the answer is no. I tried to reason with her, but she won't budge."

"So that's it? You're not gonna help us?"

"I'm sorry. If I could, I would."

Tyler shot out of his seat. "Fine. Come on Gabe, let's go. We can't waste any more time on this bullshit."

Tyler stomped out of the house, smacking the bead curtain on his way out. Heat rushed to his head as his anger went into overdrive. "That stupid old hag! I can't believe she won't tell us where those fucking ruins are! What the hell are we supposed to do *now*?"

Gabe caught up to Tyler and tugged on his arm. "Tyler, slow down. Just breathe."

Tyler spun around on one heel. "What good is that gonna do? This whole trip is *fucked*! Everyone here treats us like a disease, and if we don't find those ruins I can kiss my future goodbye."

"Well maybe that's not the worst thing. I've been thinking. If the stories I've read about these ruins are true, then others looking for them disappeared. Do you really want to find out what happened to them for yourself?"

Tyler scoffed. "It's an urban legend, Gabe! It always is with these things. What would you have us do? Pack up our stuff and go home with our tails between our legs?"

"Look, all I know is that ever since we've got here it's been one weird thing after another: the sunset curfew, the missing persons, the way people are avoiding us. Maybe coming here was a bad idea."

"The only bad idea is listening to you right now. I've been working at this for the past two years. Two *years*! And you wanna bail because of some old rumors and *coincidences*? Fuck you."

Tyler stalked off, heading back to the inn. How could Gabe just give up like that? He was supposed to be his partner in this. Their future was at stake, and if they didn't get some solid footage when they left in a week, it was all over.

Back at the inn, Tyler stormed to his suite and closed the door with a bang. He plopped onto the bed and sighed, staring up at the ceiling. He'd be damned if he was going to file for unemployment when the answers they needed were right here. There had to be a way to find those ruins, there just had to be. Something they missed, someone that was willing to talk to them.

Tyler's phone buzzed in his pocket and he pulled it out, rolling his eyes when he saw it was a voicemail from Alex. They'd only been gone a day. What could he want already? Tyler hit play on the recording and held the phone up to his ear.

Hey Tyler, it's Alex. I hope you and Gabe had a good flight and got settled in alright. How is Altalona? Hopefully by now you're finding some interesting tidbits about the town and the ruins. A lot's riding on this, Tyler. Don't disappoint me. Oh, and have fun! I'll be in touch.

Tyler threw the phone down on the bed. *Great, more pressure. Just what I need.* He put his hands to his temples and massaged them. What was he supposed to do now? Unless something miraculously changed, his career would end before it even began. Overwhelmed, Tyler turned over on his side and fell into a fitful sleep.

CHAPTER THREE

Bzzt! Bzzt! Bzzt!

Tyler groaned and opened his eyes. His cell vibrated against his leg with sharp throbs, an alarm message flashing on its screen. He swiped the snooze button and rolled over. Gabe was on the far end of the bed, sleeping soundly with his back facing him. *When did he get in?*

Tyler forced himself up, then swung his legs over the bed and rubbed the sleep out of his eyes. He wished he would've shut his alarm off earlier. It wasn't like there was anything they could do here. He'd failed, and that was that. Maybe he and Gabe should just fuck each other's brains out before going back home and settling for rehashing the popular haunted spots that had been covered ad nauseum. At least they'd go out with a bang.

He sighed and got up to use the bathroom. On the way back to bed, he noticed an envelope peeking out from under the bedroom door. Curious, he picked it up, pulled out a letter that was inside, and read over its contents.

Tyler,

Im sorry for my abuelas decision yesterday. If your serious about visiting the ruins, I will take you. Meet me at the old well outside of town at noon. It isnt far from where you are staying.

Diego

Tyler reread the letter in disbelief. Why was Diego offering to help them now? Yesterday it had been clear that only Esperanza knew the location of the ruins. Had that changed, and what might Diego want in return? Could this be some kind of trap? Wherever the truth lied, the sudden change of fortune had Tyler's heart thumping like a jackrabbit. He walked over to the bed and shook Gabe. "Babe, wake up."

"What is it?" Gabe muttered groggily.

"Someone slipped this under our door. It's from that guy Diego. Here, look."

Gabe sat up and put on his glasses before reading the brief message. When he was done, he cocked an eyebrow at Tyler. "How did he know where to find us?"

"Maybe Rosalinda delivered the message for him. She's the one who told us about Esperanza in the first place."

"Do you think he's serious?"

Tyler shrugged. "I don't know what to think. Something could've changed, but people have a habit of going missing around here. Maybe his family has something to do with it."

"Isn't that a little farfetched?"

"I guess, but any one of them could be dangerous and we wouldn't know."

Gabe grimaced, then shoved the letter back at Tyler. "Alright, so what do you want to do, go home?

"Well, no, but I--"

"Then why are we dragging out this conversation? Jesus, Tyler. Why do you have to fight with me on everything?"

"I'm not ... I don't..." Tyler stared down at his feet. Though he was only thinking out loud, Gabe had a point. He had been stressing so much lately. This trip was supposed to be fun, but all they'd done so far was fight . The terrifying possibility of Gabe breaking up with him sent a chill through his core.

Tyler put the letter down and took Gabe's hands in his. "I'm sorry, Gabe. I've been so stressed, and I shouldn't be taking it out on you. Forgive me?"

Gabe's lips curled into a faint smile. "Yeah. Let's just stop fighting, okay?"

He gestured Tyler to him, and he nestled against Gabe's side, letting his warmth envelop him. Enjoying the peaceful silence, they cuddled for several minutes before Gabe gave Tyler a light squeeze.

"So, what are we going to do now?"

"I don't think we have much of a choice," Tyler said. "If we want to find the ruins we're going to have to give Diego a chance. Maybe we should bring protection or let someone know what we're doing in case something happens."

"That's not a bad idea. I'll let Rosalinda know what we're up to on the way out and to call the police if we don't return. Why don't you text Alex and let him know if he doesn't hear from us in a couple days to contact the police and US Embassy?"

"Sounds like a solid plan to me."

"Alright, cool. What did you bring with you? Anything we might use on the trip?"

"I've got a bunch of stuff: my pocket knife, mace, some flashlights, snacks and water, and that holy water the gay priest gave to me on our first investigation. It's not a lot, but it's better than nothing."

"Fair enough. Alright, let's get ready."

Tyler texted Alex what they were up to with instructions on what to do should they become silent. Afterwards he got dressed and helped Gabe gather their equipment. On the way out, Gabe told Rosalinda their plan. She resisted at first, but with another bribe she agreed to call the police if they didn't return.

With everything settled, Tyler and Gabe headed out into the blinding midday sun. They drove their rented jeep to the outskirts of town, easily spotting the old well Diego told them about at the top of a dried out hill. As they neared Diego came into view, standing next to the rusty landmark with a beat-up pickup nearby. They parked at the crest of the hill and Diego raised a hand in greeting.

Gabe glanced over at Tyler, his hands still on the steering wheel. "You ready?"

"As I'll ever be."

Tyler and Gabe got out of the vehicle and approached Diego.

Diego smiled as they neared. "*Hola*. Thanks for meeting me."

"Of course," Gabe said. "We're grateful for the assistance you're offering, but before we do anything we have some questions."

"Okay. I'll try to answer as best I can."

"Why are you helping us? Yesterday you were translating for your grandmother and now you're going against her wishes. Why the sudden change?

Diego shook his head. "I spoke out against her yesterday in front of you. I'm guessing neither of you speak Spanish?"

"*Poquito*," Gabe said.

Tyler simply shrugged.

"I haven't been living here very long, but the location of the ruins is a closely guarded secret in this community. After my fight with my *abuela*, I went through her things and found a map that showed me where it is. You said you came all the way from the states to see them. It must be important to you, so I'd like to help. I think it's the right thing to do."

Tyler eyeballed Diego with skepticism. He might be the

nice guy he claimed to be, but no one did anything for free. "I hear what you're saying, but what do you have to gain from this? Do you really expect us to believe that you'd just help us out, free and clear?"

Diego's pleasant smile broke into a grimace. "I don't want any money, I … The reason I seek out the ruins is private. Can you respect that?"

"I guess so, but we don't know you. How do we know this isn't some kind of trap, a way to get us alone and then jump us?"

"Why would I do that? I mean you no harm, and no one else will be around because the ruins are supposedly cursed. Everyone knows to stay far away from that place … well, except for you two and me."

"I think we've heard enough," Gabe said. "Will you give us a moment to talk things over?"

"Sure."

Gabe and Tyler walked out of ear's reach.

"What do you think?" Gabe asked.

"I don't know. He seems to have good intentions, but we still don't know why he's doing this."

"Do you think the reason behind it would put us in danger?"

"How would *I* know?"

Gabe scowled. "Tyler, I told you I don't want to fight."

"This is fighting? Babe, come on. Don't be so sensitive."

"I don't want to get into this right now. Are you okay with this or not?"

Tyler scanned Gabe's face, looking for a shred of forgiveness in his stone faced expression. He didn't find any. "Yeah, let's do this."

Tyler held his hand out to Gabe, but he stomped off towards Diego without him.

Damn it! I did it again. Tyler scurried after Gabe, hoping he'd find a way to make things better before their tiffs spiraled out of control.

"We'll do it," Gabe told Diego as Tyler caught up to them. "But if you don't mind my asking, how are you so good at speaking in English? You're the first person in town we've been able to have a full conversation with."

Diego chuckled and gave them a wide, beautiful smile. "I get that all the time. I always did really well in school, and a couple years back I got an opportunity to study abroad in the United States. I spent two years there, and I loved everything about it. Even after my time there was done I kept up with all the great media. Video games, social media, comic books. I love it all."

"Wow, I had no idea," Gabe said. "I'm glad you enjoyed our culture, despite how divided our politics are."

"I don't enjoy politics, so I stayed far away from that topic," Diego admitted. "But yes, I am happy to take you to the ruins. Before we go, I have a few conditions. I have to drive us to the ruins, and you have to turn off your phones. You'll also need to put on some blindfolds."

Tyler's brows furrowed. "What? Are you *kidding* me?"

"I'm not. I don't mind taking you with me, but I have to protect the location of the ruins. I can't risk you going back to the states and telling others."

"It's a bit overkill if you ask me, but I get it," Gabe said. He looked over at Tyler, deadpan.

"Fine," Tyler grumbled.

Tyler and Gabe grabbed their packs from the jeep and threw them into the dust-covered bed of Diego's pickup. They went to the passenger side of the truck and Diego tied bandannas around their heads, double checking for tightness. After guiding them inside, Diego got in and started the car. The radio came to life, maracas, drums, and trumpets playing together in a fast, lively beat.

"What *is* that?" Tyler asked, unable to hold back a smile.

"You've never heard *cumbia* before?" Diego said, disbelief in his tone.

"Not like this."

"Well, enjoy it. It will take us a while to get to the ruins."

The pickup rolled onwards, and Tyler let the upbeat music ease the tension in his shoulders. That lasted about ten minutes before the inside of the truck turned into a sauna without air conditioning. Diego mercifully let him roll the window down a bit, and Tyler sighed in relief as the warm wind cooled his face. He rested his head against the window, closing his eyes as the gentle vibrations of the truck soothed him.

A sudden nudge woke Tyler from his unintended sleep.

"Hey, wake up," Gabe said in a flat tone. "Diego says we're here. You can take off your blindfold."

Tyler untied the covering and took in his surroundings. They were parked on the side of a narrow winding dirt path, surrounded by rainforest on both sides. Enormous trees and exotic plantlife loomed in a sea of green, the cacophony of insects, monkeys, and other animals echoing around them. Gabe and Diego stood outside the vehicle with packs on their backs.

"I don't see the ruins," Tyler said.

"There is no direct path to the ruins," Diego said. He put the map he'd been looking at in his pocket, then picked up a machete leaning against the truck's side. "This is as close as I could get by car. We'll have to hike from here, but it shouldn't be more than an hour or two."

"An *hour or two?* Jesus!"

"Stop whining," Gabe snapped. "Come on, out of the car."

Tyler got out, keeping an apprehensive eye on Gabe. He'd never chastised him like that before, even when they were fighting. He toyed with the idea of apologizing to him again, then batted the thought away. Gabe was still too upset. He'd have to hope that finding the ruins would cheer him up.

Tyler grabbed his pack from the bed of the truck, then shadowed Diego and Gabe to a small opening in the tree line.

"The forest is very dangerous, so follow me closely," Diego instructed. "This path doesn't look great, but according to the map it's the best way to the ruins."

Diego parted a curtain of green branches with his machete and pressed forward with Gabe on his heels. Tyler followed after, suppressing a gasp as he entered the rainforest. Gargantuan trees towered above, higher than any he'd ever seen before. Tropical plant life surrounded them in an emerald glow that nearly stung his eyes, and whoops, shrieks, and hollers from nearby wildlife rang in every direction, completing the majestic ambience.

Tyler's awe was short-lived as a swarm of mosquitoes flocked to him like bees to honey. He swatted at the pests with a yelp and scurried to catch up with Diego and Gabe's swift pace. As they progressed, the trees gathered closer to one another and the canopy grew more congested, blocking out more and more sunlight. Tyler was grateful for the shade, but it didn't alleviate the stifling humidity that seeped through his clothes and lined his body with sweat.

They continued onward, and as the unfamiliar terrain and conditions wore Tyler down his surroundings became little more than a verdant blur. He carried on this way, mindlessly traipsing about as his fatigue grew until he was certain he would collapse. Tyler stopped at the base of a large tree and wiped away the sweat that lined his forehead. His calves throbbed with an aching heartbeat of their own, and his feet burned like they'd been attacked by a colony of angry fire ants. How much longer did they have to go? He'd probably sweat to death before they got there.

A sudden hissing sound from above made Tyler spin

around. A large green serpent descended from a branch just a couple feet above him. It opened its mouth and hissed, revealing sharp fangs.

Tyler froze in terror. The snake reared its head to strike, and right before it launched itself at him a broad blade sliced down, severing its head. The snake's body fell to the ground with a thick thud, and Tyler yelped as he jumped to avoid it.

Diego stood next to him, machete in hand. He placed his free hand on Tyler's shoulder. "You've got to stay close. I told you it isn't safe here."

"W-was that thing poisonous?" Tyler asked, hating the tremble in his voice.

"No, that was just an emerald tree boa, but they are still aggressive. You want to arrive at the ruins in one piece, *si?*"

"Yeah."

"Then come on, and don't fall behind this time. We're almost there."

Tyler glanced at Gabe up ahead and their gazes met. Gabe grimaced and looked away, making Tyler's stomach sink. Diego continued leading the way ahead, giving Tyler no time to ponder Gabe's cold demeanor. He struggled to keep up, jumping at any sudden sounds or movements on the forest floor.

After several minutes of hiking, Diego stopped at the edge of a crowded tree line, allowing them to catch up. Tyler took advantage of the break by taking a big swig from his water bottle and drawing in ragged breaths. "Thanks for ... giving us a break."

"I didn't," Diego said. "We're here."

"Here? I don't see anything."

"Look." Gabe grabbed Tyler's chin and tilted it to the right.

Through the tightly-packed trees, Tyler glimpsed what they had been desperately searching for. An assemblage of ancient stone walls made up the hulking mass of the ruins of Ayar Kachi. Numerous piles of rubble were strewn about the expansive clearing surrounding it, covered by a swath of moss that was a sickly radioactive green. In the center of the area, a series of crumbling stone steps led underneath the ruin's central triangular archway, which had several gaps in it like a child's missing baby teeth.

Beyond, the entrance lay open, a gaping maw of darkness. Tyler shuddered. He'd been to dozens of haunted locations, some mundane, some with a lingering sensation of being watched. But as he gazed upon the ruins it felt as if something were looking back at him, seeing *through* him. He'd never felt anything like that before.

"What's wrong? Don't tell me you're getting cold feet," Gabe taunted.

Tyler forced a laugh, trying to squash the fear that had sunk into his bones. "Of course not. It just looks like it'll be really dark in there. I don't think our flashlights are gonna cut it."

"I have something you can use," Diego offered. He opened his large pack and pulled out two thick branches with cloth and wire tied to the top of one end.

Gabe grabbed one of the torches and eyed it appreciatively. "Wow, old school."

Tyler took the other for himself. "Thanks, Diego. These are perfect. Wait, you only have these two? What about you?"

Diego averted Tyler's gaze. "I'm not going in. I told you, it is cursed."

"Okay, then you'll wait outside for us?"

"Yes. Please be careful, and don't take too long."

"Of course. Gabe, let's—"

Gabe squeezed through the tight tree line into the ruinous courtyard without Tyler, lighting his torch as he walked.

Tyler lit his, then hurried after him. Dislodged chunks of stone and overgrown vines, roots, and foliage covered the ground in every direction, slowing progress to a crawl. Tyler carefully weaved his way through the hazardous terrain, stumbling several times. After a couple minutes, he broke through the worst of the natural minefield, stopping at the moss-ridden outer walls that towered several times his height.

He touched the surface gently. This behemoth had been lying dormant here for centuries. What happened all those years ago, and why hadn't anyone ever filmed this place? He followed the mountainous wall to the long set of moldering stone steps that started at its base leading inside. Gabe was already half of the way there, and Tyler ascended at a quick pace to catch up. With each step he took the temperature dropped, as if the intolerable humidity of the forest had been negated by the cold presence of this slumbering sentinel of days past. By the time he caught up to Gabe at the damaged stone archway, he was shivering.

"Are you as cold as I am?" Tyler's teeth chattered.

"You'll be fine. Let me double check my stuff before we head inside."

While Gabe attended to his pack Tyler gazed into the darkness, the hairs on his body standing on end. Though he couldn't see anything, it felt alive, like there was something within that refused to die over the years.

Tyler shuddered. He'd grown used to cliche American hauntings. People were quick to assume any location with a bad history was haunted, and most of the time they got it wrong. But this place, something was different about it.

"Whoa, check out these markings," Gabe said.

Tyler glanced over. Gabe's torch illuminated a faded pattern carved into the old stone archway. The image resembled the face of a horned imp or demon with jagged teeth and a crown atop its head. "Hmm, that reminds me of a wooden figurine I saw at the inn. Does it look familiar to you from your research?"

Gabe tilted his head. "Kind of. I'll have to check my records when we get back. You ready?"

"Yeah, I think so."

Gabe gave him a ghost of a smile, and together they walked into the darkness of the temple ruins.

CHAPTER FOUR

abe and Tyler ventured into the ruins, the inky oppressive blackness around them a living shadow hellbent on stopping them in their journey. Even with the light from their torches, Tyler could hardly see several feet in front of him.

"Gabe, these torches aren't doing shit. What should we do?"

"Look along the walls. If Ayar Kachi really created this place, he would have had some torches set up."

Tyler veered to his left and came upon a decrepit stone wall. As he walked alongside it he grasped its surface with his free hand until his fingers caught in a thick series of spider webs. He recoiled, frantically wiping his hand on his pants before focusing his torch light back on the wall. At the edge of the torch's glow an ancient torch was set in the wall, held in place with a crude metal sconce. "I found one!"

Gabe joined him and lit the old torch. "Good work. They shouldn't be too far apart from each other. Let's light the rest of them."

Five minutes later, the space was warmly lit by the several dozen torches Tyler and Gabe had found.

Tyler did a slow lap around, taking in all the details. The area was cavernous with a vaulted ceiling twenty feet high and a length half the size of a football field. Small recesses were set into the stone walls in intervals with broken ceramics, idols, and other odd tidbits stuffed in them. In the center of the room a simple stone throne sat with a high uneven back.

Tyler made his way over, joining Gabe in inspecting the seat. The stone had suffered very little erosion and had minimal cracks given its age. "This is amazing. Everything is so well preserved here."

"Yeah, it's a freaking goldmine. Just think of what a team of archaeologists would find here." Gabe continued his rotation around the throne and shined his torch on the wall behind it. "*Whoa*. Tyler, come take a look at this."

Tyler accompanied him. Hung across the wall were a strange series of strings and knots forming a semicircle, like the bottom half of a sun. The strings were tied strategically, some with multiple knots in varying places while others just had one.

"What do you think it means?" Gabe asked.

"I'm not sure. Maybe we should add it to the to-do list for later."

"Okay." Gabe took out his phone and started taking some photos.

Tyler bit at his lower lip as he watched him. As much as he wanted to get this haunted investigation underway, Gabe's attitude was still bugging him. He seemed to be warming up to him again, but the agony of not knowing what was really on his mind was unbearable. He couldn't wait any longer. He had to know now, before they drifted even further apart. "Gabe, why are you mad at me?"

Gabe stopped snapping pictures and turned to face him with a glower. "I told you I didn't want to fight."

"I'm not trying to fight. All I want is for you to be honest with me. Why are you upset with me?"

"I don't want to do this here. Let's talk about it later."

"No, not later. *Now*. You've been acting strange since we got here, so let it out."

Gabe's brows furrowed and he threw his free hand up with a huff. "All right, you wanna know the truth? You're petty and ungrateful. You take me for granted, and I can't keep doing everything for you."

"What? *Do everything for me*? I don't remember you complaining about the free trip to South America. Maybe if you understood the never-ending pressure of a paranormal travel vlog–"

Gabe scoffed. "Could you be any *more* selfish? You're not the only one who's been working their ass off. I've been taking on more and more responsibility, and you don't even notice. Instead you order me around all the time like your puppet, like some *dog*, and I'm sick of it! I think we both know who's carrying most of the workload around here."

"But we're a team," Tyler said defensively.

"No, this is a dictatorship, and you're Hitler. You're fucking Hitler, Tyler! Would it kill you to show a little humility here and there? To say thank you, to do your fair share of the work? You know what? Find your own damned Incan secrets."

Gabe stormed off towards the entrance, and Tyler followed on his heels. "Gabe! Come on, talk to me!"

"Just leave me alone!" Before reaching the entrance, Gabe took a right into another hall and shot down a set of crumbling stone stairs.

"Fine, just run away like a little kid!" Tyler shouted after him.

Gabe descended into the darkness without a word.

Tyler stood at the top of the stairs, a heaviness settling in his core as the light from Gabe's torch faded from view. How long had he been holding on to these feelings? They'd been together for a year now, but Gabe had seemed more stressed the past few months. *Ever since Alex became my agent.*

Tears blurred Tyler's vision. He'd been so focused on his vlogging career and Alex's enticing words that he'd neglected Gabe and how he might feel. God, how could he do that to him? He loved Gabe with all his heart.

Staring at the base of the stairs, Tyler held back the urge to follow him with all the willpower he could muster. Gabe needed to cool down. Once he did he'd come back up and they could talk things through. Besides, he still had a job to do.

Tyler set down his pack, got out his smartphone, and powered it on. It wasn't as good as the drone, but it would have to do. He focused the screen on himself and tousled his short blond hair, the warm ambient light making his tan skin look even more appealing. *Looking good. Okay, where to film?*

The throne was the obvious choice. It caught the eye and there was more light centered around it from nearby torches than other spots. Tyler headed over and double checked the light quality before training the phone's camera back on himself. He took a deep breath and plastered a fake smile on his face.

"Hey chill and thrill seekers. We did it! We found the ruins of Ayar Kachi and man, this place is ca-*reee*-py! I'm in a chamber that appears to have been a throne room. We were surprised to find this stone throne in such great condition. It's almost as if someone has kept this place up over all the years."

Tyler waggled his eyebrows, then moved with the camera behind the throne, getting a shot of the bizarre semicircle of cordwork. "What's even more unsettling are these strings and knots. What do they mean? Could there be more to this story than we previously thought? Stay tuned as we delve further into this ancient mys–" A dark shape in Tyler's peripheral demanded his attention. "What the–" He turned, but nothing was there.

I could've sworn ...

"Gabe?" he called. "Gabe, that's not funny!"

No one answered, and goosebumps raised on Tyler's arms and legs. That wasn't just his imagination. He knew he'd seen someone there. Could Diego be screwing with him? It didn't seem likely given the kindness he'd shown them. But if it wasn't him or Gabe, what else could it possibly ...

No, no, this place isn't haunted. Everything is just getting to your head.

The weight of the phone in Tyler's hand reminded him he was still recording. *Shit, I ruined the take. Maybe I should play it back.* Tyler stopped recording and replayed the footage.

"Let's delve further into this ancient mys– ... What the– Gabe? Gabe, that's not funny!"

Tyler smiled to himself. Actually, this might just work. It had a Blair Witch vibe to it, and lately his audience had been pushing for something with a little more edge. He made a mental note to upload the footage and show it to Gabe once they got back to the inn.

A sudden gust of warm air shrieked through a small opening in the ruin's wall, grabbing Tyler's attention. He walked over and took a peek. Through a gap in the canopy the sun still shone high in the sky, but it had begun its descent. They had maybe an hour before sunset, and Tyler had no doubt that Diego would leave them here if they didn't hurry up. The thought of spending the night in the ruins sent a sharp chill down his spine.

I better get Gabe. We can come back tomorrow.

Tyler returned to the eroded set of stairs Gabe had taken and hovered his torch over the passage, looking down. Beyond the landing he couldn't see anything besides bits of rubble strewn on the ground. He stood there for a long moment, conflicted. He wanted to go get Gabe, but his gut told him he'd be better off up here.

"Gabe, we've gotta get going! Let's come back tomorrow." Tyler waited for an answer but received none. "Gabe? Gabe! God damn it."

Tyler took a deep, steadying breath. *Just find Gabe and get out of here. There's nothing down there. You're just psyching yourself out.* With a tightness in his shoulders and a fluttery pulse, Tyler forced himself down the stairs.

A heavy dampness permeated the lower level, accompanied by a musty stale odor like wet socks that made his nose crinkle. Tyler aimed his torch left, then right. The corridor went both ways with no telling how far it reached.

"Gabe, it's time to go!" Tyler's shout echoed down the hall. He waited several moments, but there was still no response. A wave of heat rushed to his face. *What the hell is his problem? He had to have heard me that time. I know he's pissed, but this is fucked up. Is he trying to scare me or something?*

Tyler stubbornly waited at the landing for another minute before it became clear he'd have to fetch Gabe himself.

"Fuck!" he hissed. What the hell was down here that had Gabe so distracted? Whatever it was, he didn't care. He was not about to have a slumber party with a bunch of Incan ghosts or whatever rabies-infected animals lived here.

Tyler let a coin flip decide his direction and headed down the hall to his right.

As he walked, a steady chill sunk underneath his skin. He came across a number of small rooms and stopped to inspect each one. Rotted chairs, tables, and sunken frames that must have been beds at some point filled them, along with more strange half-suns of strings and knotwork similar to the one he'd seen upstairs. But no Gabe.

After several minutes of searching, Tyler reached the last room of the passage. Like the others, it was cloaked in darkness with Gabe nowhere in sight. Tyler was about to head back the way he came when something reflected off the light from his torch.

What is that? Tyler edged into the room, letting the torchlight illuminate the remnants and debris that were scattered everywhere. Slowly waving his light from left to right, the reflection caught again. Tyler walked forward and grasped the object, his stomach dropping when he realized what it was.

A dusty cracked cell phone with a pink case depicting the moon and clouds rested in his hand, a recent model from what he could tell.

How had this phone gotten here? No one would abandon their cell unless they were in a hurry or in some kind of danger. What had happened here, and where was the phone's owner? The disturbing possibilities made Tyler's pulse skyrocket. He and Gabe had to get out of here, *now.*

Tyler pocketed the phone, bolted out of the room, and raced down the hall, his torch sputtering in protest. "Gabe, Gabe! God damn it Gabe, where are you? We have to leave!"

Gabe had to be on the other end of the hall, but why hadn't he responded to him? He couldn't be mad enough to ignore him when there was a sense of urgency. Could he be in danger like the owner of the phone he'd found? Tyler picked up his pace, quickly passing the stairs he'd come down.

Sprinting past numerous unoccupied rooms, Tyler

stopped as he neared a bisecting hallway. *Great, just what I need. Which way did he go?*

Tyler froze, listening for any sounds that may point him in the right direction. Distant, scuffled footsteps echoed from the right-hand side of the passage. Further down the hall, the faint golden glow of a torch's light illuminated a doorway. "Gabe, is that you? This isn't funny! We have to get out of here right now."

Tyler stomped down the hall, his impatience soaring as he reached the room's doorway. "Gabe, I'm ser–" He stopped in his tracks.

Inside the room, Gabe stood before a large mural that covered an entire wall. Detailed scenes of warfare between two opposing groups of men were depicted with a crowned figure in the center of the mayhem, sitting upon a throne made of the bones of numerous deceased individuals. The illustrations portraying bloodshed were covered in a flaky red substance. Gabe's eyes were wide, mesmerized as he inched forward to touch the mural.

As Tyler opened his mouth to speak, movement behind Gabe demanded his attention. A tall translucent figure approached, its features blurred as if his eyes couldn't quite catch the finer details or edges of them. From what Tyler could see, it was dressed in a loincloth, cape, and sandals. Its skin was a sick, mottled gray, and a headdress sat upon its head of long black hair. Its eyes gleamed an otherworldly red as it focused on Gabe.

Tyler squinted his eyes, then blinked rapidly. *What the fuck am I seeing right now? We've got to–*

The figure surged forward with a sudden burst of speed, closing in on Gabe.

"Gabe, behind you!" Tyler screamed.

Gabe spun at the sound of Tyler's voice. The surprise on his face was replaced by confusion, then horror as the figure pounced on him. The strange presence tackled Gabe to the floor, quickly muttering foreign words in a deep gravelly voice before laying its hands on his chest. Gabe screamed in agony.

"No!" Tyler lunged forward, striking at the shadowy figure with his torch. When it made contact, the figure's form dissipated in a cloud of swirling black mist that filled the room. Tyler shouted in terror, waving his torch in every direction against the malevolent presence. Within seconds, the mist filtered away to nothing as if it had never been there. Tyler held a hand to his pulsating heart, his breathing ragged. *What on earth just happened?*

A cry from Gabe broke through Tyler's terror. He writhed on the floor, clutching his chest with his eyes clenched shut.

"Oh my god, Gabe!" Tyler dove next to him and gave him a once over. He couldn't see any injuries, but there wasn't time to mull over what happened. "Come on, let's get outta here." Tyler helped Gabe up to his feet, then draped his arm under his shoulders and grasped his forearm so he could support him.

They staggered down the hall, the hairs on Tyler's body standing on end. The air vibrated with a frantic charge, accompanied by an overwhelming sense of being watched. He ignored the sensation, trudging forward with sheer determination. *Don't look back, don't look back. Just don't fucking look back.*

As they rounded the passage with the stairs leading to the entrance, Tyler tried to speed Gabe along. "Babe, come on. We gotta hurry."

Gabe muttered something incoherently and his head drooped.

Damn it, he's getting worse.

With slow grueling progress, they reached the stairs.

Tyler dragged Gabe up with him, and they tottered their way out of the ruins to a gust of warm, humid air. Tyler scanned the immediate area, but saw no sign of Diego.

"Diego? Diego! Where are you?"

The setting sun's pale orange rays broke through the canopy, and the possibility of being lost in the dangerous rainforest at night made Tyler's legs tremble. *Fuck, fuck, fuck!* What were they supposed to do now? He looked to Gabe. His face had paled several shades, and he breathed heavily as he clutched his chest with his free hand.

Tyler guided Gabe down the crumbling stone steps, then steered him to a nearby tree and helped him settle into a sitting position.

"Let me see, babe." Tyler unbuttoned Gabe's bloody shirt without resistance and stifled a gasp at the sight of his wound.

The skin in the center of Gabe's left pectoral had been cut deep and was still bleeding freely. The flesh was an angry dark red, and the veins near the wound were visible and unnaturally dark. But what really shocked Tyler was the likeness the wound bore to the devilish carving they'd seen on the stone arch entry.

What did that thing do to you? Tears sprang to Tyler's eyes and he wiped away at them furiously. Now wasn't the time to break down. He had to be strong for both of them and get as far away from here as possible, but which direction was Altalona?

Tyler thought back to the car ride. Based on the sun's positioning when they left and the truck's trajectory, they must have gone west for a good number of miles. It wasn't enough to go off of since they could've made any number of turns while he slept, but anywhere was better than here.

With the sun steadily approaching the horizon, Tyler pulled out his compass and found east. Satisfied, he gave

Gabe a light shake. Gabe's head lolled to the side, his face paler than before.

"Babe? Babe, wake up. I have to clean your wound and then we have to get going. Do you think you can handle that?"

Gabe's eyes fluttered open and he looked at Tyler with a dazed expression. After a long moment, he gave a weak nod.

"Alright." Tyler grabbed the water bottle from his pack and opened Gabe's shirt more so his cleaning would be thorough. "Okay, on three I'm going to apply the water. One … two …"

Tyler soaked the wound with water, and Gabe moaned in pain. Tyler didn't have anything to sop up the liquid, so he used the bottom edge of Gabe's shirt. Once Gabe's pained expression had faded, Tyler buttoned up his blood-caked shirt and gave him another nudge.

"Ready to go?"

"Okay," he croaked.

"Come on, up we go." Tyler grunted as he helped Gabe to his feet. He draped Gabe's arm around his neck to support him and they headed east. The going was frustratingly slow, and as the sun set further the horror of what happened summoned a maelstrom of panicked thoughts in Tyler's mind.

What was that terrible shadow that attacked Gabe, and what had it done to him? The thing disappeared after he attacked it, but would it come back for them? Was this why the townspeople of Altalona fled to their homes at night?

After trudging on for some time, they stopped. Tyler propped Gabe against a nearby tree to catch his breath and let his muscles rest. A little bit of color had returned to Gabe's face, but his gut told him that something was still horribly wrong.

"How are you feeling?" Tyler huffed.

Gabe grimaced. "I don't know. I feel so weak, like I can hardly stand on my feet. What happened back there?"

Tyler shook his head, then handed Gabe a bottle of water from his pack. "Not now. Just catch your breath so we can keep moving. I don't want to linger any longer than we have to."

Gabe sipped at the bottle and Tyler stepped a short distance away to evaluate their surroundings. Knots formed in Tyler's stomach as he observed the thick, lush forest that stretched in every direction with no end in sight. Their car ride here had to have taken a while. That could mean hours on foot. How were they supposed to last that long? Gabe needed to get to a hospital now.

Tyler sighed. *Better keep moving.*

As Tyler headed back to Gabe, the sun made its final descent over the horizon. Shadows had begun to overtake the forest around them and the temperature had dropped several degrees, but something else gave Tyler pause. The forest's wild cacophony had grown eerily silent, enough that he could hear the rattling of leaves in the breeze. Panic shot through him and he quickened his stride, his anxiety easing when he found Gabe exactly where he'd left him.

"Gabe, are you ready? Something doesn't feel right."

"Yeah, just give me a second." Gabe groaned as he struggled to pick himself up.

Tyler moved to help, but Gabe held up a hand and shook his head.

Tyler pulled out his compass and a flashlight. The compass's pointer began to slowly spin in circles. *What the hell?* Goosebumps raised on his arms, and the feeling of being watched returned. "Shit! Gabe, something weird is happening. We need to go. Can you run?"

Gabe turned on his flashlight. "I can try, but I don't think I'll last long."

"That's all I ask." Tyler pointed in the general direction they'd been traveling. "We'll keep going that way, next to that hill that leads further into the forest. If you get too tired, we'll figure something out. C'mon!"

Gabe led the way in an unsteady jog and Tyler followed on his heels with a heavy heart. They tore through the rainforest, the sensation of being watched intensifying in icy barbs that prickled at Tyler's limbs. As the very last of the sun's rays shone down on them something passed overhead, bathing them in shadow.

Gabe slowed his pace and looked upward. "What the fuck was that?"

"Keep going! It's okay, it's all gonna be–ah!"

Tyler's feet caught on a large tree root, and his fall propelled him over the edge of the steep hill. He rolled down with chaotic momentum, snagging on rocks and tree branches with bursts of jagged, searing pain. When he finally settled, he groaned and sat up slowly. His whole body throbbed, but other than some ugly scrapes and cuts he didn't have any injuries.

Gabe! Tyler looked back up the hill, but he couldn't see him. His stomach churned as images of the terrifying figure from before flashed in his mind. He jolted to action, his body pulsing in protest as he scraped back up the hill. Once he'd clawed over the apex, Tyler searched frantically for Gabe with his flashlight, crying out when he found him.

Gabe was sprawled out on the ground ten yards away, the dark shadowy figure from before pinning him down. Somehow the details of its features were more defined now, more tangible. The being's mouth hung open and a bizarre stream of amber energy left Gabe's mouth, entering the spirit. Gabe's skin was deathly pale, and he shook violently as he stared upwards in sheer terror.

"Leave him alone!" Tyler shouted.

The spirit didn't stop or acknowledge his presence, and Tyler struggled to find the courage to act. *I've got to do something to make that thing go away, but last time my torch went right through it. Wait, that's it!*

Tyler shrugged his pack off and rummaged through it in a hurry, his hands closing around the flask of holy water he'd brought with him. He didn't know if it would work, but he didn't know what else to do.

He lunged at the spirit with a fierce cry, uncorking the flask when he was within range and splashing it around wildly. A spritz of liquid hit the spirit with a distinct sizzling sound, and a cloud of vapor erupted from it. The spirit gave a gravelly roar of pain that shook Tyler's bones and turned his insides to mush. It broke away from Gabe, shooting Tyler a murderous red glare before dissolving away in a black mist.

Once the shadow had fully dissipated, Tyler ran to Gabe. He had become deathly still and gazed forward, expressionless. "Gabe?" Tyler touched his arm. "Jesus, you're freezing!"

Gabe gave no response, and tears sprang in Tyler's eyes. "Oh god, oh god. Gabe? Gabe! Please, answer me baby!"

The only answer he received was a brief twitch of Gabe's face.

Tyler took hold of Gabe and hoisted him up with great difficulty. "I'm, *ugh*. Not. Letting you die here," he huffed.

Tyler dragged Gabe with him through the forest at a snail's pace. He shouted for help, hoping someone would hear him somehow, but quickly gave up on that. Tyler's muscles burned with a fiery fatigue as they scuttled forward, only taking brief breaks to gulp down some water or readjust his grasp on Gabe.

As he trudged onward he was both grateful and perplexed by how miraculously peaceful and silent the forest was. He would hear the sound of animals up ahead, just for their cacophony to die out upon their approach.

After what seemed like an eternity, the tree line began to thin out. Tyler staggered forward with Gabe, and together they broke free of the rainforest. The elevated ridge they were on gave a panorama of the dark countryside around them. In the distance was a small village, the few lights still on shining like glorious beacons of hope in his horrific nightmare. People were down there, people that could help.

Tyler looked to Gabe. He was still deathly pale and unresponsive, but he didn't let that squash the optimism that fluttered in his chest. "Do you see that, baby? We're going to make it. Everything's gonna be okay."

CHAPTER FIVE

Tyler sat next to Gabe in the patient room, holding his hand as the IV monitor beeped slow and steady. He brought Gabe's hand towards him and kissed it, then lowered it and rested his head against his shoulder. "Please wake up, baby."

The guilt of the situation had been eating Tyler from the inside out, and all too familiar thoughts resurfaced in his mind, playing like a broken record. How could he let this happen? He'd been the one who pushed the idea of going to Altalona. If he had just listened to Gabe's advice to slow things down, they wouldn't even be here. Now something was seriously wrong with Gabe, and it was all his fault. Tyler shifted anxiously, hoping the doctors would come by with some good news given the nightmare they'd just endured.

After finding the village near the ruins, Tyler convinced a reluctant samaritan to drive them to the nearest hospital. Gabe had been wheeled off to the ER, and after hours of poking and prodding they gave him his own room, allowing Tyler to keep him company. Since then, he'd been waiting by his side in this tiny room with only a couple of interruptions.

The first had been a call from Tyler's mom. She was a notorious worrywart, and after she chastised him for not calling to let her know they'd landed safely in Peru Tyler spilled the beans. He left out the specifics of how Gabe was injured, but assured her that they were safe and in good hands. He made quick work of the call, hoping her wishes of a speedy recovery would come true.

The second disruption was a phone call from Gabe's parents, southern bible thumpers who never approved of any lifestyle outside of their own. The hospital had notified them of Gabe's condition since they were his emergency contacts, so Tyler wasn't too surprised when they blamed him for corrupting Gabe and insisted this wouldn't have happened otherwise. But they had a point. Looking out for Gabe was his responsibility, and he'd failed. His lust for success and fame had driven them here, and Gabe had paid the price.

Unable to ignore the repercussions of his selfish actions, Tyler thought long and hard and came to a decision. As soon as Gabe was well enough to travel, they would go back to the states. He knew Alex would be furious when he withdrew from his arrangement, but he didn't care about some stupid tv show, ancient ruins, or anything else. Gabe was too important to him.

Tyler raised his head and looked at Gabe once more. His skin was bone white and his face contorted in pain as he fought whatever horrible affliction the evil spirit had set upon him. Tyler wrenched his gaze away. *God, just looking at him hurts.*

Someone knocked on the room's door.

"Come in," Tyler called.

A male doctor with tan skin and short black hair entered the room wearing a white lab coat with a clipboard in hand. "Tyler Collins?"

Tyler frowned. "Yeah, that's me. Who are you?"

"I'm Doctor Flores. Do you have a moment? I'd like to talk about the circumstances of Gabriel's condition."

"Sure. Anything to help."

Doctor Flores motioned towards the door.

Tyler got up and gave Gabe a quick kiss on the forehead. When he turned back around the doctor had an uncomfortable look on his face and he briskly left the room. Tyler followed after, annoyed at his reaction. *Great, another homophobe. Just what I need.*

The doctor led Tyler down the long hallway to a vacant consultation room and shut the door behind them.

Tyler sat before a small table in the center of the tiny room and looked to the doctor. "Do you want me to go over what happened? I already went over it with the police several times."

Doctor Flores' visibly tensed up, then steepled his fingers together. "That won't be necessary, Mister Collins. May I be frank?"

"Of course."

"While your story is entertaining, it doesn't add up, and it certainly doesn't explain Gabriel's condition."

"What are you talking about? I'm telling the truth."

"It is *fiction*, and if we are going to help your … *lover*, then we need to know the truth about what happened in Altalona. Gabriel's immune system has been severely weakened, but from the samples we took he doesn't test positive for any immune disease on record. Do you understand what that means? This has never been documented before. If this is a new immune disorder, we will have to research his condition to discover the root cause. We cannot entertain the idea of ghosts and spirits."

Tyler shot out of his chair. "I already told you what I said was true. And Gabe isn't my lover. He's my *boyfriend*, and I love him! Neither of us wanted to believe in Altalona's stupid superstitions about spirits and curses, but that didn't stop this shitshow from happening, did it? *Maybe* instead of interrogating me you should be asking the people of Altalona what they've been hiding all this time."

Tyler stormed towards the door, but before he could open it the doctor grabbed his arm. "Mister Collins, please."

Tyler shook off his grip. "Get your hands off me, you fucking homophobe. And by the way, I'll be contacting Gabe's parents to request a new doctor for him. I'm not going to put up with your prejudice, and he deserves a hell of a lot better than that."

Tyler yanked open the door and slammed it shut, then stomped down the hall with his fists clenched. God, this was such a fucking disaster. Why was everyone so awful? He plopped into a nearby chair and put his hands to his temples as tears streamed down his face.

All he wanted was for Gabe to be well again, to go home and have everything back to normal. But if what that homophobe doctor said was true, Gabe's condition was more serious than he'd imagined. They wouldn't be leaving anytime soon, and the hospital would make Gabe a living pincushion until they figured it all out. What had that evil spirit done to him, and who even was he? Mulling it over, he knew it had to be Ayar Kachi from Esperanza's story. The spirit had tried to kill the intruders of its property just like they said he would. The horrific memory of the translucent monster drawing the glowing amber energy out of Gabe flashed in his mind, making his stomach churn.

Tyler lifted his head and wiped the tears from his eyes. No. He had to be strong for Gabe. Screw Ayar Kachi, screw Gabe's family, and screw the doctors. No matter what happened, he was going to stay right here and ensure he made a full and speedy recovery.

Tyler headed back to Gabe's room, struck with an intense

longing to see him. When he entered the doorway Gabe was sitting in bed, propped up with some pillows.

"Hey baby," Gabe croaked with a weak smile.

"Oh my god, you're awake!" Tyler rushed over to his side and gave him a kiss. He broke off and looked into his eyes. "How are you feeling? Do you need anything? Should I–"

Gabe put his hand on Tyler's. "Tyler, calm down. I feel like crap, but given what happened I think I'm entitled to my fifteen minutes of meh."

Tyler smiled, happy that Gabe's condition hadn't taken away his personality, but he still had to come clean. "Gabe, listen. I'm so sorry about the way I've been acting. I've been terrible, and I should've been more grateful for all that you've done for me. I can't believe I …" Tyler's voice cracked. "Things are going to change from here on out, I promise."

"I forgive you. Honestly it's my fault too. I never said anything because I didn't want to make anything worse, but everything I bottled up was bound to explode at some point. I'm just glad you're here with me now." Gabe gave Tyler's hand a light squeeze. "Did my parents call?"

Tyler frowned. "Yeah, that was … interesting. I don't think my ears have stopped ringing from all that shouting."

"Sorry. They still don't get the whole gay thing, but screw 'em. I've got the best boyfriend around."

Tyler's vision blurred as tears ran down his face. "God, I love you."

"I love you too. Can I be honest? I'm still pretty freaked out. I can't believe what happened in those ruins and the forest. Did you see …."

Tyler nodded.

"What *was* that thing?"

"I don't know, but you're safe now and that's what matters. Don't worry, we're never going back to those ruins."

Gabe's brows furrowed. "What? But that would mean …"

"Yep, I've decided to drop my arrangement with Alex. I still want to pursue this career path, but it can't come at the cost of losing you. You're everything to me."

"Oh babe, I can't tell you how happy that makes me feel. There's something seriously wrong with that place. Did the doctor tell you what's going on with me?"

Tyler hesitated. He didn't want to freak Gabe out about his bizarre condition, but he couldn't lie to him either. A half truth would have to do. "Yeah, they said something about your immune system, but I don't think they know enough yet."

"Hmm, I guess we'll just have to see how this plays out. Hey, would you go to the vending machine for me? I'm a little hungry."

Tyler got out of his seat. "Sure, what do you want?"

"How about some Pepsi and Gardetto's?"

Tyler cocked an eyebrow. "Is that doctor's orders?"

Gabe grinned and slapped Tyler's butt. "You bet your sweet ass it is."

Tyler held his hands up, palms out. "Okay, okay. I surrender. I'll be right back, sexy."

Tyler stepped into the hall, feeling like a weight had been lifted off his shoulders. Though Gabe's condition was still a puzzle to be sorted out, he was already acting like his old self. The doctors would eventually figure out how to make him better, and then they could return home and find a new way forward together. Everything was going to be alright.

Turning a corner at the end of the passage, Tyler spotted a dingy snack and soda machine with harsh fluorescent light overhead. As he stepped up to the machines, the lights flickered on and off. He grimaced. *Stupid crappy lighting.* He got two Pepsis, then moved on to the snack machine. *Gardettos, Gardettos, where are the—Huh, no Gardettos.* Tyler pushed A5 for some Takis. It was the only thing he'd tried in the states, and he hoped Gabe would like them.

As the snack rotated, the lights flickered out. A strange prickle surged on the back of Tyler's neck, and when he looked into the glass's reflection he saw a dark figure behind him. He spun around in a defensive position, coming face to face with a middle-aged latina woman. She jumped back with a cry.

Tyler held a hand to his chest and sighed. "Jesus, don't lurk behind people like that! You nearly gave me a heart attack."

The woman stared in shock at Tyler and he grabbed his snacks before heading back to Gabe's room at a brisk pace. *God, I hate hospitals.*

Halfway down the hall, Tyler's phone buzzed in his pocket. He stopped and set his purchases down on a nearby chair so he could see who it was. Tyler groaned. Alex was calling.

He'd sent Alex an email about what happened after arriving at the hospital, but now he wasn't sure he wanted to pick up. He meant what he said about severing ties with Alex and knew the conversation would have to happen soon, but this didn't feel like the right time. What could Alex say that would make anything better? Gabe needed him now. On the other hand, Alex *had* funded their trip to South America and was the only reason they were there in the first place. On the fourth buzz, Tyler cursed under his breath and answered the call. "Hello?"

Alex's nasally voice came through. "Finally! I saw your message. Are you okay?"

"I'm fine. It's Gabe that I'm worried about."

"Oh, damn. What happened to him?"

"He was attacked by some crazy shadow thing in the ruins! I told you everything in the email I sent you."

"I skimmed it. You know I hardly read those things, especially when you ramble. So the ruins are really haunted? That's insane! Where is it located?"

"I don't know. The guide blindfolded us until we got there, then abandoned us when things went south. We're lucky we found someone to take us to the hospital."

"How bad are Gabe's injuries?"

"Pretty freaking bad. The doctors don't know what's wrong with him or how to fix him."

"I'm sure he'll be fine. And anyways, you should be proud. You made history! No one's ever filmed the ruins. Just think how significant this could–"

"I don't care! We barely made it out of those ruins alive, and all you can think about is your god damned footage. You don't give two shits about us, do you?"

"Hey, we made a deal. I fund your travels, and you record the footage. I paid good money to get you guys out there. I expect results."

"Did you not hear me? Something is seriously wrong with Gabe. I'm not leaving him alone in this condition, and I'm definitely not going back to those ruins."

"Tyler, think this over carefully. This is the opportunity of a lifetime. If you land this, you're almost guaranteed to have your own paranormal show. Throngs of fans, more money than you know what to do with, fame. I'm telling you this because your career is on the line. Finish the filming on your own. Gabe is in good hands. He'll be fine. But if you don't follow through, it's over. I don't give second chances."

Tyler clenched his fists. He couldn't believe he ever thought Alex had their best interests at heart. He only cared about the content his talent created, no matter what price they paid to get it. "You know what, Alex? Fuck off."

Tyler hung up, then turned his phone off and shoved it into his pocket. He snatched up the snacks he bought and went back to Gabe's room, plastering his best smile on his face.

Gabe's brows raised as he entered the room. "What took you so long? Did they run out of Pepsi? Oh, I hate diet!"

Just pretend everything's okay. Gabe doesn't need this right now. Tyler shook his head and showed off the spoils from the vending machine. "Nah, just thinking about things. They didn't have any Gardetto's, so I hope Takis is okay. Got any room in your bed?"

Gabe scooched over with a grimace, then pointed a finger at Tyler. "No funny business though. I'm on bedrest, mister."

"Of course." Tyler crawled carefully into bed with Gabe. They didn't quite fit, but it was close enough to not be too uncomfortable.

Gabe grabbed the remote and turned on the tv. "What's your poison? A little crime drama? Something funny?"

Tyler wrapped an arm around Gabe's midsection and rested his head on his shoulder. "Anything you want is fine by me, baby."

"Telenovellas it is!"

The tension in Tyler's chest dissipated as he snuggled with Gabe. The day had been long and terrifying but they'd made it through. They had each other, and when Gabe was better, they'd go back home and make a new life for themselves. All of this would just be a blip, a brief nightmare that would soon be forgotten.

Tyler's eyelids drooped with a sudden weight. He closed them, just for a moment.

CHAPTER SIX

The sharp buzz of static noise from the TV woke Tyler. He jolted to life, finding himself alone in the hospital bed. He grabbed the remote next to him and turned the TV off.

"Gabe?" he called. Tyler got up and went over to the closed bathroom door. He knocked. "Gabe, you in there? I'm coming in." He opened the door, but Gabe wasn't inside.

That's weird. Where did he go? He might have gotten hungry again, but it was odd that he didn't wake him up. Gabe was in no condition to be walking around on his own.

Tyler walked down the empty, dimly-lit hallway and made his way to the vending machines he'd visited earlier. No one was there, so he headed to the floor's main waiting area. It was empty, and when he checked the nurse's kiosk no one was manning the desk. Where were they? Surely they kept a skeleton crew around in case of emergencies like this.

"Damn it, where are you Gabe?" Tyler whispered to himself.

A nearby scuffle sounded, and Tyler spun around. At the far end of the large space, a masculine form with shoulder length hair rounded a corner in a hospital gown. From the glimpse he got he wasn't certain it was Gabe, but who else would be roaming the halls at this hour?

"Gabe!" Tyler chased after and turned the corner. "Baby, what are you–" The hallway was empty, and the dim fluorescent lights overhead flickered. *What the hell? He was just here!*

Further down the hall, strange dark spots spattered the tile floor. Tyler went over and knelt down close. The unmistakable coppery scent of blood filled his nostrils, making his stomach drop.

Was Gabe hurt? If these bloody splotches were from him, things could get serious fast. He stood back up, intending to follow the trail when the flickering lights above him fizzled out. *Ugh, seriously?*

Shaking his head, Tyler started walking. As he passed under the next overhead light, it too sputtered out. Perplexed, he continued, each light malfunctioning as he walked underneath. *What the fuck?*

Tyler sped up, hoping to outpace the strange phenomenon, but the darkness kept up with him. Whatever the hell was happening, he had to find Gabe and get him help pronto. Tyler rounded the corner to the next hall and increased his pace to a jog.

He continued to follow the thin trail of blood, but the failing lights were now dying out faster than he could keep up. Tyler's heartbeat drummed in his ears. Something was seriously wrong about all of this. "Gabe? Gabe!" he shouted, not caring if he woke up the other patients.

No response came as he charged down the hall, struggling to keep up with the lights flickering out. Three-quarters down the hall, the blood spatter led to a door. *Yes, gotcha!*

Tyler slammed the door open and was plunged into complete darkness.

"Shit!" Tyler's voice echoed, bouncing in a hundred directions. His hands went clammy. *Where am I?* He pulled out his phone and turned on his flashlight app. Waving the light around, he discovered he was in a stairwell. "Gabe, come on! This isn't funny!"

Cold fingers gripped Tyler's spine as he felt a familiar sensation of being watched. *Just like before …* Could the spirit that attacked Gabe have followed them here somehow? Tyler shook his head. *No, it's impossible. You're just freaking yourself out. Focus on finding Gabe.*

Tyler scanned the floor with his light. The crimson trail led downstairs, and he followed it until he reached the very bottom of the passage. He opened the door before him with a rusty squeak, revealing a basement area that was being used for storage. Unused mattresses, spare gurneys, and boxes of medical supplies lined the concrete walls with piping hanging low overhead. He still couldn't see Gabe anywhere, and the blood trail was practically nonexistent now.

"Great, just fucking great."

Tyler forced himself forward at a snail's pace, passing several cluttered passageways and a large whirring air conditioning unit with a chain-link fence around it. At the end of the main corridor, Tyler took a left. Bloodied handprints were smeared along the wall to his right and faint, indiscernible sounds from further down echoed to him.

"Gabe!" Tyler raced down the hall. *Please be okay, please be okay.* Tyler turned at the end of the corridor then forced himself to a stop, unable to keep a cry from escaping his lips.

Fifteen feet ahead, Gabe was being held against the concrete wall by the same terrifying spirit from before. Once again, its form was clearer and less blurred than the last time he'd seen it, enough to make out its features. It was a tall male with an aquiline nose, heavy brow, and long black hair that cascaded down the mottled gray skin of its bare muscled chest. Its terrible red eyes gleamed as it gripped Gabe by the neck.

Gabe's eyes were wide with terror, and his arms had deep gashes on them, his blood trickling down the wall in tiny rivers onto the ground. The spirit opened its mouth, larger than was humanly possible. Gabe's mouth opened seemingly of its own accord, and he gave a cry of strangled panic before a stream of amber energy was drawn from him, entering the evil spirit.

"Gabe, no!" Tyler screamed as he lunged at the spirit.

The spirit released Gabe, then dodged Tyler's charge with a sidestep. As Tyler spun around for another attack, the spirit grabbed hold of his collar and threw him with surprising strength.

Tyler flew through the air, collapsing onto a large box of medical supplies that caved under his weight. Dazed, he gaped at the evil spirit that was illuminated by his phone that had clattered to the ground. How had it done that? Before it had been little more than a shadow. Was it getting stronger from whatever it was taking from Gabe?

Tyler groaned and struggled to get up, but the spirit was already on him. It grabbed him by the shirt, ripping it in one swift motion. The entity put a large gray hand on Tyler's exposed chest and began to chant in a harsh guttural tone. Tyler gasped, frozen as pinpricks shot through his core. As the spirit continued its chant, Tyler's body began to pulse in response.

What is it doing to me? I can't move!

The pulse morphed into a searing heat, and Tyler cried out as a fiery burning singed his chest.

The spirit withdrew its hand and gave a hideous smile before grabbing Tyler with both hands and throwing him like a ragdoll. Tyler sailed through the air, clipping his head on the concrete wall and dropping to the floor with a heavy thud.

Tyler's head spun in circles and his skull felt lighter than air. He tried to move, and stabbing needles of pain bounced around in his head in response. *Ungh, I have to save Gabe!*

He tilted his head what few degrees he could. The spirit had returned to Gabe and continued to siphon the shimmering golden energy out of him. Gabe's pallor was deathly pale and turning a sickly gray similar to the spirit's skin tone.

Tyler watched helplessly, hot tears spilling down his cheeks. Gabe's skin was sinking deep into his face, his overly pronounced high cheekbones and chiseled jawline making him look skeletal.

Tyler's heart ached with torment. There was no way he could save Gabe; he hadn't brought his holy water with him. But if he did nothing they would both die down here. Desperate, Tyler did the only thing he could think of and hollered at the top of his lungs. His voice boomed in the concrete passage and echoed down through the halls.

The spirit halted its draining of Gabe and focused its fiery red eyes on Tyler. Tyler averted its gaze and kept screaming. Whatever influence the spirit may have over him, he wasn't going to give it the satisfaction.

To Tyler's surprise, shouts of alarm answered in the distance.

The spirit looked in the direction of the noise and gave a beastly roar that shook the walls with its strength. It shot Tyler a seething glare of hatred before dropping Gabe and disappearing in a cloud of black mist.

With the spirit gone, Tyler tilted his head toward Gabe. He rested against the concrete wall, unmoving. His features were so sunken in he hardly looked like himself anymore. He looked … *No, no, no!* Tyler scraped forward on his elbows, gritting his teeth as his head pounded in protest.

Reaching Gabe, Tyler forced himself up, stars spotting his vision. He shook Gabe. "Gabe? Gabe, wake up!"

Gabe's head lolled to one side. Tyler's vision blurred as he kept an iron grip on him to stop him from falling over. "Gabe, come on! Please, just open your eyes. You can't leave me all alone!"

The shouts in the distance were closer now, accompanied by loudening footsteps.

Tyler shook Gabe one last time, burrowing his head into his chest when he didn't respond. As the soul-shattering reality of what happened set in, Tyler let out a hoarse cry of agony. The pain in Tyler's head erupted and his vision faded into darkness.

CHAPTER SEVEN

yler stared blankly out the passenger-side window as Jessica's gray BMW rolled to a stop in the church parking lot. Even with the careful gradual deceleration, his head throbbed and he winced, bringing a hand to his head.

"Oh my god, I'm so sorry, Ty! Did I slow down too fast?"

"You're fine, it's just this stupid concussion." Tyler withdrew his hand and glanced Jessica's way, returning her worried gaze with a weak smile. Wavy black locks framed her dark dewy face perfectly, cascading over her shoulders onto her simple black dress.

It was impossible to be upset with his best friend, especially since she had convinced his overprotective mother not to attend the funeral. Ever since he got back to the states his mom had been glued to his side, attending his doctor's appointments and catering to his every whim. After the first couple days he'd had enough of her smothering, and following a long talk with Jessica she begrudgingly passed the title of caretaker to her.

"Are you sure you're okay?" Jessica asked. "It's only been a couple days. The doctor said you need at least another week of recovery before you can move around without any pain."

Tyler's head pounded in response to her question, and he fought to keep the smile on his face. "Yeah. I have to be here for–" He stopped himself. He couldn't bring himself to say Gabe's name out loud. The pain of losing him was still too raw, and he didn't want to make a blubbering fool of himself.

Jessica placed a gentle hand on his shoulder. "Hey, it's okay. I'm here for you no matter what happens."

"Thanks, Jess. Let's just get this over with."

Jessica grabbed Tyler's walking cane from the back seat and he begrudgingly accepted it. He hated the damned thing, but it had already saved him from some nasty falls. Jessica got out of the car and opened Tyler's door for him, hovering as he exited slowly.

They left the parking lot, inching along the sidewalk before arriving at the cobbled stone walkway of the church's entrance. The place of worship loomed before them, reaching toward the sky in an angular point. Large stained glass windows rested in its center in gothic style, its ornamentation further reflected in the portal's detailed stonework above the double doored entry.

The tightness in Tyler's chest constricted with each step. This was going to be a fucking nightmare, maybe more than the whirlwind that had been the past few days.

After returning from Peru, Gabe's body had been taken into custody. An investigation had been mounted to determine the cause of his death, and the investigators were stunned to discover his body had been partially mummified. Naturally their suspicions fell on Tyler, but his wounds were severe and they couldn't explain how Tyler's head had made contact at such a high point on the wall where a bloody spray remained. Unable to form a clear picture of what had happened, these odd circumstances had all but cleared Tyler as a suspect, but it didn't do anything to ease his aching heart that felt like it had been torn to pieces. Today there would be a ceremony but no body or burial, and Tyler already knew how that made Gabe's parents feel.

They'd been harassing him with phone calls ever since he got back, blaming him for Gabe's death and refusing to believe his account of what happened. Their incessant calls had become so threatening he had to block them. Now he'd have to see them face to face and hope they wouldn't cause a scene, though he understood their anger. This was his fault. If it wasn't for him, he and Gabe would still be in Dallas enjoying their life together.

Tyler and Jessica stopped at the church's double doors. He took a moment to straighten the tie that was already practically choking him to death.

"Are you ready?" Jessica said.

"I guess so."

Jessica opened the door and they entered a simple reception area. They made their way toward two clean-cut men in black suits that stood at a set of doors with pamphlets in their hands. When the men saw Tyler nearing their eyes widened and one of the men whispered quickly to the other before they forced their shocked expressions into something more cavalier.

"Hello, we're here to attend the service for Gabriel Price," Jessica said.

"Oh, um, yes," the man on the right sputtered. "The service is just about to start. Go on in."

The man handed them their program pamphlets and the other opened the door for them. As soon as they passed, the men whispered furiously to each other. Tyler knew they were talking about him, but he didn't care. Today was about Gabe, nothing else.

Inside, the vaulted chapel's wooden pews were packed with just a few seats remaining in the last couple of rows. A priest in a white robe approached the altar where a funeral portrait of Gabe sat atop a tripod next to an arrangement of white roses, lilies, and purple statice. Tyler recognized the photo. Gabe's long brown hair was swept back with several strands running down in front. He had a charming irresistible smile on his face, the one that always made Tyler's heart melt. Now it was frozen.

With a start the door behind them slammed shut, making Tyler jump and his head throb. Some members of the congregation turned their heads at the sudden outburst.

In the front pews, the fire-engine red hair of Gabe's mom Nancy caught Tyler's attention, next to the bearish hulking figure that was Gabe's dad Jim. Jim looked their way, leering as he caught sight of Tyler. He whispered something to his wife, then got up from his seat and stormed down the center aisle, his dark caterpillar eyebrows furrowed.

"What do we do?" Tyler whispered.

Jessica held her chin high. "Don't you worry, we belong here."

Jim's face was beet red as he came upon them. His thin combover had begun to unravel, and salt and pepper wisps of hair stuck out in every direction. "What the hell are you doing here? Leave, now!"

"We have every right to be here," Jessica said, unphased by his heated words. "The obituary in the paper said all were welcome, is that not true?" Jim's throat made an ugly gurgling sound as he struggled to find words, and Jessica inched in closer. "If you don't want me to cause a huge scene, you'll allow Tyler the proper rights he's deserved and let him pay his respects."

Jim's nostrils flared as he clenched his fists.

"Jim, what on earth is going on over there?" Nancy called, followed by the loud clacking of her heels. "I told you we–" She stopped beside her husband, gasping as her eyes focused on Tyler. The skin around her eyes was puffy and red, and her short fiery hair was swept back in old lady fashion. Her features contorted into a scowl of such ferocity that Tyler thought her face was going to melt off.

Jim put a hand on Nancy's shoulder. "I was just telling these two that they aren't wel–"

"Get out!" Nancy shrieked. "Get out, get out, *get out!*"

The chapel went deathly silent.

Jessica crossed her arms. "You can't just order us out of here. Tyler was a huge part of Gabe's life. He deserves to be here."

Tyler took a small step forward. "It's okay, Jess. I can handle this. Jim, Nancy, I loved your son with all of my heart. All I want is to–ah!" Searing needles of pain erupted in Tyler's head, making him double over.

Jessica caught him before he could fall. "Ty, are you okay?"

Tyler held onto her, then used his cane to right himself before doubling over again. Stars dotted his vision and the world began to spin. "Stars, spinning," he groaned.

"Come on, let's get you out of here." Jessica hauled him up and guided him back to reception, shooting Gabe's parents and the unsettled congregation a scathing glare on the way out.

Once outside, Jessica had them stop and they leaned against the outer stone wall. "Take some deep breaths, sweetie. In and out, in and out."

Tyler did as instructed, and the banging in his head seemed to fade a degree or two.

"Tell me how you're feeling. You know I have zero reservations about going back in there. Or we can just hang out here for a while if you need."

"I'm still feeling kinda dizzy, but I think I'll be–oh god!" Tyler turned away from Jessica as a rolling wave of nausea bubbled from his stomach to his throat. The contents of his stomach splattered upon the cobbled walkway, and the force from the expulsion intensified the pounding in his head. With a whimper, he slid down the wall until he was sitting on the concrete.

Jessica sat next to him. "Easy, Ty. Take some more deep breaths for me, nice and slow."

After several long moments of following Jessica's advice the nausea began to subside, only for the full gravity of his situation to take its place. Hot tears slid down Tyler's cheeks, blurring his vision.

"I'm sorry," he croaked.

"Why are you apologizing? You didn't do anything wrong."

"I wasn't strong enough. Gabe would've been strong enough."

"Hey, don't do this to yourself. You have a concussion. We knew this might happen, but it was worth trying."

"It's not my stupid concussion, it's …" Tyler stared down at the concrete, new tears spilling over. "Gabe is gone. He's *dead*, and if it wasn't for me he'd still be alive. This is all my fault."

Jessica drew her arms around Tyler. "I know you're going through a lot right now, but you can't blame yourself for this. None of this is your fault."

Tyler looked away, unable to meet her gaze.

"Come on, let's get back to the car and go home. You need to rest."

Jessica helped Tyler to his feet with some effort, then guided him back to the car. An endless void filled his core as he rested his head against the passenger seat. What did anything matter anymore? The only man he'd ever loved was gone. They were supposed to be together, grow old together. What was he going to do now? Tyler closed his eyes, hoping the tears that flowed would exhaust him enough to get some sleep.

CHAPTER EIGHT

The morning's bright light shone through the window blinds, waking Tyler from his fitful sleep. He groaned at the dull pain pulsating through his head and reached for the pills on the bedside table. Taking a chug from a water bottle and swallowing four pills, he sunk back into Jessica's guest bed.

Still real, not a nightmare.

The crushing weight of despair enveloped him, a scab that refused to heal from his incessant picking. He wanted to cry, to shout, to curse the universe for shitting all over his life, but what good would any of it do? He'd lost everything. His boyfriend, his career, his apartment. All gone.

The only silver lining besides his overattentive mother was Jessica. She'd been there to pick up the pieces: letting him stay with her, making him meals, consoling him when she wasn't working. Tyler was beyond grateful, and while he knew he'd have to tell her the truth about what happened to Gabe soon, the thought of it terrified him.

His story was unbelievable, and without any concrete evidence to back it up no one had taken him seriously so far.

If he told Jessica, would her support vanish into the void like everything else? An image of Gabe flashed through Tyler's mind, cutting at him like glass shards in his heart. When would he stop feeling like he was dying from the inside out?

A knock at the bedroom door interrupted his agony. "Ty, you awake?" Jessica's muffled voice came through the door.

Tyler wiped at his eyes. "Yeah, come on in."

The door opened and Jessica walked in wearing a black ribbed sweater and skinny jeans that accentuated her curves. Her hair was a long honey-colored ombré that fell in perfect waves, emphasizing her red lips and glowing dark skin. Her image was a masterful reflection of why she'd risen so high in the cosmetics company she worked for, but right now it just made Tyler feel like shit. When was the last time he'd combed his hair or took a shower? He bunched up the comforter between his arms, hoping it would hide his glaring imperfections.

Jessica sat on the edge of the bed. "Good morning. How are you holding up?"

"It feels like someone's been kicking my head all night."

Jessica frowned. "I'm sorry. The doctor said ten to fourteen days was the standard recovery time, so you've got a few more days of ick ahead of you. Anything I can do?"

"Put me out of my misery? God knows I deserve it."

"Hun, you know I love you, but you can't keep blaming yourself for what happened to Gabe."

"Why not? It's my fault he's gone. You didn't see ..."

"See what? Come on, Ty, talk to me."

Images of the recent past flooded through his mind's eye: him and Gabe fleeing the ruins, the monstrous spirit attacking Gabe in the forest, Gabe's skeletal face lolled to one side, unresponsive as he begged him to wake up. Tyler stared down at his arms. "I ... I can't. But I want to."

Jessica patted his hand. "I understand, it's too soon. Just

know I'm here for you, okay? I have to go to work, but maybe tonight we can Netflix and chill?"

Tyler smiled weakly. "Yeah, that would be nice."

Jessica got up from the bed and smoothed her clothes. "That's the spirit. Try and get some fresh air for a little bit if you feel up to it. The forecast says it's gonna be another sunny day!"

Jessica left the room, and Tyler listened as she left the house and started her car. When she drove off, he let out the breath he'd been holding in.

He felt terrible for not telling Jessica the truth, but how could he without sounding crazy? *What really happened to Gabe? Oh, he was killed by an ancient spirit who loves to suck the life out of people. Happens all the time.* She'd send him to the looney bin so fast it would make his head spin.

Feeling sorry for himself Tyler burrowed underneath the covers, hoping to sleep away his troubles. After some fruitless tossing and turning, he forced himself out of bed with a groan and walked over to the bathroom. Flicking the light on, he caught his reflection and grimaced. The skin around his icy blue eyes was puffy with dark circles, his tan complexion had paled to a sickly pasty shade, and he was in desperate need of a shave and a haircut.

Now he understood why Jessica had prodded him to get out of bed. He was falling apart, and she couldn't be the only one trying to put him back together. He shot himself another look in the mirror and sighed. This was gonna take a while.

An hour later, Tyler left the bathroom cleanly shaven, showered, and moisturized. He was still disappointed with how beaten down he looked, but grooming could only do so much. On his way back to the guest room he decided to attempt some outdoor time. The painful throb of his head had dulled a considerable amount thanks to the pain meds he had taken, and he hoped some fresh air would add some much needed pigment and positivity.

He put on some shorts, a tee shirt, and sunglasses, then headed downstairs and went outside. Tyler recoiled as the Texas sun's scathing light beat down on him, accompanied by a wave of sweltering heat. *Geez, when did hell take over the earth?* The day of Gabe's funeral last week was warm, but nothing compared to this blazing inferno.

Forcing himself forward, Tyler walked down the sidewalk heading south. The gayborhood was blocks away, but the hike would be worth it. Oak Lawn was a trendy area that was home to the gay population of Dallas. Tyler had always felt safe and supported there years prior to meeting Gabe.

He strolled at a leisurely pace, enjoying the blue skies and empty city blocks only a late Wednesday morning could provide. Reaching Cedar Springs Road he ambled onto the street, passing a pharmacy, the firehouse, and Round-Up, a country western night club that wouldn't be open for some time.

A middle-aged gay couple approached on the wide side-walk, holding hands. They smiled at Tyler as they passed, and a raw emptiness clenched in his gut that made him stop in his tracks. They looked so happy … He and Gabe were supposed to have that, to love each other, grow old together, to have a life worth living.

Tyler took a deep breath. *It's going to be okay. This is how the grieving process works.* He didn't believe the regurgitated words he recycled from Jessica, but he hoped it would sink in if he kept repeating it. Another sensation stirred in his stomach, this time an angry rumbling.

He glanced around and spotted Hunky's, his and Gabe's favorite burger joint. His stomach grumbled again and he headed towards the restaurant, figuring the best way to drown his sorrows was some fried pickles and a greasy burger.

Tyler entered Hunky's and was greeted by the insatiable aroma of grease, grilled meat, and fried food. He got into the short line forming at the counter, taking in his surroundings as he waited. The cooks shouted orders to each other in the background as they clanged around in the kitchen. Several gay couples sat at tables, talking to each other with loving expressions on their faces. Tyler's gaze meandered to the person in line ahead of him and his body tensed up.

The man was tall, broad-shouldered, and had long brown hair pulled up into a man bun. Even the way he slouched seemed just like …

"Gabe?"

The man turned around, cocking an eyebrow. It wasn't him.

"Oh god, I'm so sorry." The all-consuming void within Tyler reemerged with a vengeance, pulling at his core with cold, barbed fingers.

Overwhelmed, he backed out of the line and left the restaurant, heading back to Jessica's as fast as he could. What was wrong with him? Gabe was dead and he was never coming back. Did he really think this whole nightmare would end and Gabe would just magically appear out of nowhere? Coming here had been an awful idea.

With a terrible clenching tightness in his chest Tyler made it back to Jessica's, sinking against the front door once he was inside. He didn't know how to move on, but he had to do something to get some closure or he'd just keep torturing himself. Aching for something to hold onto, Tyler went upstairs to Jessica's office where he'd stored some boxes of Gabe's things from the trip and their apartment.

He cleared some space in the middle of the room, then grabbed some scissors and cut the tape off several boxes.

After digging through a seemingly endless ocean of paper documents, he found Gabe's laptop and the books he'd brought to Altalona. As he took the items out of the box, a thin object fell into his lap.

Tyler froze as he looked upon the leather bracelet Gabe had given him several months ago. The pendant in its center had a series of interlocking circles and ovals that made its beautiful, flowery shape. He clutched the bracelet to his chest, rocking back and forth gently. Finding it was like having a little piece of Gabe back. Tears ran down Tyler's cheeks as he remembered the events of that magical night, wishing it had never ended.

"KEEP YOUR EYES CLOSED," Gabe said as he guided Tyler further up the stairwell, the lively music from the bar downstairs a muffled echo.

Tyler spread his fingers ever so slightly from in front of his eyes.

"Hey, I mean it!"

"Okay, okay. Where are we going anyway?" Tyler bet Gabe wanted to surprise him for his birthday. He was always doing thoughtful and romantic things like that. Moonlit walks, picnics, and hikes with dazzling scenic viewpoints were just the tip of the iceberg, and Tyler relished all the lovely surprises that came with dating Gabe.

"You'll see. We're almost there," Gabe promised. After several more moments of blind climbing Gabe stopped Tyler by placing his strong calloused hands firmly on his chest.

"Careful babe, you're gonna get me all hot and bothered."

Gabe snorted. "Sexy time later, I promise. Alright, eyes are still closed?"

"Yep."

Gabe opened a door before them with a rusty squeak, and a warm wind blew on Tyler's face as he was led outside. "Okay, open your eyes in three. Two. One!"

Tyler uncovered his eyes and gasped. All of his closest friends were gathered before him on the large decorated rooftop of the building.

"Happy Birthday!" they roared in unison.

Tyler grinned from ear to ear. "Oh my god, you guys!" He looked at Gabe and gave him a fake jab. Several of his friends chuckled, and he gave Gabe a quick kiss before greeting them properly. After getting his fill of hugs and well wishes, Tyler returned to his boyfriend.

He looped an arm through Gabe's and they wandered the rooftop, taking in the ambience. Comfy chairs and covered tables were placed throughout the space, with colorful plants occupying the edges and corners. An overhead trellis of soft, glowing lights illuminated the area with a cozy feel, and a small bar sat at the far end where some of his friends had gathered.

"Do you like it?" Gabe asked.

Tyler cocked an eyebrow. "*Like* it? I can't believe you pulled this off."

"Well, I didn't do this *all* by myself."

As if on cue, Jessica approached them with a glass of champagne in hand. Her black hair was pulled back in an elaborate braid that made her look regal and she wore a shimmering gold dress that hugged her hourglass figure.

Tyler ran to her and gave her a bear hug.

"How did we do, Ty?" Jessica said with a wink.

"I think I'm still in shock. This is just ... "

"Amazing?" Gabe wrapped his arms around Tyler from behind, his chin resting on his shoulder.

Tyler craned his neck and gave Gabe a prolonged kiss, enjoying the bittersweet taste of champagne on his tongue.

"Thank you. No one's ever done something like this for me."

"Well, close attention must be paid. This isn't just anybody's birthday. It's yours, baby."

Jessica took a long swig of her champagne and sighed. "I need another drink. You lovebirds are making me sick!" She stuck her tongue out at them playfully before heading over to the bar.

Gabe broke his embrace with Tyler, then offered his hand. "Come on, let's go somewhere a little more private. I got you something."

Tyler gave Gabe another kiss, then let him lead him away. He didn't care what his gift was. As long as Gabe was with him, he had everything he could possibly want.

They passed several small clusters of his friends, receiving amused looks and nudges before Gabe stopped at an isolated corner.

Tyler grinned. "So, is this where you take advantage of me?"

Gabe laughed. "No, not *yet*." He pulled out a thin rectangular box from his back pocket and presented it to Tyler. "Happy Birthday, Tyler."

Tyler accepted the box and smiled. "Thanks, Gabe." As he removed the lid, Tyler took a sharp inhale. Inside was a stunning brown leather bracelet with a circular pendant in its center made of interlocking circles and ovals. Tyler removed the bracelet from the box and inspected it closely. "Wow, it's gorgeous. I love it!"

Gabe held out a hand. "May I?"

Tyler nodded, and Gabe helped secure the bracelet around his wrist. "Beautiful, just like you." Gabe's gaze lingered on Tyler, a dreamy look in his eye.

"What's that look for?"

Gabe bit his lip. "Sorry. There's something that's been on

my mind for a while now. I didn't want to take attention away from your birthday, but … hell, I can't take it anymore. Tyler, I love you."

Tyler stifled a gasp. Out of all the things Gabe could say, he wasn't expecting that. They'd been dating a little over six months and he'd been so caught up in the current of endless dates and long sleepless nights of passion that he hadn't truly considered this. Was he really ready to take this relationship to the next level?

Tyler looked into Gabe's green eyes. Gabe made him feel safe, made him smile, laugh, and forget the craziness of the world around them. But most of all Tyler knew that Gabe cared about him truly and unconditionally, and that was something he'd never known with another man. Filled with the full intensity of his feelings for Gabe, Tyler took his hand and spoke what he knew to be true. "I love you too, Gabe."

They kissed as cheers broke out all around them.

TYLER WOKE in Jessica's small office, a pillow underneath his head and his face still damp with tears. He wiped them away and sat up, eyeing the headrest. Jessica must've found him in here when she got home. Suppressing his painful memories of Gabe and the bracelet, he sat up with a groan and checked his phone.

His mom had called three times, leaving several voice-mails. Tyler rolled his eyes, imagining what she'd probably said. *Are you okay? What can I do to make you feel better? Why haven't you called me back yet?* He knew she meant well, but no matter how many times he insisted he needed space and time alone, she wouldn't listen. Resolving to call her before she flew off the handle, Tyler put his phone back in his pocket and got to his feet.

The faint aroma of food cooking drifted to his nostrils, making his stomach gurgle excitedly. Tyler went downstairs to the kitchen, a roomy rectangular space with a large serving hatch that overlooked the dining room and connecting living room. As he entered, Jessica was pulling a tray of fried chicken with toppings out from the stove.

"Hey, Jess."

Jessica glanced over as she set the tray on a thick wooden slab. "Oh, you're awake! I saw you sleeping in the office, but I didn't want to wake you. You might want to choose a more comfy place to snooze next time."

Tyler chuckled. "Yeah, I guess I didn't realize how tired I was. I was just sorting through some of Gabe's stuff. Dinner smells great."

Jessica made an exaggerated bow. "Why thank you, sir. It's your fave, chicken parm and spaghetti. Why don't you clear off the dining room table while I finish up and we can eat there?"

"Sure."

Tyler tidied up the dining table and set some plates and silverware before heading to the bathroom. He finished his business and washed up, noticing he was still wearing the bracelet Gabe had given him. He frowned, still unsure of how he felt about his earlier freakout. Maybe he should–

"Dinner's ready!" Jessica's muffled voice rang in the distance.

"Coming!" he shouted back.

Tyler went back to the dining room. A serving plate of fried chicken topped with marinara and cheese sat atop the table alongside a bowl full of steaming spaghetti. The soft, mellow tones of *Sade* carried over from the living room.

Jessica came in from the kitchen with two wine glasses in one hand and a bottle of red in the other. "I thought maybe we'd start a little early with the wine. You down?"

"Hell yeah. Oh wait, the doctor said I shouldn't drink with a concussion."

Jessica grimaced. "Damn, you're right. That was a terrible suggestion. I'm sorry." Jessica turned back toward the kitchen.

"Wait!" Jessica turned back around, and Tyler took the glasses from her. "A little bit won't kill me."

"Okay, but if you start feeling woozy I'm cutting you off."

"Deal."

Jessica poured a moderate amount of wine into Tyler's glass, then filled hers generously.

"That bad of a day, huh?" Tyler asked.

"Hun, you have no idea."

Jessica joined him at the table and they served themselves.

Tyler took a large bite of his chicken parm, savoring the sharp taste of parmesan and the succulent fried chicken. "Oh my god, this is so good. Thanks for doing dinner. We'll have to take turns."

Jessica took a swig of her wine. "Really?"

"Yeah, totally. I've got some culinary tricks up my sleeve. Wanna tell me about your shit day? I could use a distraction."

"I was hoping you'd ask. I've had the day from hell." Jessica took a bite of spaghetti, then washed it down with some wine. "So I left for work this morning heading to NorthPark, right? I was supposed to be training some of the girls there. But right when I'm pulling in to park I get a call that I've been transferred to Town East for the day. Town East!

"Now, you know I love helping everyone fine tune their application techniques and showing them what's trending, but Ty, some of these people have so little experience it's like starting from the ground up. What's even worse is Town East sales are probably the worst in the entire region. Why did they even send me there? I can't single-handedly save them!"

Jessica went on for a little while longer and Tyler nodded along to her troubles. He always loved hearing her talk about her work in the makeup industry. It all sounded so fabulous even though she wanted to pull her hair out sometimes.

Jessica concluded her rant with a deep sigh and took another sip of her red. "So that was my day. How was yours? You said you went through some of Gabe's stuff. Did you get a chance to go outside?"

Tyler picked at his fingernails under the table. "Uh, yeah. I went out for a little bit, but nothing crazy. I'll probably try again tomorrow. Most of Gabe's stuff was old junk and papers, but I found his laptop and this." Tyler displayed the bracelet on his wrist.

"Oh, I always loved that bracelet he gave you. Can I see it for a sec?"

"Sure." Tyler unclasped it and handed it over.

Jessica eyed it appreciatively, running a thumb over the pendant before giving it back. "That's a flower of life symbol, right?"

"Oh, I'm not sure. I guess so."

"Well regardless, I'm glad you found it. That night on the rooftop was so beautiful. Gabe put so much effort into making it perfect."

A flurry of images ran through Tyler's mind at Jessica's words: Gabe's irresistible smile, the tingle he'd get when he placed his hand on his lower back, the breathtaking way he kissed, like their lips were perfectly aligned, destined for one another. Tyler stifled a sob as tears spilled down his cheeks.

"Oh god, I'm such an idiot." Jessica scooted beside him. "I shouldn't have brought up all those memories."

Tyler sniffled and wiped his tears away. "I just miss him, you know? I mean, a week ago we were in Peru and now … How am I supposed to pick up all the pieces? I don't even know where to begin."

Jessica wrapped her arms tight around Tyler. "Hey, it's going to be alright. These things take time, and I meant it when I said you could stay here as long as you need. When my dad died I was devastated, but each day a tiny piece of that hurt would lift off of me until one day I was back to my normal self again. You'll get there, I promise."

Tyler rested his head on Jessica's shoulder, hoping she was right.

CHAPTER NINE

Tyler awoke the next morning with a groan, his head pounding as if he'd rushed headfirst into a brick wall. Forcing himself up in bed, he cursed his poor decisions from last night.

After dinner, he and Jessica stayed up late watching trashy reality tv shows and drinking wine. He'd snuck little splashes into his glass when Jessica wasn't looking, which got easier the more she drank. By the end of the night he was feeling dizzy, but he ignored the sensation and kept drinking. Tyler's head pulsed with a vengeance. *Ugh, never again.*

He popped a couple pain pills, then laid back in bed and fell asleep. When he awoke several hours later, his pain had diminished a considerable amount and he was brimming with energy.

Not wanting to jinx his resiliency, he got out of bed and washed up in the bathroom. As he scanned himself in the mirror, he noticed the bags under his blue eyes weren't quite as puffy and dark, and his skin not as pale and dry. Even the weight of his loss felt a bit lighter today. Whether it was just hopeful thinking or not, he decided to take advantage.

Tyler went back to his room and texted Clay, a close friend of his. When he agreed to meet him for a walk Tyler changed into some gym clothes and headed out his bedroom door, nearly running into Jessica.

"Oh, sorry!" Tyler apologized.

Jessica smiled, showcasing her glowing rosy cheeks and matching pink eyeshadow. "No worries. I was just about to let you know I was leaving for the day. I'm back at North-Park today, and–Wait, are you going to the gym or something?"

"Something like that. I woke up with all this energy, so I'm meeting Clay over at Katy Trail for a walk."

"Oh, that's great! I wish I felt as good as you do. It's gonna be a hardcore coffee day for me. Alright, have fun and I'll see you tonight."

"See ya."

Tyler left the house with Jessica, waving her goodbye as she departed her driveway. Katy Trail was just over a mile from Jessica's split-level, and with the mid-morning streets being virtually empty he made quick work of the distance.

As he neared the trail, Tyler checked his phone. Clay hadn't messaged him anything further so he took in the view. The sun's radiant light shone upon the forest of trees that lined the wide concrete trail ahead, their branches swaying in the late summer wind. Swaths of people traversed the broad passage in numerous modes of transportation, from walking their dogs to rollerblading to riding their bikes.

Watching the activity on the crowded trail made Tyler's stomach churn. What if he thought he saw Gabe again or had another gnarly flashback? Suddenly he wasn't sure this hike was such a good idea after all.

"Hey, Tyler!"

Tyler turned at the calling of his name. Clay waved as he crossed the street in short shorts and a bright yellow tank top that showcased his bulking biceps, pecs, and slim physique. His short blond curls bounced in time with his steps.

Tyler brought Clay in for a hug, feeling self-conscious for his choice of baggy gym clothes. Clay was his gay gym head friend that had fully embraced the thrill of sex. His bed hopping had become practically legendary in the past few years thanks to his build, chiseled facial features, and bright green eyes. There was no guy he couldn't have, and those that resisted him quickly caved under his charms. Tyler had always had a brotherly connection with Clay, something he was counting on now.

Clay pulled back from Tyler's embrace, his expression severe. "I heard the news. How are you holding up?"

"It's pretty rough right now. I'm staying with Jessica just trying to make sense of everything. My life had direction with Gabe. Now ..." Tears welled in Tyler's eyes and he wiped them away with a chuckle. "Now I can't even go outside without losing my shit. Same thing happened to me yesterday."

"Hey, you're allowed to cope and grieve however it comes to you, alright?"

Tyler grimaced as more images of Gabe surfaced in his mind. "Let's start walking, yeah? It'll give me something to focus on. I haven't quite recovered from my concussion so I can't jog yet."

"Don't worry about speed, baby steps are just fine. Besides, I can check all the hotties out easier this way."

Tyler laughed. "You're crazy."

Clay waggled his eyebrows. "It's the crazy ones that have all the fun. But seriously, Tyler. I'm always here if you need anything. You don't have to go through this alone."

"Thanks. Why don't you tell me what you've been up to? I bet you've got some juicy stories."

Clay cocked an eyebrow. "Oh, you have *no* idea."

They walked the trail at a brisk pace, Clay filling Tyler in with scandalous stories of manhunting Oak Lawn and other raunchy escapades. As Tyler listened, he wondered what the future had in store for him. Clay's carefree life of screwing every hot guy he saw didn't appeal to him, but neither did the solitary existence of a hermit. When would he be free from this agonizing limbo, living in the shadow of his and Gabe's love?

"Um, your phone's ringing," Clay said, snapping Tyler out of his thoughts.

"Oh, shit!" Tyler stopped walking and fished his phone out of his pocket. He didn't recognize the number but answered it anyway. "Hello?"

"Hello, is this Tyler Collins?" a woman's voice said on the line.

"Yeah, that's me."

"I'm Detective Kirby Kilgore with the Highland Park Police Department. There's been an incident, and we'd like to ask you some questions."

"An incident? What do you mean? What happened?"

"I'm not at liberty to discuss any details over the phone. Could you come by our location over on Drexel sometime today to talk?"

"Um, yeah, sure. I can be there in an hour or two."

"Alright. Thank you for your cooperation."

The woman hung up and Tyler froze in place, perplexed. Highland Park? Why were they calling *him*? He didn't know anyone from that area, did he?

"Who was that?" Clay asked.

"Highland Park Police Department."

"Really? What the hell do they want *you* for?"

"Your guess is as good as mine. They said something happened and they want to talk to me, but I don't think I have any friends that live around there."

Clay made some educated guesses from their mutual friends as Tyler mused over the strange phone call. There had to be something he was missing. Highland Park was a ritzy part of Dallas he steered clear of because of all the old conservatives that retired there. That and he could never afford to live there anyways. *Wait a sec. Old people. Conservatives.* A chill shot through Tyler's core.

"Oh my god, it has to be Gabe's parents! I have to go."

"Whoa, just calm down, will you? I'll take you. Jessica's still at work, right?"

"Yeah, but I don't wanna put you out."

"I'm helping you and that's that. Besides, I wanna know what the tea is. Come on, let's get changed and head over."

Tyler followed Clay back to his car, worry and anxiety warring inside his head. Whatever happened to Jim and Nancy, if the police were involved it couldn't be good.

CLAY PARKED his Camaro on the side of the Highland Park Police Department building. "You ready?" he asked as the engine idled.

Tyler sighed. "I think so, but it's not like I have much of a choice anyways."

"Sorry, buddy. I'm sure it'll be over in no time."

Clay killed the engine and they got out of the car. Tyler followed Clay on the sidewalk to the front of the multi-level property. The police department was an imposing structure, square, squat, and made of brown brick. Its windows were heavily tinted, providing no hint at the activity inside.

Tyler's stomach bunched up in knots as they approached the front entry. He'd never been inside a police department before and didn't know what to expect. He assumed they probably wanted to ask him some routine questions, but that didn't make him any less nervous. If something had happened to Jim and Nancy, his tense history with them could make the authorities suspicious of him.

Through the double doors they entered the main hall, a rundown corridor with cheap laminate flooring, harsh fluorescents, and old wooden surfaces. Tyler and Clay ambled to a long kiosk ahead of them where a cop with receding black hair sat behind the desk, his eyes focused on his computer screen.

He grimaced when he saw Clay and Tyler. "Afternoon. What can I help you with?"

Tyler took a step forward. "I'm here to see Detective Kirby Kilgore. My name's Tyler Collins."

"Who's that?" The cop asked, gesturing to Clay.

"My ride."

The cop shrugged, then started typing on his keyboard. "Collins, Collins. Ah, here you are. I'll let the detective know you're here."

"Not necessary, Bennett," a feminine voice called to their right.

Tyler turned. A thin woman with shoulder length red hair in a blue pantsuit stood several feet away, her vibrant blue eyes fixed on him.

"Tyler Collins?" she asked.

He nodded.

"I'm Detective Kilgore."

"Nice to meet you. This is my friend Clay. He drove me here."

"I'm sorry, he'll have to wait out here. Please, make yourself comfortable. Tyler, if you'll follow me."

Tyler looked to Clay. He shrugged, then plopped into a plastic chair set against the wall.

Detective Kilgore led Tyler upstairs and down a hallway

lined with doors. She stopped at the last door to the right and opened it, gesturing him inside.

Tyler studied the room from the doorway. Within was a simple table and two chairs with a mirror behind it. Sudden heat flushed to his face. Was that one of those one-way mirrors? Would they be listening in on their interview? Did they think he did something?

"Relax," the detective said. "You're only here to answer some questions I have. Please, take a seat."

Tyler went inside and sat at the table with his back to the wide mirror.

Detective Kilgore shut the door and joined him, her expression grave as she steepled her fingers together. "First things first, I wanted to offer my condolences on your loss. We've been working hard to figure out what happened to Gabriel."

Tyler fought to keep his expression neutral. As much as he wanted to correct her on what actually happened, he'd already argued with police several times and didn't want to stir the pot again. It wouldn't help anything, and unlike the others the detective seemed cool-headed and rational. "Um, thank you."

"That being said, I called you here because an incident occurred last night involving Gabriel's parents Jim and Nancy Price."

"What happened to them? Are they okay?"

"I'm not at liberty to give specifics. All I can tell you is that they were assaulted last night."

A sudden weight settled in Tyler's chest. "An assault? Who would attack them?"

"That's why we're here now. Mr. Collins, have you ever harbored any ill will towards Mr. or Mrs. Price?"

"What? No, of course not! Gabe's parents always gave him a hard time about being gay and I didn't like them all that much because of that, but I would never hurt them. Do you seriously think I could do something like that?"

"Please, just answer my questions as straightforward as you can. It is my duty to make these inquiries to determine if you may be connected to the event that occurred last night. Let's move on. Can you tell me your whereabouts last night?"

"Yeah. I was hanging out with my friend Jessica, Jessica Buchanan."

"Alright. And what time would you say you two were hanging out?"

"All night since she got home from work about six p.m. Right now I'm staying with her. I couldn't afford me and Gabe's old place on my own, and she offered to let me stay there until I got back on my feet."

Detective Kilgore jotted down a few notes on a notepad. "And would Jessica be able to verify your whereabouts last night?"

"Of course." Tyler gave the detective Jessica's contact information. "Is there anything more you can tell me about what happened?

"I'm sorry, I cannot." The detective glanced down at her notes. "Tell me more about your interactions with Jim and Nancy. Have you spoken with them often in the past or since you came back from Peru?"

Tyler shook his head. "Given how they felt about Gabe being gay, I never really spoke with them unless they were having a family spat and Gabe wouldn't answer his phone. They'd call me, then I'd hand the phone over to Gabe. But when I came back to the states, they started harassing me over the phone."

"Harassing you?"

"Yeah, they'd call me several times a day, blaming me for what happened to Gabe. I understood where they were coming from. I mean, they're his parents. They want all the answers, and so do I. I tried to reason with them. I told them the authorities were trying to figure everything out, but they wouldn't listen and kept harassing me so I had to block them. After that, I had a runin with Jim and Nancy at Gabe's funeral. It didn't go very well."

Detective Kilgore cocked an eyebrow. "Oh?"

"They said I wasn't welcome there. I get that they couldn't really understand what Gabe and I had, but it really hurt that they wouldn't even let me pay my respects, ya know?"

Detective Kilgore frowned. "I can understand how frustrated that would make you feel. Were you still feeling the effects of your concussion at that time?"

"Yeah, I could hardly get around at that point. We started arguing, but I had to leave because I became ill. I'm lucky Jessica was there to get me back home in one piece."

The detective wrote down some additional notes on her legal pad, then fixed her gaze back on Tyler. "Do you know of anyone close to the Price's that may have wanted to do them harm?"

Tyler shrugged. "I honestly have no clue. I always stayed away from them and their circle. The whole bible thumper thing isn't my cup of tea."

The detective's head lowered slightly, and her lips pressed tight into a grimace. "Alright, thank you for your time, Mr. Collins. I think we're done here for now. I'll see you out and will be in touch should we need anything further."

Detective Kilgore led the way out of the interview room to the main hall downstairs where Clay waited. After a curt handshake, she gave him her business card. "If you think of anything else, please give me a call."

The detective went on her way, and Tyler and Clay vacated the building.

Once they were back in Clay's car, Clay's gaze was laser

focused on Tyler. "Okay, give me all the deets. What happened?"

"They really didn't tell me much of anything. All I know is that Gabe's parents were attacked last night."

"What? By who?"

"That's what they're trying to figure out."

"Okay, but they don't think you did anything, do they?"

"I don't think so, but it doesn't look great either. I was present when Gabe died, and his parents were attacked shortly after I came back from Peru. God, this is such a hot fucking mess. What am I supposed to do?"

Clay put a hand on Tyler's shoulder. "Nothing, just let them do their job. You were with Jessica last night, so focus on your recovery and moving forward, yeah?"

"Okay. Can you take me back to Jessica's? I'm so over this day."

"Of course, buddy."

Clay started the car and Tyler stared out the window, flustered.

Gabe's parents may be obnoxious bible thumpers, but what could they have done to warrant an attack from someone? Part of him wanted to ignore the whole incident. It was none of his business, and he needed to concentrate on moving on with his life. On the other hand, he worried that Gabe's parents were in real danger. Should he check on them, or would that just exacerbate things? Tyler's thoughts spun in circles as he tried to make sense of the awkward situation.

～

TYLER PEERED through the oven door's window, resisting the urge to open the door to check on the stuffed bell peppers again. He wasn't the greatest cook, but he'd made

90

this dish so many times with Gabe he'd memorized the recipe. Cooking turned out to be a great distraction from the day's stressful events, and with the addition of some soothing tunes in the background he was feeling a lot better.

The oven timer blared and Tyler quickly turned it off. Just as he was putting on oven mitts, the front door to the home opened, followed by the clack of Jessica's high heels.

Tyler took the food out of the stove and hurried over to the preset dining room table, placing the tray of stuffed peppers next to the spanish rice and black beans. He straightened the frilly apron around his waist that he'd borrowed from the hanging rack and assumed a silly over-stated pose.

As Jessica entered the living room she glanced his way and beamed. "Oh my god, Ty, you cooked!" She walked over, set her purse down, and gave Tyler a hug. "Thank you so much. This smells great."

"Of course. I told you I had some culinary tricks up my sleeve. How do you like my getup?" He waggled his eyebrows.

Jessica slapped his butt. "You can be my wifey any day. Okay, so I don't wanna kill this good vibe you've got going, but on the way home I received a call from the Highland Park Police Department. They asked me to verify you were with me last night. What's going on?"

"You might wanna sit down for this. Let's fill up our plates, then I'll get into it."

The two of them sat down and loaded their plates. After taking a couple bites of their meal, Tyler went over the day's events.

"Alright, so I met Clay out at Katy Trail for a walk, but while we were out there I got a call from the Highland Park Police Department. Gabe's parents were attacked last night."

Jessica gasped and set her fork down. "Oh my god. Are they okay?"

"I don't know. They wouldn't tell me anything."

"Jesus, this is insane. What are you going to do?"

"I don't know. I kinda don't wanna get involved, but I'm worried that Jim and Nancy are really in danger. I wasn't planning on ever talking to them again after what happened at Gabe's funeral and I don't want to make anything worse, but I can't do nothing either. It's such a clusterfuck."

Jessica placed a hand on Tyler's. "It's a tough situation. I trust your judgment, whatever you decide to do. You've been through so much already with Gabe, and I–Sorry, is it too soon to talk about him?"

"No, it's okay. I think I'm ready. I've been hesitant to say anything because of how unbelievable it is. I didn't want you to think I was crazy."

"Ty, I'm here for you. I won't judge you."

"You're sure?" With a nod from Jessica, Tyler explained the events of what happened in Altalona. He left out no detail, starting with his and Gabe's bickering and the strange actions of the townspeople before moving on to the terrifying attack at the ruins and what happened at the hospital.

When he finished Jessica sat in stunned silence.

"Well?" Tyler prodded.

Jessica started to speak, then stopped herself. "I … Jesus, I don't know what to say."

"I told you you'd think I was crazy."

"I don't, it's just … it's a lot to take in. I thought you didn't even believe in that stuff."

"I didn't until all this shit happened."

Jessica sighed. "I don't know. Are you absolutely sure about this? Maybe there's another explanation."

Tyler's brows furrowed. "You don't believe me?"

"That's not what I'm saying. I'm just interpreting things

differently. I do believe you came into contact with some-thing in those ruins that did a number on you and Gabe, but maybe it's more rational than you think. You said those ruins were ancient and no one ever goes there, right? There's no telling what kinds of germs, bacteria, or airborne particles exist there that could've affected your mind. And since no one has been there in ages there's no way for anyone to verify what really happened."

"Then how can you explain the doctors not being able to figure out what was wrong with Gabe? Or how he was partially mummified? Or the fact that I was marked with this?" Tyler pulled down his shirt, revealing the scar that Ayar Kachi had given him. "Ayar Kachi gave me this scar before he forced me to watch him kill Gabe."

Jessica's eyes went wide with shock. "Oh my god. He did that to you and Gabe? What did the police say when you told them?"

"Most of them thought whoever attacked us did it to mark their victims, which I guess isn't far from the truth, but some of them thought I did it to throw the scent off of myself. Either way, they weren't able to prove anything so they had to let me go. The whole experience just left me feeling numb. Gabe meant everything to me ..." Tyler's vision blurred as tears sprang to his eyes.

Jessica scooted over and wrapped her arms around him. "Oh, Ty. I had no idea."

They sat there in silence for a long moment, the raw emotion of Tyler's loss filling his being until it began to wane. He slowly pulled away from Jessica's embrace. "Thanks for not thinking I'm crazy. I know I've been really emotional, but I still don't even know how to process all of this."

"You have every right to feel whatever you need to feel. Your whole life was torn away from you, and no one has been listening to you and what you've been through. Is there anything I can do to help?"

Tyler gave a weak smile. "You've already done so much for me, but just asking helps. After what happened today, I'm not really sure what I should do. Part of me wants to move forward, but I have this gut feeling that I should call Gabe's parents and make sure they're okay. I know it sounds strange given our history, but I think it's what Gabe would've wanted, and it feels like the right thing to do. Maybe it'll even help me move on."

Jessica gave Tyler's hand a squeeze. "I think that's a great idea. It's such a gracious thing to do, and I hope it gives you the closure you need to move on."

Tyler squeezed her hand back in response. "Me too, boo. Me too."

CHAPTER TEN

The next morning, Tyler sat at the dining room table with Jessica after grabbing some coffee and a granola bar.

Jessica took a large sip from her steaming mug. "Good morning. How's your day starting out?"

"Eh, it's a mixed bag. I'm hardly feeling any pain from my concussion, but Jim and Nancy haven't answered my calls. I was thinking of stopping by their house. Maybe they'd be willing to talk."

"Are you sure that's the best idea? They haven't responded to you, and if they were just attacked they probably won't be too happy to have any unexpected visitors, especially you. No offense."

"What other choice do I have? Worst case, they'll tell me to screw off. Best case, they tell me what happened and I can help them sort things out, maybe even mend the rift between us. Either way, if I do this I can wipe my hands clean knowing I did everything I could to make things better for Gabe and his family."

"I don't know, Ty. At the very least I think it would be

better if I took the day off and went with you. You don't have a car right now."

Tyler waved her off. "Don't worry, I'll just get an Uber. I can text you updates if it makes you feel better."

"Alright, if you insist. Just be careful." Jessica glanced down at her phone and jolted, setting her mug on the table. "Oh my god, I'm gonna be late! I have to go. Do you mind?" She gestured towards her empty plate and mug.

"I'll take care of it. Go, before you upset the makeup gods."

"Okay, I'll see you later. Good luck." Jessica gave him a quick hug, then hurried out the door.

Tyler finished his breakfast and put their plates in the dishwasher before going upstairs and changing into some decent clothes. Afterwards he paced his room, trying to make a final decision on whether he would go through with his idea or not.

Jessica had made some valid points. The Prices hadn't answered his attempts at communication, and having just been attacked they wouldn't be very appreciative of him dropping by their house unannounced. Still, Tyler's gut told him there was something more to their situation, and the more he fought the feeling the more insistent it became.

Unable to shake his unwavering intuition, he pulled Uber up on his phone and ordered a ride. He tapped his fingers against his leg as he watched the vehicle's slow progress on his screen, hoping this encounter wouldn't be a repeat of his last run in with Gabe's parents.

Tyler glanced out the window as his Uber rolled up to the end of the long cobbled driveway of Gabe's parent's house. Jim and Nancy's two-story french country home exuded success and wealth. Its stone exterior looked freshly washed, and every detail seemed meticulously thought out, from the sloped roof and shutters that complimented the stone's natural hue to the second floor patio outlined by ivy with not a leaf out of place.

"Everything okay?" the driver asked.

"Yeah, sorry." Tyler tipped the driver on his phone and exited the vehicle. As it sped off Tyler faced the house again, his gut churning. *I can't believe I'm doing this.*

Tyler had only visited this place once before when Gabe and him got serious. Tyler was Gabe's first long-term boyfriend, and from Jim and Nancy's cold reception it was clear that they hoped Gabe's homosexuality was a phase he'd grow out of. Once their awkward visit was over, Gabe promised they wouldn't have to come back, and they never did. It had bruised Gabe's relationship with his parents, but Tyler never blamed himself for that. They were just being who they were. Here and queer, take it or leave it.

As Tyler started down the cobblestone driveway, his phone buzzed in his pocket. "Jesus Christ," he muttered when he saw that it was his mother. Suppressing his irritation, he answered the call. "Hey mom."

"It's about time you answered!" she cajoled.

"Sorry, things have been really crazy."

"How was the funeral?"

"Not good. Gabe's parents were upset that I showed up and it turned into this whole thing."

"Do you want me to talk to them?"

"No mom, let's just leave it alone. They have their reasons."

"Really, I don't mind. If you give me their address, I could whip up some baked goods and drop by, explain to them how important Gabe was to you–"

"Mom, no."

"And honestly, I'm curious to see the place. You always made it sound so fancy."

Ugh, she's smothering me. I don't want her advice, I don't need her help. I just need to figure this out myself! "Mom! Will you just drop it?"

His mother went silent.

"Listen, I just need some space. This is all too much for me."

Tyler heard a sniffle on the other line and his stomach dropped.

"I understand," his mom croaked. "I'll give you some space."

"No, mom, wait–" The line went dead, and Tyler cursed at himself for hurting her feelings. He'd have to make it up to her later, but for now he had to focus on the present.

Tyler continued down the cobblestone driveway at a slow pace. He hadn't considered what would happen once he got here. Which one of Gabe's parents would answer the door? Would they slam it in his face? Was he a total hypocrite for trying to help Gabe's family when he'd just lashed out at his own mother?

Trying to calm himself, Tyler focused on the shaded surroundings of the property. A sea of flowers in every color of the rainbow lined the driveway, with wrought iron fencing bordering the two acre lot. A large pool house stood on the right hand side of the property that hadn't been there the last time he'd visited.

Tyler arrived at the wooden front door that was over-shadowed by a rounded stone archway. He gave the door three sharp knocks and waited with no response. He was just about to knock again when the door opened.

Nancy stood before him in a burgundy sweater, a floral shirt, and tapered black pants. Her eyes were puffy and bloodshot, and her short red hair was in tangles. When she recognized him she scowled. "I'm going to scream."

"Wait, Nancy, please. I talked with the police yesterday. They told me you and Jim were attacked."

Nancy's eyes widened, but her hostile gaze didn't falter.

"I didn't want to bother you but the more I thought about it, the more I knew it was the right thing to do."

"What do you want?"

"I want to help. I know that you're going through a lot and that this assault is none of my business, but Gabe would want me here if it meant supporting his family in a time of crisis."

Nancy held her austere expression for a long moment before it fell away, revealing an intense sadness in her reddened eyes. She stepped aside, opening the door just enough to let him through. She silently led the way through the marble-floored foyer into the living room. The space was enormous and vaulted, with extravagant paintings covering the walls and opulent vintage furniture spread throughout.

Nancy gestured to a stiff-looking couch and Tyler took a seat. She sat on a chesterfield sofa across from him and fidgeted, looking uncomfortable.

"Is Jim going to join us?"

"He can't, he's … in the hospital." Nancy's face crumpled and she leaned over her seat, plastering a hand over her face. Her shoulders shook with muted sobs as Tyler stared, unnerved by her sudden shift in behavior. She seemed fragile and broken, a sharp contrast to the unshakeable christian warrior he'd always seen.

Tyler got up and sat beside Nancy, warily placing a hand on her shoulder. "I'm sorry to hear that. Is he going to be okay?"

"I don't know," she sniffled. "He's still under observation."

Tyler grabbed a tissue from a nearby end table and handed it to her. "Here."

Nancy blew her nose loudly, then composed herself enough to sit up straight and wipe at her wet eyes. "Thank you. I feel like I'm losing my mind. No one will listen to me."

"What do you mean?" Tyler asked.

Nancy glanced over at him with bloodshot eyes.

"Sorry, I'm being nosy. It's none of my business."

"No, it's alright. I … I need to know that I'm not crazy. The authorities think I have PTSD and hallucinated everything. Even the members of my church won't talk to me after I told them."

"Nancy, I'm not here to judge you. You can trust me, I promise."

Nancy nodded weakly. "It happened in the middle of the night, around 3 a.m. Jim and I had gone to bed a couple hours earlier, but he kept getting up. Jim has an overactive bladder, so I assumed he was having a rough night. After the first couple of times I asked him if he was feeling alright. He told me he was fine, but something didn't feel right. When I asked what he meant, he said he thought we weren't alone. He checked our surveillance system but didn't find anything, so we went back to sleep."

"What happened after that?"

Nancy's eyes got watery, and her hands began to tremble. She intertwined her fingers to stop the motion.

"It's okay," Tyler reassured her. "Focus on your breathing."

Nancy took a couple deep breaths to calm herself. "I woke up to Jim screaming from across the room. I've never heard him cry out like that before. That was when I realized he was right. We weren't alone. I …" Nancy shook her head, then stifled a sob with her fist against her mouth. "I'm sorry, maybe you should just go. No one believes me. Why would you?"

Tyler placed a hand on hers. "Nancy, in the past few weeks I've seen things that defy all reason. If I can't believe your story, I wouldn't be able to believe my own. You're not alone in this."

Nancy took a shaky inhale, and her posture relaxed a bit.

"You said someone else was there. What did you see?"

"A man. He was tall with long hair, and he stood over Jim with a hand on his chest. He was speaking in a strange language with a horrible booming voice. But his eyes ... they glowed a hateful red, like burning coals. Oh god, it was so terrible!"

An icy chill spread through Tyler's veins. *No, it can't be.*

"Jim kept screaming. I didn't know what else to do, so I hid underneath our bed. After a minute Jim's screams stopped, but when I crept to the edge of the bed the strange man vanished, just disappeared before my eyes! He was gone, like he was never there. But Jim, his face ... what did that man do to him? I can't lose Jim, he's all I have left!"

Nancy sobbed, and a high-pitched ringing flared in Tyler's ears that drowned everything out.

He couldn't believe this was happening. Somehow, by some hellish misfortune, Ayar Kachi was here. Why was he attacking Gabe's family, and how had he traveled thousands of miles in such a short time? It was unthinkable, and yet Nancy's account of the attack left nothing to debate. It had to be him, and if Ayar Kachi was here then he wasn't done with his reign of terror and death. A tingling sensation spread through Tyler's chest. He couldn't let this happen again. He had to find a way to stop Ayar Kachi or he would keep coming back until Jim and Nancy were dead. But how could he pull that off when their time was already short? Maybe there was a clue in the rest of Nancy's story.

The ringing in Tyler's ears dissipated, replaced by Nancy's weeping, which had reached a fever pitch of misery.

Tyler grabbed hold of her shoulders. "Nancy, Nancy. Please, calm down. Can you do that for me?"

Nancy's sobs leveled out over several long moments. She sniffled, then nodded.

"I told you I'm here to help, and it's a good thing that I came. I know who attacked you and Jim. It may be hard to accept, but I believe this all started with me and Gabe."

"Gabriel was involved in this?" Nancy croaked. "How? If you know something, tell me."

Tyler told Nancy of the grim course of events that occurred in Altalona, from their seeking out the ruins and the horror of the evil that lurked within to their unsuccessful attempt to flee.

When he finished Nancy seemed remarkably calm. "So this Ayar Kachi is some kind of demon?"

"Yeah, something like that."

"It all makes sense now," Nancy said pensively.

"You believe what I told you?"

"What other conclusion is there? There are far too many similarities between your story and mine to ignore, and I saw what that demon did to Jim. But what does that change? If it wasn't for you, my baby would still be alive. *You did this*."

Tyler's stomach bunched into knots. "You're right. I was selfish and greedy, and Gabe died because of it. The guilt of it all has been tearing me up inside, and I know that it's not enough, that nothing will ever be enough because it can't bring Gabe back. I will have to bear that burden for the rest of my life. But none of that changes how little time we have. Your and Jim's lives are on the line, and Ayar Kachi won't stop until he kills you both."

Nancy's severe gaze held a long moment before softening the tiniest degree. "Yes, it appears I'm stuck with you no matter how much I'd like to throw you out right now. So how do we stop it? How do we destroy Ayar Kachi for what he's done to Gabriel and Jim?"

Tyler grimaced. "I've told you all I know, but Gabe was conducting research when we were in Peru. Maybe if I dig through his records I can find something useful. Figuring out how Ayar Kachi operates may provide clues at how we can stop him. I'll have to move fast."

"What can we do to avoid Ayar Kachi in the meantime?"

"The only thing I've used that repelled him was holy water. Do you have any here?"

"No, but my church should."

"Alright. Go there and get plenty of it just in case. Also, you should probably stay with Jim. He can't defend himself right now, so you'll have to do that for him. If Ayar Kachi appears, spray him with the holy water. It should force him away long enough to buy us more time."

"What about you? Aren't you just as vulnerable as I am right now?"

Tyler smiled. "Thanks for your concern, but I have some holy water at home from my paranormal vlogging. I should be fine as long as I head right back to Jessica's."

"My concern isn't for you. I just want to survive the mess you've made, and you're the only shot Jim and I have."

"Understood. I promise I'll do everything I can to help you." Tyler got up from the rigid sofa. "I'll be in touch once I find anything that'll help, and if you think Ayar Kachi is near, call me. I'll come right over. Take care of yourself."

"I will." Nancy escorted Tyler to the door.

Tyler left the house and ordered an Uber ride on his phone. He'd just begun his descent of the cobbled driveway when Nancy's voice made him turn around.

"Tyler? Be safe."

Tyler nodded and continued his walk down the driveway,

his heart hammering as the reality of the situation sank in. Ayar Kachi was here, and it wouldn't be long before the spirit attacked Jim and Nancy again. He had to figure something out quick. Otherwise, their blood would be on his hands.

CHAPTER ELEVEN

"Thank you!" Tyler scrambled out of the Uber and rushed down the short driveway to Jessica's house. He let himself in, slamming the door closed after himself. "Jessica? Jessica!"

He hurried into the living room and spotted her. Jessica was heading his way from the dining room with a large brown paper bag in hand. She wore a form-fitting white tee, dark jeans, and her hair was a mahogany ombre that spilled over her shoulders in undulant waves.

"Hey Ty. I saw your messages and told work I wasn't feeling well so I could come home. What's going on? I got us Chinese for lunch."

Tyler shook his head. "Fuck the Chinese food. You're gonna want to sit down for this."

Tyler sat with Jessica at the dining room table next to the fragrant takeout bag. He explained everything that Nancy had told him about the attack and the unmistakable conclusion that Ayar Kachi was hunting them down. By the time he finished, Jessica's good mood had vanished and her good posture crumpled.

"Wow … okay," Jessica said, staring blankly at the glass table. "Ayar Kachi is here, and he's going to kill Jim and Nancy if we don't find a way to stop him."

"Whoa, hold up. What do you mean, *we*?"

"Don't you need my help?"

"With small stuff, sure. But Jessica, lives are at stake now. Ayar Kachi killed Gabe and attacked Jim without hesitation or remorse. What do you think he would do to you? I can't let you get more involved than you already are. It's too dangerous."

"And who's gonna look out for you, huh? I'll be damned if I'm gonna let you go on some crazy suicide mission without backup. I've always looked out for you and that's not going to change now, end of story."

"God damn it, Jess. I don't want to see you get hurt!"

"And I refuse to just let my best friend die! Don't you know how much you mean to me?" Jessica's voice cracked, and tears spilled down her cheeks.

"Oh, Jess." Tyler reached out to her.

"*Don't.* I won't lose you, and I'll do whatever it takes to stop this asshat if it means protecting you. Face it, you're in over your head. Let me help you figure this out so we can save Jim and Nancy. Do you really think Gabe would be okay with you going through this alone?"

Tyler frowned as he mulled over Jessica's plea. He hated how much sense her argument made. Gabe wouldn't want him throwing his chance at life away if he could tip the scales in his favor, however little that may be. There was strength in numbers, and Jessica was a smart, resourceful woman. He also didn't have any leverage in this dispute. He had nowhere else to stay, and once Jessica set her mind to something it would take an act of God to make her change her mind. Giving a heavy sigh, he made his choice.

"Okay, you can help. But if Ayar Kachi shows up at any time I want you to get the hell out of dodge."

"No, *we'll* get the hell out of dodge. No one gets left behind," Jessica said, stone faced.

"Alright, alright. Partners. Now can we move on?"

Jessica gave a triumphant grin. "Gladly. So what's the game plan? Is there anything we can use against this bastard?"

"I don't know. The only thing I've used that repels him is holy water, and those effects were only temporary. Gabe was doing some research on his laptop, so I'm hoping to find some answers there, but we have to move fast. Very little time passed between the first and second time Gabe was assaulted, and if that's any indication then Jim and Nancy don't have long."

"Alright, let's not waste any time then. Fill up a plate and we'll go sort through Gabe's stuff upstairs."

Tyler and Jessica dumped some food on plates, then headed upstairs to the study where all of Gabe's things were. Inside, boxes were strewn haphazardly around the room with piles of Gabe's belongings littering the floor.

"Yikes, where do we start with this mess?" Jessica asked.

"Sorry, I should've cleaned this up the other day. I'll get on Gabe's laptop and try to locate what he was researching. Maybe you could sort through everything else and see if there's anything related to Ayar Kachi?"

"Alright, sounds good."

Tyler and Jessica found empty spots on the floor, took a couple bites of their food, and got to work.

Tyler fished Gabe's laptop and charger from the heaping masses before them. As he set the device on his lap a mental image of Gabe manifested in his brain; he sat on their bed in Altalona with the laptop, his hair tied back with his sexy professor glasses resting upon his nose. Tyler took a slow deep breath. *It's okay, you can do this.*

He plugged the computer's charger into the nearest outlet. Once the laptop booted up, Tyler logged in and brought up a browser to begin his search. Locating Gabe's recent search history was easy, and as he scrolled down the list he found several articles centered on the tale of Ayar Kachi. The first had an illustration of Ayar Kachi's likeness that was so accurate it made his blood run cold. Fighting his pangs of residual fear, Tyler pored over the details of the articles.

According to South American legend, Ayar Kachi and his seven siblings were believed to be responsible for laying the foundation of the Incan empire. They were sons and daughters of Viracocha, the supreme creator god of the Incas.

Together the family traveled the countryside in search of fulfilling a grand destiny. Unlike the others, Ayar Kachi was supernaturally strong, which made his brothers and sisters jealous. In a cruel twist of fate, they tricked him into exploring a cave and locked him in with a giant immovable stone. Ayar Kachi's screams of anger made the earth tremble, but they did not release him from his plight. After days of fruitless attempts to escape, Ayar Kachi begged the gods for mercy. They granted his wish and freed him.

Once liberated, Ayar Kachi sought vengeance against his brothers and sisters. As he traveled he gathered a following and planned to create an army worthy of their destruction. His crusade led him north, where he established a stronghold in the rainforest. However, his growing influence had poisoned his mind, and in a moment of great hubris he declared himself a god among men. The gods who had given him a second chance were deeply offended. Supay, the god of death, carried out the condemnation by cursing Ayar Kachi, and he and his followers were never seen again.

Tyler's shoulders slumped after he finished reading the articles. Though the legend of Ayar Kachi's fate was intriguing, it hadn't shed any light on what the curse had done to him or how he could be stopped. Thinking back, he recalled Gabe mentioning stories of explorers and others disappearing when they found the ruins near Altalona. He was able to locate the articles, but the details behind their disappearances were too vague to indicate that Ayar Kachi was responsible.

Tyler set the laptop aside with a grunt and took a large bite of his cold chinese food.

"That bad, huh?" Jessica asked as she sorted through several pieces of paper in her hands.

"Yeah, I'm not getting anywhere. I found the legend of Ayar Kachi and his siblings. The god of death named Supay supposedly cursed him, but I can't find anything that explains what that means. How are you coming along?"

"No better than you. Nothing I've found has anything to do with Ayar Kachi. It's all just details of your trip and old documents and bills." She tossed the papers she'd been inspecting into a box, then grabbed a cracked cell phone with a pink case from the remaining pile of Gabe's stuff. "Hmm, is this Gabe's? It doesn't seem like his vibe."

Tyler's heart skipped a beat as he recognized the dusty moon and cloud design on the phone's back. "Oh my god! That's not Gabe's, it's the phone I found in the ruins."

"What? Why didn't you mention it earlier?"

"I honestly forgot about it until just now. It didn't seem important with Gabe's funeral and everything else that's been going on. Are you thinking what I'm thinking?"

Jessica nodded. "If we can find more information about what happened to the owner of this phone, we might be able to piece some things together about Ayar Kachi."

"Exactly. Look at the phone's charging port. Do you think you have one that might fit it?"

Jessica inspected the phone's port closely. "Yeah, I think so." She left the room, quickly returning with several phone chargers.

Tyler joined her at the nearest outlet. The first charger didn't fit, but the second snapped into the port without resistance.

"Yes!" Jessica whooped.

Tyler snatched Gabe's laptop and told Jessica he'd take notes, then settled close to her as she powered the phone on. When the phone booted up, the background image of a smiling little girl surrounded by half a dozen latina women and balloons flashed to life.

Jessica sighed with relief. "No password protection. Thank god."

"What now?" Tyler asked.

"It's impossible to tell who the owner is from this wallpaper. Let's look at their media files." Jessica scrolled through the owner's videos and pictures. Based on the majority of images that populated, the owner was an attractive latina woman with long black hair and bangs. She'd been on the right hand side of the wallpaper photo. "This is definitely the owner, whoever she is."

"Try playing one of the videos," Tyler suggested.

Jessica tapped the first video in sight. The owner of the phone had the device facing herself with the little girl from the wallpaper sitting on her lap. A cat nose and whiskers had been painted on the woman's face, while the little girl had butterflies painted on hers. A necklace with a pendant of the moon hanging from the woman's neck caught Tyler's attention, distracting him from the colorful border of balloons that surrounded them with the words *'¡Feliz cumpleaños!'* centered below.

The woman bounced the little girl on her knees as she made meowing sounds, making the little girl giggle.

"¡*Feliz cumpleaños*, Isabel!" she said.

The little girl turned around, placing her small hands on the sides of the woman's face. "*Te amo*, Eva."

"Aw, *gracias chica. Yo te quiero.*" Eva gave the girl a kiss on the cheek and a big hug before the video ended.

"Fuck, she seems so nice," Tyler said. He felt awful knowing that this endearing woman had somehow become a victim of Ayar Kachi's.

"All the more reason to make Ayar Kachi pay. At least we know her name's Eva now. Let's keep going."

Jessica resumed her search through the media files and was about to start the next video when Tyler stopped her. "Wait, what's that?"

Jessica tapped the picture he referred to. It was a missing persons poster of an older woman who looked to be in her sixties. Her bulbous nose, hairline, and facial structure was very similar to Eva's. Under the portrait of the woman was the name Anita Mendoza, with what was most likely her description in Spanish below.

"Do you think that's Eva's mom?" Tyler asked.

"That or a close relative. The resemblance is unmistakable. But does it have anything to do with Ayar Kachi?"

"I guess we'll just have to see."

Jessica continued to peruse through the media files, stopping at a picture of a large indoor funeral ceremony for Anita Mendoza. A large portrait of her was propped and centered on the stage of a crowded church near a closed casket with an assortment of flowers atop them. Eva stood at a podium, shadowed by a young man and older gentleman. Something about the young man seemed familiar to Tyler, but he couldn't quite grasp the connection.

"This is definitely raising a red flag for me," Jessica said.

"Anita goes missing, only to be found and buried–" Jessica compared the dates on the photos. "Three days later. What do you think?"

"There are some differences in this situation, but Ayar Kachi could still be behind it."

"Agreed. Oh, here's another video."

The next video started with Eva facing the camera. Her hair was disheveled and her eyes were puffy as if she'd been crying. She began speaking at length in Spanish, when Tyler had Jessica pause the video.

"This is no good. Do you still have that translator app on your phone?"

"I think so. Ah yeah, here it is."

"Alright, I'll type the translation for the video. Go back and let's try again."

Tyler activated the translator app and Jessica restarted playback of the video.

Eva's message came through clearly this time. "Hey everyone. I'm sorry to keep posting about this, but some strange things have been happening since my mother passed away and they're getting worse. I keep feeling like someone is watching me, and now I'm seeing this man. He's tall with dark hair and he's got this awful gray skin and glowing red eyes like fire. I don't know what to do. Has anyone ever heard of something like this? How do I make him go away? Please, I just want some relief. I feel like I'm going crazy." A noise sounded off camera and Eva jerked at the sound before the video ended abruptly.

"Ayar Kachi," Tyler muttered, goosebumps raising on his arms and legs.

"Yeah, this is bad," Jessica agreed.

"How long was that from Anita's funeral?"

"Two days after."

"Damn. Okay, let's keep going with the next clip right there."

The succeeding video began in a crowded parking lot. Lively music and a cacophony of voices echoed faintly in the distance. The camera shook with each step before stopping abruptly.

"Hello? Who's there?" Eva called out shakily. The camera veered left to right, but nothing was in sight. "I know someone's there!" Again, there was no answer or movement.

Eva muttered something under her breath then continued to bee line across the parking lot between cars, this time at a brisker pace. She was halfway across the lot when a guttural cry of rage bellowed close by. Eva yelped, then started running, the camera view bouncing violently.

The deep roar crescendoed, and as it came upon Eva the phone flew from her grasp, landing on the pavement with a skidding clack. The camera now provided a view of the asphalt, only the audio hinting at what was happening.

Eva screamed at the top of her lungs as an all too familiar gravelly voice began to chant in indiscernible words.

"Get off me! Someone help me, please!" she begged desperately.

Ayar Kachi venomous words didn't relent, and Eva shrieked in agony when a distinctly male voice called out, "What's going on over there?"

"Hey, get off her!" another cried.

"Help me! I'm over here!" Eva wailed.

Ayar Kachi gave a robust cry of fury as hastened footfalls pounded closer, his shout withering away as he retreated. Eva sobbed uncontrollably, and as the good samaritans spoke to her in soothing tones the video cut out.

"Shit, do you think that was when he marked her?" Jessica asked.

"Yeah, that or later on. He's … persistent." Tyler shuddered as an image of Ayar Kachi forced itself to the forefront of his mind's eye: his tall imposing form, his fiery red eyes, his vicious sneer that emanated his pure hatred for the living.

"You okay?"

"Yeah, yeah, I'm good. Sorry, just hearing that brought me back to when Gabe and I

were attacked. Is there anything else?"

"There's one video left, but that's it."

"Okay, let's get this awfulness over with."

Jessica started the last video, which appeared to be nothing more than a static black screen. Just as she was about to fast forward the footage, short rapid breaths became audible.

"Hello? Hello!" Eva called out, her voice echoing in the dark.

The flashlight on Eva's phone came to life, illuminating a long stone passageway. "Where am I? How did I get here? Hello! Is anyone there?"

A deep, savage growl answered her call from further down the tunnel.

Eva cried in alarm and ran in the opposite direction, the camera's view shaky as she bolted. She passed a number of dark openings in the corridor on her way and soon came to the end of the passage, a flat wall of stone.

"Damn it!" Eva grunted as she slapped her hands against the immovable stone, her frustration fading into a whimper as she was forced to turn around.

Another menacing snarl traveled down the passageway, closer than before.

"No, no, no, no, no," Eva muttered to herself. Her camera jerked in every direction, settling on one of the rooms on her right.

She raced inside, hiding behind a large, rotted mass that may have once been furniture before shutting her flashlight off. Once more, her surroundings were shrouded in absolute darkness.

A tremendous roar boomed from the hall, and Eva's breath hitched.

"Oh god, he's coming!" The light tinkle of metal sounded, then Eva began to chant quietly. "St. Michael the Archangel, defend us in battle. Be our defense against the wickedness and snares of the Devil."

Another inhuman howl of malice pierced the air, but it didn't deter Eva.

"May God rebuke him, we humbly pray, and do thou, O Prince of the heavenly hosts, by the power of God, thrust into hell Satan, and all the evil spirits, who prowl about the world seeking the ruin of souls. Amen."

With Eva's whispered prayer finished, everything went deathly silent. The seconds dragged on, and no more sound came from the hall. After several long moments, Eva mustered enough courage to speak. "My prayer worked, I can't believe it! Maybe if I go back the way I came I can–ah!"

Eva screamed frantically, pleading with the heartless monster Tyler knew all too well. Her requests were answered by grisly shouts of rage, and her cries faded into nothingness as Ayar Kachi hauled her away. Within the next minute all sound had dissipated, the static black screen unchanged.

"Is that it?" Tyler asked.

Jessica fast forwarded, rewound, then repeated the process before stopping the video. "Yeah, it looks like it kept recording until the battery died."

"Damn. I was hoping she would make it somehow, that someone had actually survived Ayar Kachi."

"I know hun, but look on the bright side. This timeline of events gave us a lot of good information. Now we can try to put this all together."

Tyler offered a weak smile. "You're right. Thanks boo."

"Do you want to start? You're the expert between the two of us."

"Sure. Let's start from the beginning. From what we've seen, this all started when Eva's mother Anita was taken by Ayar Kachi and killed."

"Right, and Ayar Kachi kills by draining the life out of people. But why is he doing it? Is it just for some sick pleasure, or is there more to it than that?"

"There's definitely something deeper going on. The first time I saw Ayar Kachi he was little more than a blurry shadow, but after he attacked Gabe I could see him more clearly."

"Okay, so he's getting some kind of sustenance from killing people. If that's why he does it, will he fade away if he doesn't feed?"

"I'm not sure, but each time I've seen him it feels like he gets stronger and stronger. He won't be fading away anytime soon if he gets to Jim and Nancy. I also noticed that he only seems to attack at night. The people in Altalona plan their day around it. The second the sun starts to set, they lock themselves indoors."

"Why do you think Ayar Kachi only hunts at night?"

"I can't be sure, but I'm fairly certain he has some kind of sensitivity to sunlight. Either that or something else we haven't considered. Let's move on. Several days after Anita's funeral he came for Eva and marked her, but she was saved by some good samaritans. My thought is that since Ayar Kachi found Eva so quickly without marking her, he must be able to track those closest to his latest victim somehow. He did the same thing with Jim and Nancy."

"Yeah, there's definitely a pattern there. Do you think his ability to track his victims is connected by blood, or could a significant other be tracked just the same?"

"Based on what we've seen we can't be sure, so let's not count out that possibility. Alright, so after Eva was marked, she started seeing Ayar Kachi more and more, which makes sense since he was circling in for the kill. But that last video confused me. How did Eva wake up not knowing where she was? I guess she could've sleepwalked, but that seems like a stretch."

Jessica nodded thoughtfully. "Good question. Did you notice anything like that with Gabe?"

"Hmm, that last night at the hospital was strange. Gabe was supposed to be in his bed, but he was roaming around the hospital. I never saw his face while he was walking around, but it feels similar to what happened to Eva."

"Maybe he's drawing them to him somehow? I'm no neurologist, but maybe a dormant mind is easier to influence."

Tyler grimaced as his stomach churned.

"What is it?"

Tyler put a hand on his left breast over the scar that resembled the bizarre figurine he'd found at the inn in Altalona. "Jim was marked by Ayar Kachi, but I was too. It's already night time. Is … is he going to come for me too?"

The color drained from Jessica's face. "I don't know, but I'm not going to let anything happen to you. Still, if there's any silver lining to the situation, it's that you don't seem to be Ayar Kachi's priority at the moment. You haven't seen him since you came back, and he seems to be focused on Gabe's family."

"I guess you're right, but it's just a matter of time. What are Jim and Nancy supposed to do? We haven't figured this out yet."

"Ty, breathe. There's no way we were going to decode Ayar Kachi in one night. We'll just have to keep trying, and you'll have to trust that Nancy can protect herself and Jim with holy water. It's all gonna be–"

As if on cue, Tyler's phone rang. As he read Nancy's name on the screen, his heartbeat raced. He grabbed his phone and answered the call. "Nancy? What's going on?"

"Tyler, I think something's happening!" Nancy said, her voice strained. "Jim got up from his bed and was trying to leave the room. He kept fighting me and the nurse I called, so they had to sedate him."

"Oh my god. Are you okay? Did you see Ayar Kachi?"

"I'm fine and I didn't see him but … I don't know. I have a strange feeling that he's nearby. Can you come by the hospital? I … I'm scared."

"We'll be right there. What floor and room are you at?"

"We're on the fourth floor, room 412."

"Got it. Until we get there, lock the door to the room and grab your holy water, okay?"

"Alright, please hur–" The line went dead.

"Fuck! Jessica, we've gotta go. Ayar Kachi's coming for Nancy and Jim."

Jessica and Tyler scrambled to leave the house. As Tyler raced downstairs he couldn't shake a sinking sensation in his gut. Ayar Kachi was coming for Jim and Nancy, and if he and Jessica couldn't save them, he'd be coming for him next.

CHAPTER TWELVE

Tyler clutched the grab-handle for dear life as Jessica's BMW roared down the busy Dallas streets, veering around slower moving vehicles with mere inches between them. Jessica swore as she was forced to brake hard for a red light, making them both bang against the back of their seats from the sudden stop.

"Jess, I want to save Jim and Nancy as much as you do, but could you get us there in one piece? You're going to kill us driving like this."

Jessica frowned and eased her vice grip on the steering wheel. "Sorry, I'm just freaking out. Why does traffic have to be so insane the second we have an emergency?"

"Well, it's Friday night. Let me try reaching Nancy again." Tyler called Nancy's number but it went straight to voice-mail. He hung up and dialed the hospital, however, their emergency line gave him a busy signal. "Damn it. Nancy and the hospital aren't answering."

"Sounds like we could use a little boost to get us there faster," Jessica said, giving Tyler a hopeful cocking of her eyebrows.

Tyler relented with a heavy sigh and resumed his tight grip on the grab-handle. "Fine. Step on it, but be careful."

"You got it. Jim and Nancy, here we come!"

The traffic light turned green and they blazed forward. After several minutes of sharp turns, sudden stops and starts, and one too many close calls they arrived at the hospital, screeching to a halt in front of the emergency room entrance. They got out of the car and bolted for the hospital entryway, slowing when they saw the lights flickering inside.

"What the hell is going on here?" Jessica said. "Do you think Ayar Kachi is doing this somehow?"

"It's got to be him. It's too similar to what happened at the hospital after Gabe and I escaped the ruins. Come on, let's get moving."

The automatic doors opened partially for Tyler and Jessica before stopping, forcing them to squeeze themselves through into the dimly lit emergency lobby. Nurses and the occasional doctor scurried around panicked patients, shouting orders to one another and darting in a dozen different directions. Formidable looking security personnel roamed the area, severe expressions stamped on their faces.

Tyler grabbed Jessica's arm and led her to a darkened corner where they wouldn't be sighted.

"What now?" Jessica whispered.

"We've got to find a way to Nancy and Jim. They're on the fourth floor, but with what's going on, they're probably not allowing visitors right now, so we'll have to sneak up there."

"Yeah, those security guards don't look so happy." She looked in their direction, squinting her eyes. "I think I see a stairwell over to the left. Do you see it?"

Tyler glanced in the direction Jessica indicated. "I think so. We'll have to wait until they're distracted to make a move, then we can make a run for it."

Tyler and Jessica stuck to the shadows, and after several

long moments one of the guard's walkie talkies came to life in a string of static babble. The man engaged in a quick back and forth over the device and gestured to the other nearby guards. Half of the guards slammed open the stairwell they'd been meaning to take, while the rest rushed into the halls of the emergency department away from the lobby.

"Okay, now!" Tyler said.

Jessica and Tyler dashed forward. They shot to their left, banging open the door to the stairwell. Once the pounding of footsteps from the guards above subsided, they sprinted up four flights of stairs to Jim and Nancy's floor. They arrived on the far end of the floor where a service elevator and vending machines sat idly, the lights overhead spasming with a strobe-like effect.

"Fuck! We're on the wrong end of the floor," Tyler said. "We have to keep moving. Keep an eye out for room 412. With any luck–"

A sudden blood curdling scream echoed in the distance, followed by shouts and the distinct boom of gunfire.

Terror gripped Tyler's spine with icy fingers. "Oh god, he's already here. Come on!"

Tyler led the way through the labyrinth of hallways, the heightened sounds of violence guiding them. They rounded a corner to a long corridor. Chaotic beeps and static drones echoed from the rooms within, and several terrified nurses ran towards them, looking over their shoulders as they escaped from whatever unspeakable horrors Ayar Kachi was responsible for.

Tyler and Jessica sprinted down the passage. They took a right into the hall the nurses had fled from and stopped at the sight of the carnage before them.

Several nurses and security guards were splayed across the floor several rooms down amid miscellaneous medical equipment, small pools of blood surrounding them. The door handle to room 412 had been ripped out with large splinters of wood taking its place. A high-pitched scream came from inside the room.

"Nancy!" Tyler charged forward, slamming the door open.

Ayar Kachi stood in the center of the litter-strewn patient room holding Nancy up by her neck with little effort. Streams of amber energy vacated her mouth entering his, and her skin was so sunken in she looked skeletal.

"No!" Tyler shouted.

Ayar Kachi leered at Jessica and Tyler's intrusion, his piercing red eyes filled with hate. He threw Nancy's gaunt form against the wall with a sickening crack, then took a step towards them.

Ayar Kachi's display of power made Tyler's legs stiffen like they were superglued to the floor. The evil spirit was stronger than ever, and his once blurry form was now opaque with a blue luminescent glow around the edges. How much more powerful could he get? Would his holy water even work now?

Unfazed by Ayar Kachi's strength, Jessica ran forward with a cylinder of holy water in hand. She uncapped the container and thrust it at him, splashing water in a dozen directions. A small river hit Ayar Kachi's face with a hissing sizzle, and he gave a monstrous roar that shook the room like thunder. The room's window burst into a thousand tiny shards from the force of the resounding boom, and Jessica and Tyler backed away with their hands over their ears.

Before Tyler could get his wits about him Jessica made another lunge towards Ayar Kachi, but just when she was within reach his form dissipated into a large cloud of black mist. The amorphous cloud swiftly exited through the deci-mated window into the night.

In Ayar Kachi's absence, the terror holding Tyler in place

vanished, and he sprang to Nancy's crumpled form on the floor. Her neck was bent at an unnatural angle, her cadaverous face frozen with the horror of her last moments. "She's dead," Tyler croaked as tears blurred his vision.

Jessica knelt beside Jim's body nearby on the floor and felt for a pulse. "I'm sorry, Ty. Jim didn't make it either. I'm going to find another–"

A loud scream interrupted Jessica. A nurse stood in the doorway, abject horror written on her face. "What … what was that thing?"

Jessica approached the nurse with her hands held up. "Please, you've got to help us. Call the police."

The nurse remained still as if she hadn't heard her. Jessica closed the distance between them, trying to get the nurse to calm down and get help.

As the reality of what took place processed in Tyler's mind, he collapsed against the wall, burying his face in his hands. They'd failed to save Jim and Nancy, and now he was probably next on Ayar Kachi's hitlist.

TYLER SAT ALONE in the interview room, rubbing his hands on the backs of his arms against the frigid draft that spewed from the AC vent above him. He'd been sitting there for what felt like an eternity, the only way of telling time the tapping of his shoes on the crappy laminated floor.

Once Jessica calmed the nurse who saw Ayar Kachi down they called the police, and Tyler and Jessica were placed into their custody. Jim and Nancy's deaths had been unexplainable just like Gabe's, but their presence at the time of their demise had raised some serious questions. After being separated from Jessica, Tyler had been interrogated numerous times throughout the night, and now his anxiety and exhaustion were through the roof, warring for dominance.

The room's only door opened and Detective Kilgore entered in a huff. She scowled as she stomped to the table Tyler sat at and slapped a manilla folder on it. Unlike her tidy appearance from the first time they'd met, her blue suit was crinkled and errant red hairs split out from her sloppy ponytail in every direction.

"What exactly do you think you're doing?" Detective Kilgore demanded. "I can't help you if you keep implicating yourself like this."

"I know it doesn't look good, but I was trying to protect Jim and Nancy."

"You deliberately involved yourself in a police matter!"

"What was I *supposed* to do, huh? I couldn't let them die at the hands of that monster, not that it made a difference anyway."

Detective Kilgore rolled her eyes. "Please tell me this isn't about the 'evil spirit' you mentioned in your police reports."

"His name is Ayar Kachi, and like I've told you and everyone else he is responsible for everything that's happened. I know it sounds crazy, but he's real and he won't stop killing. The hospital staff saw him, Jessica and I saw him, and so did Gabe and his family before he murdered them. If you don't do anything anyone could be next. Then what will you do?"

Detective Kilgore glared intensely at him, faltering after a long moment. "Alright fine, I'll level with you. You know as well as I do that this case has numerous deaths attached to it with a perpetrator no one can get their hands on. It won't be long before some crappy tabloid or news station catches wind and blows it all out of proportion. Just like it did with …"

Her eyes went watery, but before a single tear could be

shed she sniffled and straightened her posture. "There is a reason I am handling this case. This isn't the first time something like this has happened, and unless I figure it out it won't be the last. Last year my friend Jill and her daughter Andrea went to Peru. Jill is an archaeologist, and she always takes Andrea on whatever explorations she can. They traveled all over Peru and were supposed to return to the states in the next day or two, but they decided to follow some rumors they heard about a hidden ruin of significant importance.

"No one ever saw them again, and when the press got word of it there was a media circus given her influence in her field. It tore her family apart, and I don't want that for you. I don't want that for anyone."

"I … I had no idea," Tyler said. "Do you think there's a connection between what happened to them and Gabe and his family?"

"I don't know, but I'm determined to solve this case before anything else happens. That's what I need your help with. I need to hear your account of things. There could be leads in your story that I haven't considered. And while I don't believe in this Ayar Kachi you keep mentioning, I'll do my best to keep an open mind if it means justice for Gabe, Jim, Nancy, and any other victims this monster has murdered in cold blood. Does that sound fair to you?"

Holding back a rebuttal, Tyler nodded. He wasn't in any position to fight Detective Kilgore, and the sooner he got out of here the faster he could get back to work on stopping Ayar Kachi before things got even worse. With a heavy heart, Tyler told the story of his hellish past couple weeks.

Detective Kilgore made notes throughout his recollections, and by the time he was done her eyebrows were scrunched up in concentration as she analyzed her scribblings. "Thank you, Tyler. You've given me a lot to think about. You are free to go, but I want to warn you. If you continue to involve yourself in this matter any further there will be consequences. It's a felony to interfere with a police investigation. I'm talking about serious jail time here. Do you understand?"

"Yes, I understand."

Detective Kilgore led Tyler out of the room and headed towards the lobby. On the way, she stopped at a door marked 'Property' and told him to stay put. She went inside, returning with a small zipper bag of his personal items that she handed over to him.

"Thanks,"Tyler said.

"You're welcome. Your friend Jessica is waiting in the lobby. Remember what I told you, and stay safe."

Detective Kilgore went back the way she came and Tyler headed to the lobby feeling lousy. He knew it was impossible to stay away from Ayar Kachi and the death that followed, especially now that he and Jessica had pieced some of the puzzle together. Ayar Kachi hunted those he marked before moving on to their immediate family and any other marked prey. If that assumption held true, then he would be coming after Tyler next since he was marked right after Gabe was. How long did he have before Ayar Kachi came for him, and what would he do then? Even if he thwarted his next attack he couldn't keep it up forever, especially with his mounting strength.

Tyler entered the lobby. As soon as he spotted Jessica she shot up from the chair she was sitting in, rushed over, and enveloped him in a bear hug.

"Oh Ty, I was so worried! Are you okay?"

"I feel like shit," he croaked. "Can I have my lungs back?"

Jessica released her hold on him and took a step back. "Sorry, that was a dumb question. Of course you're not okay. Let's get out of here. The police impounded my car so we'll have to pick it up, then we can keep trying to figure this out. Sound good?"

Tyler smiled weakly, then gave a nod. They left the building and were greeted by a pale gray sky with coral rays that peeked out from the bottom of the horizon.

They came to a stop at the curb and Jessica pulled out her phone, bringing up her Uber app. Tyler gave her a once over while she was preoccupied. Her hair was wild, her eyelids droopy, and her skin lacked the usual glow it always had.

As much as Tyler wanted to vocalize his guilt for involving her, he knew it would just stress her out, especially with everything they'd just been through. Still, it didn't keep his emotions from tearing him up inside. Jessica didn't deserve any of this. She was just being a good friend. He wished he could throw in the towel, that he could whisk him and Jessica away from this nightmare, but until he knew exactly how to stop Ayar Kachi it wouldn't end. Their lives and that of their families potentially stood in the balance.

Just as Jessica was about to book a ride, Tyler stopped her. "Wait. I know someone that'll give us a ride. Let me give them a call. It'll save us some money."

Jessica shrugged. "Okay."

Tyler got on the phone, and ten minutes later Clay's Camaro pulled up to the curb.

The passenger window lowered, revealing Clay in a vibrant yellow tank top and some aviators. He lowered his glasses expertly and smiled. "Get in the car, biotches."

Jessica and Tyler piled in, and loud electronic dance music suddenly sparked to life, pulsating around them.

Jessica grimaced and put a hand to her forehead. "Can you turn that down?" she shouted over the noise.

Clay frowned but did as she wished. "No problem. Where are we headed?"

Jessica gave him the address of the impound lot and he set the coordinates into his GPS before starting the drive.

"So uh, what happened to you guys last night? No offense, but you look like shit."

Jessica sighed and pinched the bridge of her nose at Clay's remark, so Tyler piped up. "It's a long story, but we're running on no sleep. Mind if I give you the details later?"

"Yeah, that's fine. The impound lot is twenty minutes out, so try and get some shut eye and I'll wake you guys up when we get there."

"Thanks, Clay."

Tyler leaned back against his seat's headrest and closed his eyes, sleep taking him in mere moments. What felt like seconds later, a light jostling woke him up.

"Hey Tyler, wake up," Clay said from the driver's seat. "We're here."

Tyler rubbed his eyes, noticing the seat next to him was empty. "Where's Jessica?"

"She's paying the bill. Shouldn't be more than a minute or two. So, what happened last night?"

Tyler grimaced. "Can we talk about this some other time? I gotta use the restroom."

"Yeah, no problem. See ya later buddy."

Tyler exited Clay's car, happy to have avoided his probing questions. The less Clay knew, the better. He couldn't stomach endangering anyone else. He joined Jessica at the dingy little office where she was finishing up her payment. When they were done they walked across the lot to Jessica's car and got in. Jessica ignited the engine and sat there for a moment, staring blankly forward.

"Thank you," Tyler said.

"You're thanking me? For what?"

"For being so brave last night. If it weren't for you I don't know if we would've survived. Seeing Ayar Kachi again after what happened to Gabe, it shook me. I put your life in danger, and I'm sorry. I won't let myself freeze up again."

"Ty, no one's perfect. If anything, I'm not half as brave as you've been. I don't know how you got through the hell of these past couple weeks, but I'm glad to have your back. When I saw that bastard I just thought of all the people he's hurt. Gabe, you, Eva, all the others before. I got so mad I just charged at him."

Tyler took Jessica's hand and gave it a light squeeze. "I couldn't be more grateful to have been saved by such a beautiful badass. Thanks again, bestie."

Jessica grinned. "Of course. So … I know we have more work to do, but do you mind if we head home? I'm exhausted."

"Yeah, let's go home. I'm beat too. We'll feel better after we get some rest."

Jessica drove them back to her house, and after dragging themselves to their rooms, sleep took them easily.

Several hours later, Tyler woke up feeling refreshed. He shuffled over to the guest room window and took a peek outside. A storm had rolled in; dark clouds smothered the horizon like a blanket of smoke that refused to dissipate. He put on some gym shorts and a shirt and headed down stairs to the dining room. Jessica sat at the table in her pajamas with a steaming mug of coffee and an extra one for him.

"Morning," Tyler muttered.

Jessica returned his half-hearted greeting.

Tyler took the empty mug and went to the kitchen to fill it with steaming coffee. The strong nutty scent tickled his nostrils as he returned to the table and set it down to let it cool.

Jessica took a slow cautious sip of her brew. "Pretty bleak out there, huh?"

"Yeah. I would give anything for a rainy Netflix binge right about now. Did you sleep okay?"

"Not really. I kept having nightmares about the asshole who shall not be named. Speaking of which, what are we gonna do now? You had a plan, right?"

Tyler's stomach bunched into knots. "More like some educated guesses I came up with in between interrogations. My first thought was that someone's gotta know more about Ayar Kachi in Altalona. If the legend is true, he's been around for centuries. There's no way a small town would've survived this long without figuring out how to protect themselves or repel him. Then there's his sensitivity to holy water. There has to be a connection there that can shed some light on how to stop him."

"Alright, so what do you want to do?"

"I think I should start by calling the inn I stayed at in Altalona. The lady managing it might know more, and she's helped me before. Could you handle a search of catholic churches near us while I do that? A priest may be able to provide some insight, and we can stock up on holy water while we're there. I have a feeling we're going to need it."

"Sure."

Jessica got her laptop and started searching and Tyler went into the living room to look up the inn's information. Once he had it he called the number, cursing as the call went straight to voicemail. "Rosalinda? This is Tyler Collins. I stayed at your inn a couple weeks back and … listen, I need your help. My friend and I found the ruins of Ayar Kachi, but we were attacked by his spirit. He killed my friend, and now he's followed me back to the states. I don't know how long I have before he comes for me, but please, *please* give me a call back as soon as you can. I don't know how long I can keep him away." Tyler recited his phone number, then hung up the phone and went back to the dining room. "It went straight to voicemail. We're gonna have to deal on our own until she calls back. Are you seeing anything promising?"

"Yeah, there's a catholic church close by that looks well established. I pass it on the way to work sometimes depending on where they send me. Should we stop by?"

"I don't see what else we can do at the moment. To be safe, let's pose as a couple. We need the holy water too bad to risk getting ousted if they're homophobes."

"Sounds good to me."

Jessica and Tyler changed into some nicer clothes, then got into Jessica's car and drove to the Catholic church she'd located. They parked, fussing over their attire one last time before walking towards the looming white brick building. St. Thomas Aquinas Catholic Church stood in gothic style with an enormous circular stained glass window in its center under layered, pointed stone arches. They entered through the large wooden double doors, a raised statue of St. Thomas Aquinas between them.

Inside, they filed through the small, empty reception space to the worship area. The nave was vaulted with a green marble tiled floor. Arched, open passages stretched on the far left and right, leading to the altar where a large statue of Jesus and other holy figures were depicted. A dozen parish-ioners were scattered throughout the pews, heads bowed in prayer.

Tyler gulped, trying to swallow his anxiety. He hadn't been to a church in a very long time and his troubled past didn't make him feel any better. Raised as a baptist at a young age, he'd learned firsthand of the inherent homophobia and hypocrisy of the church. When his parents gave that up around his fifteenth birthday he was overjoyed to be free of Sunday services, religion, and all the baggage that came with it.

However, his father clung to the homophobic ideals with

gusto, demeaning Tyler in any way he could. His mother always overcompensated for his father's prejudice, but the soured situation had driven a growing wedge between him and his family over the years.

Being back in this kind of setting forced his fears to the surface. Would this church really be willing to help them, or would they sniff out his gayness right away and shoo them out like pariahs?

Jessica nudged him. "Hey, you okay?"

"Yeah, sorry. I haven't been to a church in forever. I'm kinda nervous."

"It'll be okay, just remember our story and focus on the task at hand."

"Alright. Do you think we should try to find a priest?"

Jessica smiled. "Looks like one already found us."

Walking down the center aisle from the altar was a short old man with a white combover. He wore a black clergy shirt and some slacks and had a pleasant smile on his face as he approached them.

The priest extended a hand to Tyler, then Jessica. "Welcome to St. Thomas Aquinas. I'm Father Edwards. Are you new to the church? I don't believe I've seen you here before."

Jessica gave a delighted chuckle. "Were we that obvious? We've never seen such a beautiful church like this before."

"Well, we always welcome new parishioners to our congregation. We have mass every day except for Monday with varying confession times. You can find all of our information on our website. Outside of that, is there anything I can help you with today?"

Tyler grimaced. "Actually, I have to apologize, Father Edwards. We didn't come just to see the church. We came because we need your help."

Father Edwards's gray eyebrows squished together. "My help?"

"Yes. We have a situation on our hands, and we didn't know where else to turn. We're being followed by some sort of … demon."

The priest's pleasant smile faded. "I … see. Please, let us speak in private. I'll lead the way to my office."

Father Edwards led them out of the worship area from a side exit into a long hall. At the end of the passage, the priest opened the last door on the left and gestured them inside. The priest's office was small but cozy. In its center was a small desk and chair with two additional chairs on the other side. Portraits of saints were hung upon the wall with a large cross on the opposing wall and a half bookcase underneath.

The priest waved them in and had Tyler and Jessica sit across from him at his desk. Together, they told their story and what they'd learned, sticking to a version where Gabe was portrayed as Tyler's friend and Jessica as Tyler's girlfriend in case the priest was homophobic. By the time they finished their rendition of events, the priest had an intrigued, thoughtful expression on his face.

Tyler leaned forward in his cushioned chair. "I know it sounds crazy, but all of this really happened. Gabe and his parents were murdered by this entity, and we fear this will all start over again soon." He grasped Jessica's hand in his. "I didn't want to include Jessica in any of this, but I don't think I would've gotten this far without her. Please, there's got to be something you can do to help us."

Father Edwards grimaced. "If what you've told me is indeed true, then I am concerned for your safety. The Catholic Church acknowledges the existence of demons and uses exorcisms to purge the evil spirits. We perform quite a lot of them with our group of exorcists, and only in extremely rare cases do exorcisms result in a death. But what troubles me is that you've already witnessed three deaths to this entity. Even more perplexing is that what you are experiencing is not a possession."

"What? Is Ayar Kachi not a demon?" Jessica asked.

"I'm not completely sure. Most demons desire to inhabit the bodies of the living. However, this Ayar Kachi can keep corporeal form, which allows it to hunt for the life force that keeps it alive. You said you have been marked by this demon. Could you show me please?"

Tyler nodded, then unbuttoned his shirt enough to reveal the deep scar Ayar Kachi had carved into his flesh.

Father Edwards frowned at the sight. "May I take a picture of the scar for further study?"

"Sure," Tyler said.

Father Edwards pulled out his smartphone and took several photos before gesturing for Tyler to conceal his wound again. "This is worrying. I do not know what the symbol on your chest means, but if the spirit made this mark, then I would guess that it has linked itself to you and may be able to track your whereabouts."

Jessica frowned. "What can we do, Father?"

Father Edwards steepled his fingers together. "Based on what you've told me, there aren't many options. You could stay on hallowed ground like this church. This demon's aversion to holy water implies a weakness to divine or sacred objects and locations, which is important. As the exorcist for the Catholic Diocese of Dallas, if you decide to accept my assistance I'll need you to complete a questionnaire and agree to work with me and my pre-team, which consists of a psychologist and medical doctor. They will have to evaluate you."

He held up a hand to stop Tyler and Jessica's coming protest and continued. "I understand your concerns with a timely resolution , but you must understand that this is a process and doesn't happen overnight."

Tyler and Jessica looked at one another and frowned.

"If it's any consolation, I believe you and I want to help, but these things take time."

"How long?" Tyler asked.

"I can't say. I must work with my team and learn more about what we are dealing with. Given the complexity of this entity a decisive plan of action could take weeks or months. We may need to observe the spirit in action."

"I'm sorry, but I can't put other lives at risk, especially when we're not fully sure what Ayar Kachi is capable of and how he operates. Also, Jessica would have to put her entire life on hold and that's just not doable. Is there anything else we might try?"

"The only other thing I can think of is to contact individuals you interacted with at the entity's place of origin to seek resolution. You mentioned the people of Altalona may know of a way to stop Ayar Kachi or keep him away more effectively. Seek that out. If this phenomena has been occurring since his death, they must know of something that can help you."

Tyler's shoulders slumped and his hands went clammy. He already tried that and still hadn't received a response. As fortunate as they were to have the offer of assistance from the church, dragging this out weeks or even months would make the situation that much more dire with no promise of stopping Ayar Kachi. How many more would die if he took that path? He couldn't put Jessica and the church through that.

A desperate thought entered Tyler's mind, making his stomach curdle. What if he went back to Altalona? The last thing he wanted was to relive the hell he'd already been through, but without any other viable plan it felt like his only real shot at ending this. He and Jessica had failed to save Jim and Nancy, and every minute that Jessica or anyone else stayed around him they were in danger of being marked.

Tyler rose from his seat. "I know what I have to do." He shook the priest's hand, avoiding Jessica's gaze. "Thank you for your advice, Father."

"You're welcome. I am always happy to help." The priest took a business card from the holder on his desk and handed it to Tyler. "If you need anything else, anything at all, please give us a call."

"Thanks again. Before we go, may we have some of your holy water?"

"Of course. I'll have some bottled up for you. Follow me."

Father Edwards led them out of the room and back to the worship area, and Tyler did his best to ignore the perplexed looks Jessica gave him along the way.

After they entered the chapel Father Edwards called a nearby priest to him. Brief words were spoken, and the man left the space at a brisk pace. "He'll be right back with the holy water. In the meantime, feel free to say a quick prayer before you leave. You may need it. Good luck, Tyler, Jessica."

Father Edwards left the worship area, and Tyler walked towards the altar. He couldn't remember the last time he prayed. Would it matter if he did? With nothing else to lose Tyler sat in the second row pew, steepled his hands together, and closed his eyes.

Hey God, or whoever's out there listening. I know it's been forever, and you certainly don't owe me anything given how much I've screwed up in my life. But please, if you have any mercy in you that you can spare, please protect Jessica. She didn't ask for this, and I couldn't bear it if something happened to her. My greed started this. Give me a chance to end this and bring some peace to those who have lost someone to Ayar Kachi.

Unsure of what else to say Tyler repeated his message in

his head, desperately hoping that the crazy thing he was planning to do would work.

CHAPTER THIRTEEN

As soon as Jessica and Tyler left the church with their supply of holy water, they came face to face with the worsening storm outside. Torrential gusts of rain pelted them, and they bolted for Jessica's car. Even with their quickened pace they were soaked through by the time they slammed the doors closed.

Jessica wrung out her long black hair before starting the car and heading back home.

Tyler stared out the window blankly, uncertain how he would tell Jessica about what he had planned for the next step of his journey. As much as he needed and appreciated her assistance in figuring out how to stop Ayar Kachi, he couldn't keep letting her do it, even at the risk of her throwing him out. He'd be damned if any more lives were lost because of his past mistakes.

"What did you mean back there?" Jessica asked.

Tyler glanced over at her. She was stone faced as she concentrated on the road. "What are you talking about?"

"With Father Edwards. You said I know what *I* have to do. What was that supposed to mean?"

Crap, why did I say that?

"Jess, listen. We have a good idea of what Ayar Kachi's attack pattern is, and he'll be after me soon if he isn't already. I need to go to Altalona and end this. The distance should delay Ayar Kachi like it did when I left Peru the first time, and that'll give me enough time to convince the townspeople to help me figure out how to stop him. But most importantly, you'll be safe."

Jessica snapped her head in Tyler's direction, her nostrils flaring. "Are you fucking kidding me? After everything that's happened you're just going to run off and sacrifice yourself? Ty, I love you, and I meant it when I said I'd do anything to help you through this, but I refuse to stand by while you throw your life away because you feel guilty."

"It's not even about that anymore! At least, not just that. Gabe and his family paid the price for my actions, and now that I've seen what can happen I can't let others make the same mistake. I'm not going to Altalona to throw my life away. I'm going to find out how to stop this once and for all so people don't keep dying in vain. That's why I can't let you get any more involved in this. Ayar Kachi didn't mark you, and if he did it would ..." Tyler's voice cracked. "It would kill me if anything happened to you and your family, and I can't promise that it won't if you go with me. So please, don't let me lose you. You're everything to me."

Jessica swiped at the tears that now brimmed over her eyes. "I didn't realize how strongly you felt about this. Let's put the brakes on this conversation for now, okay? We can talk about it at home over some brunch. Sound good?"

"Yeah, let's do that." Tyler returned his gaze to the passenger window as they sped down the road.

He had no intention of acquiescing to Jessica. If it came down to it he'd leave in the middle of the night, but when he did go it would be his last shot at stopping Ayar Kachi. Failure meant certain death.

"Ah!" Jessica's scream cut through his thoughts and the car suddenly swerved, nearly colliding with another vehicle going the opposite direction. She righted the vehicle with a jerk.

Tyler yanked on the grab handle and glared at Jessica. "Jesus, Jessica, what the hell was that?"

"Sorry, sorry! It wasn't me. I ... I could've sworn I saw ..."

"Saw what?"

Jessica looked at him, her big brown eyes wide with fear. "I thought I saw Ayar Kachi. He appeared right in front of the car, but that's impossible right? Every instance of an attack we know of has been at night."

Tyler's stomach sank as he eyed the menacing dark skies of the storm outside. "Maybe it's not as black and white as we thought. It's so damned dreary right now that whatever effect daylight has on him might be diminished, maybe enough to give him the balls to attack us. We've gotta get home, quick!"

Jessica cranked up the speed, nervously tapping her pink manicured nails on the steering wheel. "Damn it, what are we going to do? He's just going to follow us!"

"I don't think we have any other option at this point. We'll have to take Father Edwards up on his offer of protection, at least until we can figure out another solution. If we stop by your place quickly we should have enough time to pack some bags and get back to safety. Fuck, I thought we had more time."

"I did too ..."

The tense and silent car ride to Jessica's townhouse wracked Tyler's nerves as they drove through the Oaklawn area, not just due to the dangerous situation but because of the double-cross he would be forced to execute. He didn't know how he would shake Jessica off once they got back to the church, but he'd have to figure something out. Getting the church involved could mean more victims for Ayar Kachi, even with his weakness to holy water.

As they neared Jessica's home he looked up flights to Peru and lucked out in finding one that left in several hours. He booked the flight on his credit card then kept a stern eye on their surroundings, not seeing any hint of Ayar Kachi.

Hesitantly trusting their good luck, they made it home and hurried inside.

Jessica went straight to her laptop that she'd left in the dining room and shoved it into a tote before getting on her phone. "I'm letting work know I'll need some time off, then I'll get my things together."

"Alright, hurry up. I'll go pack upstairs."

Tyler left the dining room and jogged up the stairs to the guest room. He pulled out his black duffel bag, threw it on the bed, and started cramming things inside.

He was banking a lot on the flight he'd booked to South America. It would buy him the time he needed to sort things out in Altalona, meaning once he got there he needed a game plan. The obvious choice was to seek out Rosalinda and Esperanza. In some way they'd both helped him before, and he hoped they'd have some answers for him. But if they didn't would he just be killing time waiting for death to take him? No one else in the small village had been helpful.

Tyler shook off his pessimistic thoughts. *Stay positive. They've got to know something, they've just got to.*

Making quick work of packing his duffel, Tyler zipped it closed with a sigh. Once Jessica was packed up they'd be good to go. Tyler laid on his bed for a moment, staring at the ceiling as he relished what would probably be one of the last calm moments for a while. As the seconds ticked by, he noticed how quiet the house had become. Uneasy, he got up and edged to his doorway. "Jessica? Is everything alright?" he called.

A scream echoed to him from downstairs, followed by the crash of breaking glass.

"Jessica!"

Tyler barrelled down the stairs to the living room. He found Jessica in the kitchen, facing the partially-broken window that overlooked her small backyard with shards of glass scattered all around her. She was visibly shaking, and there were numerous cuts on her arms and legs. Tyler sped over, slowing when he neared to avoid any glass shrapnel. "What happened? Are you okay?"

"Ayar Kachi … I saw him watching me from the backyard and then the glass broke. I–he's still there!"

Jessica pointed, and Tyler looked outside. A shadowy figure lurked underneath the shade of a short oak tree. It emerged from the darkness, and Tyler's heart pounded in his ears as he recognized Ayar Kachi's tall menacing form. The evil spirit gave a wicked smile before charging towards them at a frightening speed.

"Get away from the window!" Tyler yelled.

He pulled Jessica into the dining room and they ducked behind the serving hatch when the remainder of the window erupted in a whirlwind of glass. Tiny sharp projectiles rained down everywhere, and Tyler lifted his arms over his head to cover himself and Jessica as shards slashed at his arms.

After all the glass had fallen, Tyler dared a peek into the kitchen. A cloudy black mist was drifting through the oblit-erated window, amassing in the center of the kitchen among the fragments of broken glass.

"He's coming. Quick, get the holy water! I'll hold him off."

Jessica scrambled to her feet and out of the dining room, heading through the living room towards the bottled holy water they'd left near the front door.

The black mist in the kitchen had now formed Ayar Kachi's silhouette, and within seconds he'd be ready to attack. Tyler eyed his surroundings for something that could be used as a weapon, settling on the knife block resting under the kitchen access hatch. He leapt up from his hiding place and yanked a butcher knife out of its slot just as Ayar Kachi's form fully materialized.

Tyler backed towards the center of the dining room, holding his knife in front of him protectively as he sized up the ancient spirit before him.

Since last night, Ayar Kachi's presence had become even more defined. The aura haloing his form had deepened to a golden hue, and his red eyes were so bright it almost hurt to look into them. His once mottled gray skin was now a healthy bronze tone, and his chest and ab muscles looked solid as a rock.

Ayar Kachi stared back at Tyler with an amused grin.

Tyler bared his teeth and clutched his knife tighter. "Come at me, fuckhead. Let's see how smug you are when this knife is sticking out of your throat."

Unphased, Ayar Kachi took a step toward Tyler. Tyler mirrored his movement and stepped back with the briefest of glances towards the front door. Damn it, where was Jessica? She had to have the holy water by now. He'd have to stall Ayar Kachi in the meantime, but would attacking him even work? He'd never tried to harm him physically.

Tyler gauged Ayar Kachi's slow methodical advance, and when he saw an opening he lunged forward knife first. Despite the spirit's corporeal form, he and the knife failed to make contact and passed through with a frigid shock that chilled his veins. Instantly he was grabbed, spun around, and lifted up by the collar of his shirt.

Tyler flailed and kicked fruitlessly as Ayar Kachi's blood red eyes burned into his. "Let me go, you sick bastard!"

Ayar Kachi sneered, then opened his mouth until it was stretched wider than humanly possible. Within was a void of absolute darkness that had a draw, an intangible pull to it that wrenched Tyler's mouth open like a souped up magnet hungry for his life force.

Tyler thrashed even more violently. *No, no, no! I can't die like this!*

Just as Tyler's life force began to vacate his mouth in a golden stream of energy, Jessica appeared behind Ayar Kachi from the dining room armed with a bottle of holy water. She sprayed the water wildly, and a cloud of steam erupted from Ayar Kachi's back as it made contact. He roared in pain, dropping Tyler to the ground before spinning around and striking Jessica.

Jessica cried as she soared into the air and crashed into the glass dining room table. It broke under the impact with a sharp clatter.

"Jessica!" Tyler scrambled back against the wall. From the partial glimpse he'd gotten due to Ayar Kachi blocking his view, she wasn't moving.

Ayar Kachi advanced towards Jessica, and a chilling jolt made the hairs on Tyler's arms stand on end. He couldn't let Ayar Kachi mark her, but how could he stop him? When he attacked him with the knife he'd gone right through him.

Tyler looked around frantically, his gaze settling on the fallen holy water bottle a few feet away. Ayar Kachi was stronger now, but holy water still affected him. If he doused the knife in it, could that pierce his otherworldly defenses?

Ayar Kachi stood over Jessica now. His gravelly voice boomed, reciting the same ominous foreign words he always spoke before sealing his next victim's fate.

Tyler's heart thrashed in his eardrums as he crawled forward and grabbed the holy water, then doused the knife with it. Forcing himself to his feet, he lunged forward and plunged the knife deep into Ayar Kachi's back. It stayed there, wedged tight as if his body had suddenly gained tangibility.

Ayar Kachi let out a terrible roar of agony before his form erupted into a giant cloud of darkness. Tyler yelped and covered his face with his arms against the blackness swirling all around him. The particles shot away, clustering together as they filtered out of the dining room, through the kitchen's broken window, and beyond Jessica's backyard.

Tyler took a deep, ragged breath to calm his heart's frantic beating, but it quickened once more at the sight of Jessica. Her crumpled form lay amid a bed of jagged spikes of glass, metal, and wood. He bolted to her side and scanned her body, gasping when he saw a large glass shard protruding from her stomach. Blood poured from the wound in tiny rivers.

In a panic, Tyler dialed 911.

"911, what's your emergency?" a female voice answered.

"Yes, there's been a break in and my friend is hurt badly. We need an ambulance." Tyler gave the operator his address and Jessica's information while clinging to her still arm with his free hand.

The operator assured him an ambulance would be sent over immediately and he stayed on the line, praying help would get there before it was too late.

CHAPTER FOURTEEN

Tyler sat in a cushioned chair next to Jessica's hospital bed, the heartbeat monitor dinging in a steady, healthy rhythm. Her chest rose and fell lightly, and the grimace on her face made his stomach bunch up in knots. He hated seeing her like this, almost as much as he hated himself right now.

She'd just had surgery on her abdomen. The damage from the glass shards wasn't extensive, but the wound was deep and she'd have to spend a day or two in the hospital. Her recovery afterward would take weeks, maybe months, and there would be permanent scarring.

Tyler eyed the folded note he'd written to her in his hand. Jessica would be furious that he was leaving her here on her own, but he hoped in time she would understand. She was vulnerable in this state, and the only way to keep Ayar Kachi away from her was to follow through with his plans to go to Altalona.

Tyler placed the note in her hand and closed her fingers over it. He then stood up, leaned over, and kissed her on the forehead. "I'm so sorry, Jessica. For everything."

After giving her one last glance, Tyler grabbed his duffel and left the room, feeling a small weight lift off his shoulders knowing she would be safe. He headed down the hall, and just as he neared the elevator it dinged and the doors opened.

The world tilted on its axis as he observed Detective Kilgore speaking to a nurse. Their gazes were set on each other as they stepped onto the hospital floor and Tyler scrambled, shooting down the nearest bisecting hallway so he wouldn't be spotted. He held his breath until their footsteps echoed past him.

What the hell was she doing here? She must've been alerted somehow after Tyler had called 911. However she'd found out, he had to get out of here if he wanted to make his flight that left in an hour, but he'd have to wait until she was out of eyeshot.

The nurse and Kilgore's footsteps continued briefly, then stopped. Tyler dared a quick peek. They were standing in front of a kiosk he'd passed on the way to the elevator where another nurse had just taken a seat.

"Hello, I'm here to visit a patient," Kilgore said. "Jessica Buchanan. I'm Detective Kirby Kilgore. I called earlier?"

The nurse manning the kiosk typed some quick commands into her computer and glimpsed the results. "Ah yes, of course. Go on in. It's room 214."

"Thank you, and thank you Lacey," she said to the woman who had accompanied her on the elevator.

As Tyler watched Kirby walk down the hall, his gut clenched as a sudden realization dawned on him. If she went into Jessica's room, she'd see the note he'd given her. Then she'd know what he was planning. *Shit, shit, shit!*

Tyler darted over to the elevator and pounded the down button frantically. The elevator doors opened and he bolted inside, hitting the lobby and close door button in quick succession. He nervously tapped his sides, waiting for the doors to open on the ground floor. If he didn't make it to the airport in time, he'd be stuck in Dallas with Kirby on his tail. And once he was in police custody without any way to protect himself, he was as good as dead.

~

TYLER DRUMMED his fingers on the rear passenger door of his Uber ride as the vehicle approached the congested airline terminal. With so much at stake, he'd been mulling over what to say the entire ride to the airport, but he didn't have any more time. He pulled out his phone and placed a call to his mother. When the call went to voicemail his heart sank, but he hoped his message would help mend the rift between them if he made it back to the states alive.

"Hey, Mom. I know things aren't great right now between us, but I wanted to say I'm sorry. I never should've snapped at you like that. There's been so much happening in my life, but that's no excuse for how I treated you. I know you only want the best for me, and I appreciate all you've done. There's something I have to do, and I have to go away for a while. I know you can't understand right now but … when I come back I want to make things better. I love you."

Tyler let out the breath he'd been holding in and watched the sea of red brake lights around him as the car inched towards his gate. *What's the deal with all this traffic?* His flight at JFK was supposed to leave in twenty minutes, and even if he blasted through the lines, he'd be cutting it close. The car idled for another minute before Tyler opened his door and took his black duffel bag with him.

"Hey!" The driver shouted at him.

"Sorry, I'm gonna miss my flight!"

Tyler slammed the door shut and raced between cars toward his gate. Angry horns honked at his disturbance, and after a couple close calls he made it to the sidewalk. He took a deep breath before hurrying inside the terminal.

Amid the hustle and bustle, Tyler located his gate entry not far away. He speed-walked ahead, keeping a wary eye on his surroundings. He didn't see Ayar Kachi anywhere, and after thinking on the subject for a moment he relaxed a bit. He'd injured him earlier in their scuffle, and judging by the spirit's speedy exit he must have really done a number on him. That had to have bought him some time, and even if Ayar Kachi had the strength to keep pursuing him, he wouldn't expose himself so carelessly in front of so many people, would he? Tyler hoped he was right.

Rushing into his gate's long entry line, Tyler spotted a black female TSA officer moving through the line and looking over other passengers' boarding passes. He waved frantically to get her attention, and she reluctantly made her way over to him with a pinched expression.

"Yes?" she said, lacking any hint of enthusiasm.

"I'm gonna miss my flight to Peru. It leaves in twenty minutes."

"I'm sorry, but that's not my problem. You'll have to speak with your airline about making other arrangements."

The broad-shouldered woman turned to leave, and Tyler nearly screamed in frustration. This woman was his last shot to make his flight. There had to be something she could–Tyler's heart skipped a beat as a small rainbow clip pinning the woman's shoulder-length hair back caught his attention. Was she gay? If she was, maybe he could convince her this was an emergency. But what would he say? Precious seconds ticked away as she walked, and Tyler left the line, quickly catching up to her.

"Miss, *please*," he said.

The woman turned around and placed her hands on her

hips. "Did you not hear me the first time? There's nothing I can do to help you. Talk to your airline."

"Please, this isn't some vacation. It's an emergency. My husband went missing in Peru. I know who took him, but the authorities won't listen to me."

The woman's lips twisted as she mulled over his plea.

"He's the love of my life. If I don't make this flight, I don't know what will happen to him. He could *die*. The last three years of our life together will have meant nothing. "

After a long moment, the woman cursed to herself. "You better not be lying to me. I could lose my job for this."

"I'm not, I promise. His name is Gabriel Price, and–"

"Show me your boarding pass," she demanded.

After inspecting Tyler's pass she escorted him to the front of the line and passed him off to another agent. He thanked her profusely as she left, and the TSA at the checkpoint rechecked his information before telling him to move ahead. As Tyler passed into the security screening area, he faintly heard his name being called. He turned around to see a redheaded woman resembling Detective Kilgore running towards his gate from a distance.

Tyler's pulse thundered in his ears and he spun back around, hoping she hadn't seen him. *Damn it! She must've booked it the second she read my note.*

He fidgeted impatiently as the line moved at a sluggish pace. No matter what, he couldn't let Detective Kilgore stop him. If he was put in police custody Ayar Kachi wouldn't hesitate to kill him and continue his massacre with his parents and possibly Jessica. Finally, Tyler arrived at the body scanner. He stepped inside and stood in place. As he raised his arms, Detective Kilgore's tense voice carried over to him from the front of the gate entry. *Damn it, she's close!*

The body scanner finished its function and Tyler moved on just as Kilgore entered the security screening area and called for him again. He ignored her, grabbing his duffel bag from the conveyor belt and entering the inner gate. As he walked briskly forward, the intercom announced his flight was doing its final boarding call.

Shit! His flight was at the far end of the gate. If he didn't pick up the pace he'd miss it, but he'd also risk catching the detective's attention. Tyler dared a look back. Detective Kilgore had just cleared the security screening area. She looked his way, locking eyes with him.

Tyler bolted, and Detective Kilgore shouted after him above the din of the inner gate. He darted between other patrons in a tight formation, hoping to put distance between him and the detective. He was halfway across the gate when two large crowds of offboarding passengers began to converge towards one another, nearly blocking the path ahead. If he could worm his way through, it may delay Kilgore long enough for him to get on the plane.

He rushed forward, straining for speed. Just in time, Tyler wedged himself between the two converging crowds and was jostled with shouts of protest. Ignoring their frustration, he pushed his way through. When he broke free of the throng, the gate for his flight came into view. Two flight attendants were about to close the large metal doors for onboarding.

"Wait!" Tyler called, waving his arms.

He showed the irritated attendants his mobile pass and they let him through, telling him to hurry down the ramp. He started his descent, giving them one last glance as they shut the doors. Right before they closed, he caught a glimpse of Detective Kilgore and smiled to himself. *Better luck next time.*

Tyler sped down the jet bridge and got onto the plane just as they were about to retract the bridge. Sitting himself in one of the only spots remaining in the far back, he exhaled deeply to calm his panicked pulse. Getting onto the plane and ditching Detective Kilgore was a close call, but he'd pulled it off.

Knowing the detective's persistence, this was far from over. She or the authorities in Peru would certainly be looking for him once she told them about the situation, but he had a head start and he was going to make it count. Besides, he had bigger fish to fry. This was his last chance to end Ayar Kachi, and he was going to find out how or die trying.

CHAPTER FIFTEEN

yler brought his crappy car rental to a stop, a cloud of dust rising in its wake. As the particles settled, the squat nondescript inn he and Gabe stayed at several weeks ago came into view, the midday sun bathing it in blinding light. Tyler grimaced and rubbed at his chest. Ever since landing in Peru, there was a strange tightness in his chest that had only worsened as he approached Altalona.

Cursing his poor decision to shovel down shitty airline food, Tyler grabbed his duffel, got out of the car, and headed to the inn. As he neared the entrance he noticed a ceramic stepped cross in vibrant colors nailed above the front door. *Was that there last time?*

He shrugged it off and stepped inside. Upon entry, his scar from Ayar Kachi throbbed in searing pain as if someone had reinflicted the wound. Tyler sucked air through his teeth to stop himself from swearing. What just happened? He hadn't felt any pain like that since getting the injury.

Fighting through the bizarre sting, he observed his surroundings. The tiny lobby was just as he remembered, with exotic plants hanging overhead in worn baskets and old framed pictures mounted on the wall. At the check-in counter, Rosalinda stood with her back turned toward him, her nose in a book.

Tyler approached the desk, speaking up when she failed to notice his presence. "Hey, Rosalinda."

Rosalinda jolted at the sudden intrusion. *"Dios mio!"* She spun around, her eyes widening at the sight of him. "Tyler Collins? What are you doing here?"

"Well, I didn't have much of a choice when you didn't return my call. I need your help. Something terrible happened in the ruins I was searching for. My friend was killed by the spirit of Ayar Kachi, and now he's after me. If I don't find a way to stop him he's going to kill me too. Please, you've got to help me."

Tyler awaited Rosalinda's response, unsure how she would react. Maybe she would yell at him for leaving her crazy voice messages, call the cops on him for flying thousands of miles to harass her, tell him to lay off the booze. Instead she crossed her arms, cursing under her breath as she stared hard at Tyler. *She does know something!*

After a moment, she gave a heavy exhale. *"Lo siento,* I cannot help you."

"But you have to! This is life or death. Come on, I know you know something." Tyler fumbled around in his pockets, pulling out several wadded up bills. "I have money!"

Rosalinda scowled at him. "Your money is no good here."

Tyler reluctantly stuffed the money back in his pockets. "Okay, then can I at least rent a room while I'm here?"

"You cannot stay here," Rosalinda said, pointing to Tyler's chest. "You are *maldito.*"

What? Tyler glanced at his torso. The wound on his chest had reopened and was bleeding through his shirt. *When I entered the inn, that pain I felt ... What the hell is happening?*

"If I let you stay, I put everyone here in danger. I am sorry that you came all this way, but there is nothing I can do for you. Please leave."

"Are you kidding me? Where am I supposed to go?"

"I don't care, I said leave!" Rosalinda commanded, her sudden austere tone making Tyler flinch.

A tall man with cropped hair and a muscular physique entered the lobby from the hallway to the right. "*¿Hay algún problema aquí?*"

"No. Senor Collins was just leaving." Rosalinda gave Tyler a stern, expectant look.

Tyler's body tensed at Rosalinda's hypocrisy. "No, I'm not. The only reason I found those ruins is because of you, and now you just want to wipe your hands clean? I don't think so. I want answers, and I want them now!"

Tyler took a step towards Rosalinda's kiosk. The bulky man blocked his way, but that only made Tyler more furious. "Get out of my way!" Tyler threw a punch at the man's face, but he blocked it with his forearm, countering with a sucker-punch from his other muscled arm to his gut.

The air collapsed from Tyler's lungs and he fell to the floor, struggling to catch his breath in ragged croaks. The bulky man mercilessly lifted him from the floor and carried him to the entryway before throwing him outside. Tyler hit the ground with a thud, a cloud of dirt and sand rising around him.

"*¡Y no vuelvas!*" the man shouted. He tossed Tyler's duffel bag out before shutting the front door with a loud bang.

Tyler curled into a fetal position, the sun's searing heat beating upon him as he hacked and coughed his way back to healthy breaths. Finally, he was able to force himself into a sitting position.

How could Rosalinda toss him out knowing Ayar Kachi was coming for him? Would it have hurt her to lift one fucking finger? Tyler closed his eyes, refocusing on his mission to stop Ayar Kachi. Rosalinda may have refused to help him, but there was still Esperanza. Although she'd been against helping him find the ruins in the first place, she might take mercy on him and give him some useful information.

Tyler picked himself up and headed down the street, desperately hoping this would work. There were no other viable options, and he was as good as dead if this didn't pan out.

He entered the market area with its makeshift displays and smorgasbord of colorful merchandise. It was more crowded than the last time he'd been there. Dozens of towns-folk engaged with one another, perused the offerings, and haggled with the vendors. As he walked by the locals stared at him, keeping a wide berth. Tyler trudged forward, uncaring of their opinion of him. None of that mattered now.

In minutes he found himself outside of Esperanza's small house. He stepped through the beaded curtain entrance, his mark from Ayar Kachi throbbing in pain as he nearly ran right into Diego. The sight of his dark mop of hair and pock-marked face sent a wave of furious heat through Tyler's veins like hot needles. The traitorous bastard had left him and Gabe high and dry when they needed him the most. If he would've stayed like he promised, they could have gotten away free and clear. Gabe would still be alive. He wouldn't even be in this dumpster fire of a situation.

Tyler grabbed Diego by his t-shirt and shoved him against the nearest wall, sending wood and bone baubles crashing to the floor. *"You!"*

Diego yelped, and Tyler slammed his fist into his stomach before pushing him to the floor. "Do you have any idea of what you've done? *Do you?* My whole life is completely fucked because of you!"

A clatter sounded from the adjoining room, followed by shouting and quick, heavy footsteps. Esperanza entered the tiny foyer, her gray eyebrows furrowed and her nostrils flared. *"¡Deténgase! ¿Qué está pasando aquí?"* Her eyes narrowed when she saw Tyler.

"Vino a mí de la nada," Diego groaned as he struggled to prop himself up on his elbows.

Esperanza smacked him upside the head. *"Tú y él nos encontramos en la sala principal. ¡Ahora!"*

Esperanza shot them a lingering glare before stomping back into the main room.

Diego got up to his feet and edged away from Tyler, eyeing him apprehensively. "She wants us to meet her in there. We need to talk."

Tyler clenched his fists but reined in his anger. As much as he wanted to keep beating on Diego for abandoning him and Gabe, he knew his emotions had gotten the better of him. Diego wasn't at fault for him coming to Altalona. His own greed for fame and success had done that. At the same time, he couldn't bring himself to apologize to him. He still bore some responsibility for what happened. Tyler followed Diego into the main room, a calming woody scent filling his nostrils.

Nothing had changed since the last time he'd been there. Cabinets lined the room's perimeter, filled with crystals, stones, and jars of herbs. Innumerable dried plants hung from the ceiling, and oddly shaped bone, wood, and feather trinkets were hung on every spare inch of the walls. Esperanza sat in a wooden chair next to a round table with two empty seats. She met Tyler's gaze stone faced and gestured for him and Diego to sit.

They did as instructed, and Diego stared down at his lap with a guilty look on his face until Esperanza spoke up, jolting him to attention. *"Pide disculpas y explícate."*

Diego's brown eyes settled on Tyler. "Tyler, I'm so sorry for what happened. I never should have shown you and Gabe the ruins."

Tyler frowned. "Look, we don't have to do this. Gabe and his parents are dead, my friend Jessica is in the hospital, and I'm running for my life. There are more important things to talk about."

Tears welled in Diego's eyes and his lower lip quivered. "I understand, but please, let me explain. I owe you that much."

Tyler scrutinized Diego for a long moment before acquiescing with a reluctant nod.

"When I met you and Gabe outside of Altalona I told you that I hadn't been living here long, but I didn't tell you everything. I came here because I was looking for my mother. She disappeared around this area like so many others and I had to find her, so I stayed with my *abuela* hoping someone in town had seen her or knew more.

"No one did, and after a while I lost hope until you and Gabe showed up looking for the ruins. I knew about the legend. Everyone in town said they were haunted by an evil spirit, but I didn't believe it. I had already asked Esperanza to take me there, but she refused. I became desperate. The ruins were the only place I hadn't looked for my mother, so I took matters into my own hands. I went through Esperanza's things and stole a map that showed where the ruins were.

"That was when I left you the note saying I could take you there. I had to find my mother, but I wanted to help you too. I never meant to hurt you or Gabe in any way. I'm so sorry, for everything."

Tyler's stomach fluttered as Diego's head drooped. He pitied him for his sad predicament, but the last part of Diego's explanation clawed at him. "Hold on a second. You said you were looking for your mom. If that's true, then why did you leave us and abandon your search?"

Diego shifted with a grimace. "Once you and Gabe entered the ruins, I started looking around outside. I found this."

He pulled an old brass necklace from his pocket and showed it to Tyler. The circular pendant attached to it depicted a full moon on its face with an upraised craggy crescent on the left hand side. Something about the pendant seemed familiar to Tyler, but he couldn't quite place it.

"My mother always wore this wherever she went," Diego explained. "Once I saw it, I knew the legends were true and that Ayar Kachi had killed her. I didn't think. I ran to my truck and drove back here as fast as I could. Esperanza had me return the next day to look for you, but by then it was too late. For Eva, for Gabe, for you …"

An icy jolt gripped Tyler, raising the hairs on the back of his neck. "Did you say Eva? Eva Mendoza?"

"Yes, how do you know her?"

Tyler took out his duffel and rummaged through it, pulling out Eva's phone and presenting it. "I found this inside the ruins. It belonged to her."

Tyler handed the phone over. Diego cradled it to his chest as tears spilled down his face.

"The pictures and videos in Eva's phone helped me and my friend Jessica figure out a few things about Ayar Kachi's curse, but things still fell apart. That's why I'm here now. I need to find a way to stop Ayar Kachi for good. I don't know if that's possible, but there's got to be something I can do."

Diego sniffled and wiped away his tears. "I don't know how to stop him, but I'll do anything I can to help you. That *pendejo* killed my mother and her family, and I won't let him get away with that."

"I could really use the help, but something still doesn't make sense to me. Why didn't Ayar Kachi come for you after he got your mom? I thought he could track the loved ones of those he marked."

Diego opened his mouth to speak several times, but stopped himself each time.

"What is it?" Tyler pressed.

"I, well … What I'm about to say isn't going to make much sense."

"Nothing has made any sense for a long time. Just tell me."

"Alright, but don't say I didn't warn you." Diego held out his right arm, presenting a leather bracelet on his wrist with a small pouch in its center. "You see this?"

"Yeah."

"When I first came here, Esperanza made me wear this bracelet at all times. I didn't question it or the strange looking crosses hung above all the houses in town because my mom always told me how superstitious people were around here. But once I returned from the ruins, she told me the reason behind it all.

"Ayar Kachi has been killing the people of Peru for ages. Every year people and their families go missing, never to return. After a while the community had enough, so they banded together to find a way to prevent these killings. My *abuela*, she's been making items like this for a long time. They're made with herbs grown on sacred land to repel Ayar Kachi. The crosses above the entries to homes do the same thing but they're more powerful."

"How do they work? Don't tell me it's magic."

Diego shifted uncomfortably.

Esperanza's low alto voice broke the silence. "It's alright, Diego. I'll take it from here."

Tyler and Diego both looked to Esperanza, mouths agape.

"*Abuela*? You can speak English?"

"I apologize for the secrecy *nieto*, but I had to be sure of the situation before I truly revealed myself and what I know.

Tyler, you've been through so much in such a short time, and your journey is not over yet. The world you live in is not as it seems. Gods, magic, monsters, they all exist. I am a *bruja*, and with the assistance of a network of covens, we have been protecting this town and many others from Ayar Kachi and other supernatural threats.

"Together, we came up with the idea of the sacred herb pouches and blessed crosses to slow Ayar Kachi down. The pouches protect those who haven't been marked, but their power is limited. That's why the townsfolk stay in their houses after sundown. The crosses are more powerful and prevent Ayar Kachi from entering a household so long as we keep the talismans charged. Combined, these precautions help break the cycle of death and limit Ayar Kachi's power. But when outsiders discover the ruins and are marked, it allows Ayar Kachi to go on a killing rampage and amass his power because they don't have these protections.

"I also need to point out that the presence of those who have been marked inside a blessed household interferes with that protection. That makes us vulnerable, so we have to move fast. A prophecy has been foretold that one day a marked one would survive Ayar Kachi's bloodlust long enough to challenge him and end this horrible cycle of death and despair. This individual would be able to expose Ayar Kachi's true weakness and destroy him. I believe that marked one is you, Tyler. No one else has survived close to how long you've held out."

Tyler put a hand to his head and sighed. "Magic, prophecies, gods and monsters … It sounds crazy, but from what I've already seen I guess it makes sense. It's just a lot."

"I understand. Most people live outside of this dark reality that we keep hidden, but your situation warrants the exposure. Here, let me show you." Esperanza got up and retrieved a nearby pot. She filled it with soil, then buried several seeds underneath before sitting back down. "Watch."

Esperanza's hands hovered over the pot and she closed her eyes, chanting in a low, indiscernible murmur. Tyler gasped as verdant sprouts rose from the soil, quickly blossoming into mature flowers with vibrant petals in red, blue, and purple hues.

"I … I can't believe it. You're really doing this."

Esperanza smiled, her dimples showing at opposing corners of her mouth. "My gift lies in botany. I can influence plants' ability to grow and speed up or slow the process."

"And this network of covens, they can do stuff like this too?"

"Yes. We all have different talents, none of which can defeat Ayar Kachi single handedly."

"Why not? Can't you and the other witches just join forces and, you know, magic him away?" Tyler said with a wiggle of his fingers.

Esperanza sighed. "It's not that simple. The gods' mercy on Ayar Kachi has corrupted his spirit. He is an aberration that cannot be stopped by simple means. If you accept this responsibility, I must send you to The Sisters of the Four Moons. They're the most powerful coven in Peru, and they can give you the answers you seek while guaranteeing your safety. I don't see any other way you can survive this than to seek their counsel in stopping Ayar Kachi once and for all."

Tyler stared down at his lap, mulling over his situation. He still didn't know how he felt about this unbelievable bombshell. Everything he thought he knew about the world was a lie. Magic, monsters, gods. They were real, hiding behind the thin veil that had been his and so many others' reality. Could he really trust Esperanza? It seemed every step of his journey so far had been destined for disaster. On the other hand, if he refused, would he be able to accomplish anything before Ayar Kachi found him?

Tyler locked eyes with Esperanza. "Okay, I'll do it."

"I'm going too," Diego said.

Esperanza's gray brows furrowed at Diego's statement. "*Nieto*, no. It is too dangerous."

"*Abuela*, I have to do this. I may not be completely responsible for what happened to Tyler and Gabe, but I played a part. I have to make amends for that, and if I can avenge my family and save innocent lives at the same time, then it's worth it. Besides, who is going to take Tyler to the sisters? He doesn't know the roads like I do."

Esperanza mulled over Diego's words for a long moment before acquiescing with a tiny nod. "Your argument makes sense, but I still don't like you putting yourself in harm's way. Our family has lost too much to lose you too. Promise me you'll be as safe as you can."

"I promise."

"Are you sure about this?" Tyler asked. "There's no guarantee we'll come back from this. You haven't even dealt with Ayar Kachi before."

"I have to do this. You can fill me in on the way, can't you?"

"Yeah, of course. Well, I guess this is it then. Where are we going, Esperanza?"

Esperanza got up and rifled through the cabinets behind her, returning with a map and a wooden token with the image of a plant carved into it. She sat back down and spread out the map. "You'll be heading for Ayabaca. Once you arrive, go to this location." She circled a block on the village's western borders with a pen and wrote down a house number. "When you get there, present this token to the coven. I've imbued it with my essence so they'll know to trust you. *Do not* lose it. Do you understand?"

Tyler nodded. "Yes, I understand."

Esperanza handed over the sand-dollar sized token, and Tyler stuffed it into his pocket.

"I'd better go grab my things," Diego said. He rose from his seat and left the room, leaving Esperanza and Tyler alone.

Tyler tapped at his thighs with his fingertips, nervous to be isolated with Esperanza after all the nerve-wracking things she'd told him about the world and his uncertain future.

Esperanza glanced his way and patted the chair beside her with a small smile.

Tyler hesitated. If tradition here was similar to what he'd experienced with his latinx friends' moms, refusing this simple request would be an insult. He got up and sat next to her, curious what she wanted to discuss.

"Your mark is still bleeding. I have some salve that should help. Take off your shirt."

"Uh, sure," Tyler said, fighting the heat that rushed into his cheeks. He removed his shirt as she rifled through her cabinets. She returned with a couple rags, a small bowl, a short cylindrical canister, and a glass jar filled with clear liquid.

Esperanza removed the lid from the jar and doused the rag with it over the bowl. As she neared his scar with the rag he tensed.

"It's just water," she reassured him.

"Sorry."

She smiled and soaked the wound with the wet rag.

It stung a little bit, but it felt good.

"It's perfectly normal to feel overwhelmed," Esperanza said in a gentle tone.

Tyler let out the breath he'd been holding in. "Over-whelmed is an understatement. How am I supposed to deal with it all, knowing there's so much awful stuff out there?

Even if I make it through this, I don't know how I'm going to adjust. I feel so … insignificant."

Esperanza removed the wet rag from his skin and tossed it in the small bowl. She grabbed the unused rag and carefully dried his inflamed skin. "Don't doubt yourself, Tyler. You are stronger than you give yourself credit for. You survived this long, did you not?"

Tyler smiled weakly. "Yeah."

She dropped the dry, slightly blood stained rag into the same bowl and unscrewed the lid from the canister. Inside was a pea-colored cream he assumed was the salve. Esperanza scrubbed her hands with some nearby hand sanitizer before scooping up a moderate amount of the substance with the end of two wrinkled fingers. As she massaged the salve into his skin, a warmth spread through the contact site, followed by a soothing coolness.

"Few have ever been able to fend off Ayar Kachi this long, and I am confident you will see this through. As for what happens after, take it day by day. The knowledge you have can be a burden or a gift depending on how you look at it, and you will adjust with time."

"Thank you, for everything. You helped me when no one else would."

"You are welcome. Just promise me that you'll look after Diego. He can make his own decisions, but sometimes I worry."

"Of course."

Esperanza stopped her application of the salve, giving his scarred flesh one last look. "All done. You can put your shirt back on now."

"Thank you.It already feels a lot better."

"Good. It's not a permanent fix, but it should help with the pain."

As Tyler pulled his shirt back on, Diego reentered the

room with a large bulking knapsack. "Alright, I'm ready. Are we all set?"

Tyler got out of his seat. "Yep, we're good to go. Thanks again, Esperanza. I won't forget what you've done for me."

Esperanza nodded, then drew Diego in for a hug. Diego gave her a kiss on the cheek and led the way to the foyer when Esperanza came tottering after them.

"Wait, wait!"

"What is it, *abuela*?" Diego asked.

"A blessing, before you venture into harm's way." Esperanza stood before Tyler. She closed her eyes, brought the fingertips of her hand together, then kissed them. "*Fuerza. Destreza. Valentía. Sabiduría.*" She opened her eyes and placed her hand on Tyler's chest with force.

A light, tingly feeling spread through his core that dispersed in seconds.

Esperanza repeated the process with Diego, then waved them goodbye as they left.

Tyler and Diego walked across the street to Diego's beat-up red pickup. After setting their bags on the floor of the interior they set out, leaving the tiny town of Altalona behind in a trail of dust.

Tyler watched the expansive green backdrop of forest recede in the rearview mirror. Esperanza was betting a lot on him and Diego, and despite her optimistic words he still had no idea what this coven wanted from him or how they were going to stop Ayar Kachi. What could he do that they couldn't with their powers? Whatever it was, he hoped their plan would work. His life and so many others depended on it.

CHAPTER SIXTEEN

*D*iego clutched the steering wheel, his knuckles white with tension. "Come on, come on, come on."

Tyler watched nervously as smoke continued to spill out from under the pickup's hood. It started just a few minutes ago, and with nothing but dried out hills, trees, and shrubs along the paved road they didn't have much else of a choice but to keep going.

The vehicle gave a sudden sharp sputter, and a large plume of black smoke erupted from the hood. Diego kept his foot planted on the gas pedal but the vehicle slowed to a stop, forcing him to veer to the right hand side of the road.

Diego slapped the console. "*¡Joder, joder, joder!*"

Tyler tried to think of something optimistic to say, but couldn't find the words. "What should we do? I'm no good with car repairs."

Diego rested his forehead on the steering wheel. "Neither am I. *¡Hijo de puta!*" He smacked the dashboard again.

Tyler rummaged around the floor of the car and found the map they'd been using. "Let's look and see where we are.

We can't be that far away, can we? We saw that sign for Ayabaca a couple miles back."

Diego lifted his head from the steering wheel, red faced, and gave Tyler a feeble smile. "Yeah, okay. Sorry for getting riled up."

"It's alright. Happens to the best of us."

Tyler eyed Diego warily as he took the map and spread it out before them. As he told Diego of his encounters with Ayar Kachi on their drive to Ayabaca he'd become increasingly upset: heavy breathing, clenching his jaw, muttering to himself. Tyler had felt the same anger when he lost Gabe, but he worried it might make Diego too impulsive when caution was needed, especially if they had to fight him soon.

"We're on this road here," Diego said, pointing to their current location. "So if we keep going south we'll hit Yacupampa, then Ayabaca. That's only a little over a kilometer, and once we reach the center of town we can go west at the plaza. Our destination is a couple streets over from there."

"That sounds simple enough, but how are we going to get there?"

Diego pulled out his phone, entered some commands, and frowned. "By the time the nearest Uber gets to us we'll have nearly made it on foot. Let's grab our stuff and head out."

"You're just going to leave your truck here?"

"There's no time and I don't have money for a mechanic. I can figure it out later."

"Alright, if that's what you want. Lead the way."

They gathered their things and headed down the road. The overgrown trees and shrubs threatened to overtake the pavement before giving way to a scattering of boxy dwellings and establishments. The small residential area tapered off until they passed a shabby hospital and swathe of clay houses half a mile further. The residences had rusty tin roofs and were painted in dull shades of white, blue, and pink. Some of them had been converted into makeshift shops selling miscellaneous knicknacks, clothing, and other accouterments.

The road widened over the next few blocks, opening into a large square under the full light of the scathing afternoon sun. Droves of townsfolk were scattered throughout the streets going about their business, and a sense of calm washed over Tyler as he watched the everyday hustle and bustle.

Diego took a right at the next intersection of streets where a large yellow building with two elaborately designed towers at its front loomed on the left.

"Whoa, what's that?" Tyler asked.

Diego made the sign of the cross. "That's the *Templo del Señor Cautivo*. It's a famous church people come to visit every fall. They come from all over: Ecuador, Colombia, other parts of Peru. They usually travel on foot and it can take them months to get here."

"Why would they do that?"

"To pray at the Land of the Captive is a great privilege. The journey here is a sign of their devotion and faith."

"Hmm, that's pretty cool I guess. I'm not religious, but knowing gods exist kinda makes me wonder if I shouldn't at least consider the whole thing."

Diego smiled and shrugged. "You'll get no judgment from me. I was raised Catholic, so it's pretty much programmed into my head. Oh hey, let's stop over here for a bite. I'm starving."

They came to a halt at the side of a white building under a banner that read *Restaurante El Carbón*. Tyler peered inside the establishment's open door. A couple simple tables and plastic chairs filled most of the small dining area with a little bar at the back wall. Spicy scents drifted from inside the eatery, making his stomach gurgle.

"Okay, but let's make it quick."

Diego and Tyler sat down and ordered a meal of *Pollo Saltado*, a Peruvian chicken stir fry, and *Lomo a lo Pobre*, a cousin of steak, eggs, and potatoes.

Once the server disappeared from view, Tyler leaned back in his plastic chair and nudged his feet out of his shoes with a groan. "Ugh, my feet are killing me."

"I'm guessing you don't walk very much where you're from?"

"I mean, I'm not out of shape, but in Dallas everything is pretty spread out so I usually have to drive around."

"I've never been there, but I stayed in Austin while I was abroad. I loved all the music festivals there. My mom would've loved it …" He frowned.

"What was she like?"

"Amazing. She was a kind, gentle person. She always had something nice to say about everyone. She loved to sing, and she got so good she was able to perform at some local places."

"Wow, that's awesome. Any chance you inherited some of her singing skills?

Diego chuckled. "Nope, not at all. If I sang in the truck you probably would have begged me to let you walk here."

Tyler laughed.

"What about you? How did you get into ghost hunting?"

"My grandma. After she died me and my parents visited her old house to get a couple things. When I went into her room I had this weird sense that she was still there, even though I knew she was gone. I was so freaked out by the feeling that I ran out of the house. When I went to sleep that night she visited me in my dreams and told me not to be scared, that everything was alright and she was in a better place. Ever since then I was fascinated with the paranormal and started making videos on tours of local haunted places. It turned into this whole thing."

Diego smiled. "Whoa, that's so cool. I'm sure your grandma is proud of you."

"I hope so."

The server arrived with their food and they made quick work of their spicy, flavorful meal. They left the small restaurant in a noticeably better mood and took a right onto Arequipa Avenue, following the winding path west. Squat, dingy residences resembling the ones they'd passed earlier lined both sides of the street in faded colors. They walked on for a while, and Tyler felt a buzz of concern when he noticed there hadn't been a soul in sight for some time.

"Are you sure we're headed in the right direction?" Tyler asked. "It's kinda weird that no one's out here."

"Don't worry so much. It's the middle of the afternoon. People are working. We'll be there in just a few minutes."

"Alright, if you say so."

They proceeded down the deserted road, the condition of the houses getting shabbier as they went along. Rounding an unremarkable corner, Diego came to a sudden stop. Before them stood a cluster of residences that formed a dead end. He pulled out the map and scrutinized their surroundings, his brow furrowing.

"What is it?" Tyler asked.

"I think we went too far. Let's back up a little."

Tyler and Diego reversed course, carefully retracing their steps.

"Okay, that pink house is 215, and over there is 219, meaning 217 is ..." Diego frowned as his gaze focused on a large dilapidated residence with busted windows and craters in its walls. "This doesn't make any sense. Why would my *abuela* send us to an abandoned house?"

"I don't know. Maybe she wrote down the wrong

address?" Tyler stepped towards the crumbling building, flinching back when he felt a strange charge to the air. "Wait, Diego. Come here."

Diego shuffled next to him. "What is it?"

"Do you feel that? It's weird, almost like the air's been electrified or something."

Diego reached forward with his free hand, his eyes widening. "Whoa, what is that?"

"I have no idea. Do you think our eyes could be tricking us or something? I mean, they're a coven. They probably want to keep a low profile. Maybe this is how they protect themselves from intruders."

"You think so?"

"There's only one way to find out. Stay here."

Tyler walked toward the rickety front door. The electrified sensation intensified, making the hairs on his arms stand up on end. "It's getting stronger," he called back to Diego. He continued onward, stopping a couple feet from the ramshackle entrance. The thin flimsy door looked like it might succumb to the slightest gust of wind.

Here goes nothing.

Tyler grabbed the door's knob. On contact, a massive burst of energy shot through him, sending his body flying back. He hit the pavement with a hard thud and rolled to a stop on his stomach. As he settled, every orifice throbbed with prickling, searing pain as if he'd been electrocuted.

"Tyler!" Diego cried.

Tyler tried to push himself up but the agonizing sting throbbed, sending him back to the ground. When he attempted to rise again, cold metal pressed against his throat. Tyler froze in place, sharing a shocked expression with Diego who had stopped several yards away.

"Either of you move and I'll slit his throat," a deep female voice threatened. "Who are you and why are you here?"

"Please don't hurt him," Diego pleaded. "My *abuela* Esperanza sent us here. I'm her grandson, Diego Mendoza."

"Oh really now? And how am I supposed to believe that?"

"Esperanza gave us a token containing her essence to prove who we were. My friend Tyler has it in his pocket. He can hand it over to you."

A bead of sweat ran down Tyler's forehead as he struggled to maintain his uncomfortable position and tolerate the ebbing pain from the door. "Is that okay or are you going to gut me in the street? I'm about to cramp up here."

The woman silently relented as the cold steel was released from his skin. Tyler eased himself back down to the pavement and took several deep breaths to recover.

"Slowly reach into your pocket and remove the token. Don't do anything stupid."

Keeping the rest of his body still, Tyler moved his right arm down to his pocket and retrieved the wooden token. He held it out and the woman snatched it from his hand. Several seconds passed.

"Huh, I guess you're right. You can move now."

Tyler's pain from the boobytrapped door had diminished a considerable amount, and he managed to pull himself to his feet without too much difficulty. The woman who threatened him stood before them with an irritated look on her face, a long broad knife still in her hand. She had a long black pixie cut and was clad in jeans and a t-shirt with a tan leather jacket over it.

"Why has Esperanza sent you here?" she demanded.

"We need your help," Diego said. "Tyler was marked by the spirit of Ayar Kachi a couple weeks ago. Esperanza said there was a prophecy that a marked one could expose his weakness and help destroy him. She thinks Tyler is the one mentioned in the prophecy and sent us your way."

The woman's green eyes widened. "You want us to help you vanquish a centuries-old aberrant spirit?"

Diego and Tyler looked at each other and nodded.

"Yes," Diego confirmed.

The woman scoffed. "Esperanza sure has a strange sense of humor. There's no way that's going to happen, but you may as well come inside. Rafaela is not going to like this."

The woman headed back to the derelict building, and Diego and Tyler followed after her. She stopped several feet from the front door and thrust her free palm towards it. "*Desarmar.*"

The door's surface rippled like a lake disturbed by a stone before resuming its shoddy appearance. The woman opened the door and glanced back at them, gesturing for them to enter.

Tyler and Diego remained fixed on the spot. Beyond the crappy door was a large warmly lit space that was the complete opposite of the building's exterior.

The woman sighed. "Are you coming or not? I don't have all day."

Tyler forced himself to place one foot in front of the other, fighting his shock at everything that had transpired in the past several minutes. Witches were powerful, and they could affect the world more than he ever could've imagined. If anywhere was safe from Ayar Kachi, it was here. He just hoped this coven would be strong enough to help stop him too.

CHAPTER SEVENTEEN

Tyler stepped inside the house, taking one last look outside before the door shut of its own accord. He found himself in a clean, vaulted foyer with tan stucco walls. Crosses and oddly-shaped baubles made of clay, bone, and feathers adorned the walls like Esperanza's house.

The woman with the long pixie cut led the way beyond the rounded arch that marked the foyer's end to an expansive living area. Open cabinets filled with herbs of all kinds lined the perimeter, and dark furniture atop ornate rugs occupied the far end of the space. Three other women were present, all of them seemingly preoccupied and unaware of their presence.

"What is this place, and how is it so spacious in here?" Tyler asked. "The outside looked so much smaller."

"This is our covenstead," the woman remarked casually. "The space has been augmented magically so we can work more comfortably. What you saw outside is a glamour, an illusion to avoid unwanted attention. We may have to strengthen our spell if you two were able to fight through it."

They neared the center of the living area where a woman

sat in a lotus position on the floor with long beachy black hair. As they approached she acknowledged their presence with a soft smile and rose from her spot to amble towards them. She wore a loosely fitting shirt with draping sleeves, and her eyes were a stunning aquamarine that looked almost unnatural. When her gaze fell on Tyler she stopped in her tracks, the color in her face paling as if she'd seen a ghost.

"Tyler, you're alive."

Tyler gaped at her. "What? How do you know my name?"

"I've been keeping an eye on Ayar Kachi and his victims. I saw many possibilities for you, very few in which you survived. I'm glad you're still in one piece. Someone must be looking out for you."

Tyler took a step back. "I, what?"

"Doria, now's not the time," their guide grumbled. "These two need to speak with Rafaela."

Doria grimaced. "There's nothing wrong with being friendly, Carmen. Besides, if they have something to say about Ayar Kachi, we all need to hear it."

"Whatever, I'm just following protocol. Come on, Tyler, Diego."

Carmen led Diego and Tyler to the far end of the room where the remaining two women sat on a pair of brown couches near a circular coffee table. The one on the left was donned in flowy bohemian garb with brown curly hair piled atop her head that cascaded down in perfect ringlets. The other wore a drapey beige top and matching pants with her jet black hair pulled in a bun so severe it looked like it hurt.

"Rafaela, Rubi, we've got guests," Carmen announced. "Esperanza sent them." She handed Esperanza's wooden token to the woman in a tight bun.

She glanced at the token in her hands, then eyed Tyler and Diego with a cold, piercing gaze. "I see. And why did she send these disheveled young men our way?"

"We need your help," Tyler blurted out. "Please, help us destroy Ayar Kachi."

The bohemian garbed woman burst into uncontrolled laughter, and the woman in the tight bun shot her a dirty look. "What, Rafaela? It was funny!"

"Ayar Kachi is no laughing matter. He's killed dozens of innocents over the past year alone. Entire *familias*, gone like that," Rafaela said with a snap of her fingers.

Rubi rolled her eyes.

Tyler took a small step forward. "Erm, right, that's why we're here. Esperanza told us about a prophecy that one day someone marked by Ayar Kachi would survive long enough to fight him and stop him for good. Esperanza believes I'm that person." Tyler lowered his shirt and presented the scar on his chest that had recently scabbed over again.

Rafaela shot up to her feet with a vicious sneer. "*¡Qué mierda!* Did you know about this, Carmen? You know how dangerous a marked one is! Ayar Kachi could come knocking on our door at any moment."

"It doesn't matter," Carmen said. "The wards will hold, and Esperanza was right in sending them here. We are their best shot at survival. The least we can do is tell them what we know."

Rubi and Doria nodded at Carmen's words, and the three of them looked to Rafaela. Her angry expression deflated as she sat back down in a refined manner. "Alright then. Everyone take a seat and let these men tell us what they know about the prophecy."

The four women gathered snugly on one couch, and Tyler sat next to Diego on the other, feeling self-conscious as their gazes settled on them.

"Honestly, Esperanza didn't say much more than what I already told you. Right, Diego?"

Diego prodded his lower lip with his forefinger as he

thought it over. "I think the most important part was that the marked one is supposed to be able to locate and expose Ayar Kachi's true weakness, whatever that means."

"Oh yeah, right." Tyler glanced back at the four women. "Do you know what that means? I've faced Ayar Kachi several times and the only thing that drives him away is holy water, but its effect on him seems to be weakening with each kill. I'd hardly call that a weakness."

"Your assumption is correct," Rafaela confirmed. "Although blessed objects can weaken or repel Ayar Kachi temporarily they cannot destroy him, and the effects lessen as he amasses power. He is something of an enigma, spiritually speaking. I assume you are familiar with the tale of his demise?"

Tyler and Diego nodded.

"Good. When Ayar Kachi blasphemed the gods' mercy, Supay, the god of death, cursed him. It transformed his spirit into the aberration it is today. Your mark bears the weight of that curse."

Tyler struggled to keep his expression neutral. The crazy looking wooden figurine in the inn, the similar symbol on the stone arch in the ruins, his scar. It was all connected to the god who cursed Ayar Kachi.

Rubi leaned forward in her spot on the far left, resting an elbow on the couch's armrest. "From what we gathered in our research, when Supay took Ayar Kachi's life and cursed him, he intended for the blasphemer's spirit to waste away in agony. But somehow he found a way to drain the life force from the living to sustain himself before that happened. This has allowed him to live for centuries.

"Ayar Kachi's spirit remains in a constant state of flux. He must continue to feed in order to survive or he will fade to nothing. We have seen him at his strongest and weakest, and in all instances he has managed to draw an unsuspecting victim to him before we could intervene. All that being said, he still has one crucial weakness."

"His physical body," Carmen said. She rose from her perch on the opposing armrest and stood beside the round coffee table to face them all. "Ayar Kachi's body was never found, and we have reason to believe that his body lies somewhere within the ruins he protects. If a marked one can lead the way to his remains, his body can be blessed and given proper funeral rites. We believe this will supersede Supay's curse and force his spirit to move on."

Tyler's heart fluttered in its cage. Finally, a way to stop Ayar Kachi's reign of terror, but still … "I like what you're suggesting, but how did you figure this out?"

"It's … complicated. We've only witnessed this a couple of times since we started monitoring the situation, but those marked by Ayar Kachi seem able to locate the ruins with no prior knowledge of his resting place. We believe that this is due to the bond that Ayar Kachi creates with his victims.

"When Supay cursed him, a connection was created between them. In order for a curse to work for this long it would have to be rooted in a physical anchor. The only tangible thing left of Ayar Kachi is his remains, so that has to be it. We also believe that the bond he depends on to hunt can be used against him. The victims we've been able to communicate with in the past described the sensation of this connection as a pull in their chest that guided them. Have you experienced this?"

A chill shot down Tyler's spine. He'd felt a tightness in his chest ever since landing in Peru. "Yes. Ever since I came back there's been a weird pull in my chest. I thought it was because of the crappy food I ate on the plane, but you're telling me that feeling is my bond with Ayar Kachi?"

Carmen nodded. "That's right. How is the feeling in your chest now?"

Tyler grimaced. "It's still there but it's a lot fainter than when I was in Altalona."

"That makes sense given how much further we are from the ruins."

"Okay, so what are Diego and I supposed to do now? Can someone show me how to use this bond thing inside of me?"

Carmen frowned. "I'm sorry, but that's impossible. By the time we located the last marked ones, Ayar Kachi was too hot on their trail. They were killed before we could get them to explain how the pull worked for them in more detail."

"Didn't you try to protect them?"

"Of course we did, but at that point Ayar Kachi was too powerful. We were forced to retreat."

Tyler sighed and pinched the bridge of his nose. "So let me get this right. This weird tightness in my chest is supposed to lead me to Ayar Kachi's remains, but there's no one to show me how to use it and no guarantee that it even does what you think it does?"

The four women stared back at him blankly.

"How the hell are we supposed to defeat Ayar Kachi like this?"

His hosts looked to one another nervously before Rafaela spoke up. "We never said we would help you destroy Ayar Kachi."

"What?" Diego said. "Tyler is fighting for his life, and my family deserves retribution!"

Rafaela's shoulders drooped and her expression softened. "Believe me, we understand the point you are making, more than you know. But it's not that simple."

"What about this *isn't* simple?" Tyler challenged. "If you don't help us Diego and I are going to die trying to find Ayar Kachi's body. And that's not counting the fact that neither of us know how to bless a corpse or give it funeral rites. It's suicide."

"You have no idea what you're asking. Our coven is the most powerful in Peru. There are millions of innocents in our care. Abandoning our duty to accompany you could risk all of those lives. The needs of the many outweigh the needs of the few."

"Needs of the *few?* Diego's family was killed by Ayar Kachi and so was Gabe's. Mine will be too if you do nothing. Didn't you guys say that dozens were killed this year? This awful spiral of death is just going to keep happening. Can you really sit back and let this go on?"

Rafaela scoffed. "You have no idea of the boundless threats we protect Peru from day in and day out. This world is plagued with ungodly terrors and horrors beyond your imagination; monstrosities that would shatter your soul, abominations that would make you claw your eyes out and beg for merciful death. We have to draw the line somewhere, and I place it at the safety of our innocents."

Rubi scooted forward in her seat and leered at Rafaela. "That's not the entire truth. Sure, there are terrors we battle beyond any mortal's comprehension, but the situation is complicated because The Pentacle wasn't convinced that Ayar Kachi's threat to humanity was enough to warrant assistance."

"The Pentacle? What's that?" Diego asked.

"Our governing body. Think of them as management of the grand design of the world. But what I'm really trying to say is that I agree with Tyler and Diego. We've seen the damage Ayar Kachi is capable of inflicting time and time again, and we have to act now if we want to put a stop to all of this."

Rafaela's brows furrowed. "You would defy The Pentacle's edict? You know that if you do there will be consequences."

Rubi shot out of her seat. "We don't have a choice, can't you see that? By the time The Five agree to hear us out it'll be too late. I'm sick and tired of letting that evil *bastardo* get away with murder because the body count falls beneath The Pentacle's radar." Rubi turned to face Tyler and Diego. "I'll help you, even if it means defying The Pentacle and leaving this coven."

"But what about our patrols?" Carmen argued. "Everything will be in complete chaos. What if something happens?"

Rubi cocked an eyebrow. "I think you're being a little dramatic. There are plenty of capable acolytes willing to take our place should anything happen, ones that have already expressed a desire to be more involved. I won't put a price on a life. They are all worth the same, whether it's the many or the few."

"I want to help too," Doria muttered, her gaze focused on the floor as she avoided eye contact. "The visions of terror I've seen through the eyes of Ayar Kachi's victims, it's unimaginable. We have to do something."

Rafaela threw her hands up in the air. "I can't believe this. Carmen, do you feel the same way?"

Carmen looked away, long ebony strands obscuring her face. "I … I don't know. Doria, can you try and glimpse the future?"

"Sure." Doria moved from her spot on the couch to the floor. She criss crossed her legs and rocked back and forth gently. A cloudy whiteness took over her eyes, and she went still. Several moments later the milky substance drained from them, her pupils and aqua irises re-emerging as she came to. "I'm sorry. The future is too hazy for me to make out. It's too uncertain."

"Thanks for trying, but I won't disobey The Pentacle's edict without a better idea of our odds. Why don't we try expediting an audience with The Five? Maybe they'll hear us out in time."

Rubi shrugged. "You can try, but I'm not going to wait around while you cut through all the red tape."

"Me either," Doria muttered.

"Um okay, so what happens now?" Tyler asked.

Rafaela straightened her posture, recovering her austere composure with an imperious look on her face. "While we may not agree on this decision, the situation is undoubtedly complicated. I agree with Carmen that we should urge The Pentacle to reconsider their stance on Ayar Kachi given the number of fatalities, but that will likely take more time than you are willing to wait.

"Rubi, Doria, thank you for all that you've done, but I still have to report this defection to The Pentacle. I'll advise of your decision to leave the coven first thing in the morning and reach out to our most promising acolytes to fill the gap. With the sun about to set, I suggest you all stay here for the night and head out tomorrow. Carmen and I will reinforce the wards in case Ayar Kachi attempts an attack."

Carmen and Rafaela left the communal space, and Rubi and Doria watched them go before rising from their seats.

"Come on, we'll show you to your room so we can talk more and you can get some rest," Rubi said.

Diego and Tyler shadowed the women as they walked to a nearby door on their left. Doria opened the door and ushered them in. The room was decorated in soft blue hues that gave it a comforting, beachy feel. A large bed was positioned against a wall with big fluffy pillows, and several chairs and a small table sat in the far corner.

Tyler wandered into the room, making a full roundabout to take it all in. "Wow, this is nice. Very relaxing."

Doria's cheeks turned a light shade of red. "Thank you. I designed this room."

"Are you sure everything's okay? Things seemed pretty tense back there."

"Of course," Rubi said with a flick of her wrist. "Rafaela is upset. She doesn't hide her emotions very well, but she's a passionate and reasonable leader. She knows we aren't going to budge on this, and we're not afraid of The Pentacle's judgment. Their former ruling on Ayar Kachi was highly divided and a big hot button issue here in Peru. We're just doing what is right for our innocents."

"Thank you for helping us." A gentle breeze blew in the room, shifting the hairs on Tyler's arms. He glanced around, but there weren't any windows or vents for air conditioning. "Um, where is that wind coming from?"

"It's a breeze enchantment I had Rafaela set up," Doria explained. "Please, make yourselves comfortable."

Diego took a seat on the edge of the bed. Tyler went to the other end and plopped down, leaning against a big pillow and grabbing another one to hold in his arms. It was cool to the touch and helped him relax from the strained conversation that had just taken place.

Doria took a central spot on the floor, while Rubi dragged a chair over and sat on it backwards with her head resting on her forearms.

Tyler squeezed his comfort pillow. "You two are putting a lot on the line for me and Diego, especially when there's no guarantee this will work. Actually, how is this going to work? It seems extremely dangerous to bring the fight to Ayar Kachi."

"We're used to dangerous situations, and this is the greatest chance we've ever had at destroying Ayar Kachi," Rubi said. "The effort is worth the risk. Things will get a little tricky once we're inside the ruins, but without us protecting you it would be impossible to find his tomb and perform the necessary rituals."

"Are the rituals complex?" Diego asked.

"In essence, no. Like we said earlier it's really just a matter of blessing the body and baptizing it to force the spirit to move on. The real challenge will be what happens once we start the blessing. Ayar Kachi will manifest to protect his body then."

"How are we going to deal with him when that happens?"

Rubi snapped her fingers. A spark ignited and hovered in the air before her, growing to an apple-sized orb. "With a little magic."

Tyled gaped at the sight. Despite what Esperanza had shown him and Diego, magic was still shocking to see, especially with the ease Rubi had summoned it.

"*Whoa*," Diego remarked, echoing Tyler's thoughts.

"Hey Doria, catch!" With the twitch of a finger, Rubi's orb suddenly went hurtling towards Doria.

Doria's eyes widened, and as the fiery globe neared her a wall of water appeared before her, dissolving the fireball with a sharp sizzle. "Watch it! You know we aren't supposed to be flaunting our gifts like that."

"Oh, come on. I'm just illustrating a point. I've got firepower, and you can protect us."

Tyler scooted to the edge of the bed next to Diego. "This is all very illuminating, but can your powers even affect Ayar Kachi? I tried attacking him, and unless I douse something in holy water nothing will make contact with him."

Rubi tapped a finger to her lips pensively. "How do I explain it … Ayar Kachi is a spirit, right? Everything he does to affect the physical world around him consumes his reservoir of spiritual energy. Magic is much the same. It uses spiritual energy. Therefore, Ayar Kachi operates on the same level that we do. If I throw one of my fireballs in his face he's definitely going to feel the burn. I can't wait to test it out," she said with a wicked gleam in her eyes.

"*Rubi*," Doria said, a warning in her tone.

"Okay, okay, I'll calm it down. I'm just saying that he's got this coming."

"All the more reason to be careful."

Rubi shot her a beaming smile. "You got it, *hermana*. Now, why don't we give these two some space?"

Doria got up from the floor, and Rubi set her chair back in its proper place before heading for the door.

Just before they left, Rubi turned around. "It'll be night soon. Get some rest. You're going to need it for the journey ahead. Let us know if you need anything, and we can talk more about our big battle in the morning."

Tyler and Diego thanked them as they shut the door.

Tyler eyed the bed apprehensively, then looked to Diego.

"It's okay, I'm not going to bite," Diego said.

Tyler smiled and eased himself onto the bed. Diego followed suit, keeping a respectable distance from him.

"How are you feeling about everything?" Diego asked.

Tyler turned onto his side and looked at Diego. "Nervous. What if I screw this up?"

"I get it. It's got to be nerve-racking not to fully understand what's happening to you or have someone to guide you, but I'm sure you'll do fine. You've made it this far, and you already know what to expect from Ayar Kachi."

"Yeah but once we get to the ruins, finding him is all on me. If I fail … The last thing I wanted was to endanger more lives."

"I understand where you're coming from, but we volunteered out of our own free will, Tyler. We've all seen the evil that Ayar Kachi is capable of and we believe in a future where innocent people and their families don't have to die for nothing. For what it's worth, I think Gabe would be proud of you. You're doing the right thing, and that takes a hell of a lot of *cajones*."

Tyler smiled. "Thanks, Diego."

"Of course, man. You tired yet?"

"Yeah."

"Alright, let's get some sleep."

They changed into some more comfortable clothes and Diego turned off the lights.

"Sweet dreams," Diego said.

Tyler settled into a relaxing position on the bed, hoping this would all be over soon with no more innocent blood on his hands.

CHAPTER EIGHTEEN

shrill chime screeched to life, jolting Tyler from his slumber. He groaned and opened his eyes as the sound filled the room in an incessant repetition. Diego sat up in bed next to him, his shaggy black hair shooting in every direction.

"What the hell is that noise?" Tyler shouted over the din.

"I don't know, but something's happening and I don't think it's good. Let's get dressed and go see, quick!"

Diego threw his clothes on in a hurry and Tyler followed suit, pulling on a fresh t-shirt and finding his shoes. Muffled shouts carried from the main room that filled Tyler's core with dread. What was happening? Was Ayar Kachi attacking, or could it be one of the other threats the witches mentioned?

"Tyler, come on!" Diego urged.

"Yeah, sorry." Tyler finished tying his shoes and shot out of bed to follow Diego out of the room.

Inside the cavernous living area, the shrieking alarm blared louder and faster. The air was charged, alive as it crackled with energy. Tyler spotted the Sisters of the Four

Moons gathered before the rounded arch that led into the foyer. They chanted frantically with their gazes focused on the front door.

"What do we do?" Tyler said loudly.

"I'm not sure. Let's head over there in case they need our help or something."

"Okay."

Tyler and Diego edged towards the coven.

Tyler doubted they'd be able to help them in any meaningful way, but as much as he didn't want to interrupt what they were doing he wasn't sure what else they were supposed to do.

As they neared the witches a massive force hit the front door, revealing a bright purple hexagonal grid that wasn't there a moment ago. Sparks shot from the translucent glowing mass and the door held, but the impact rattled the house's foundation and made the ground tremble.

The four women visibly cringed at the assault, and Tyler steadied his feet as his heart pitter pattered. "What the hell was that?"

Rafaela glanced back at Diego and Tyler, her face covered in sweat. "It's Ayar Kachi, stay back! *Hermanas*, keep reinforcing the wards!"

Tyler's stomach dropped into his worn shoes at Rafaela's words. Ayar Kachi was here, and he wasn't leaving until he found Tyler and killed him.

Tyler and Diego backed up as the four women continued their chanting in increasingly desperate tones, the strange purple grid growing brighter from the concerted effort.

Another resounding boom shook the door, and Carmen cried out as the shield faded in color and opacity. "*Mierda*, he's too strong! What do we do?"

"Fall back, but don't stop your work with the wards yet," Rafaela instructed. "Spread out, and on my word we'll surround and trap him within a new set of wards long enough to escape."

Inch by agonizing inch, the witches retreated until they were in the center of the room and spread out from one another. With each step, the chiming alarm picked up in pace and pitch until it was practically screaming in protest at Ayar Kachi's assault. The front door continued to take hits from Ayar Kachi with increasing frequency, and the protective purple grid encasing it steadily diminished to a thin ghostly veil.

After an especially rough battering, Doria fell to one knee and struggled to recover. "We can't keep this up, Rafaela! The wards are going to break!"

"*¡Maldita sea!*" Rafaela spat. "Okay, release your hold on my mark! *Tres … dos … uno!*"

All four women visibly relaxed as they released whatever intangible energy they had been contributing to the wards. At the same time the front door cracked, then blew apart in a showering spray of splinters and dust that filled the room.

Tyler scurried back with Diego, hoping they'd be camou-flaged by the thick haze. All was silent as they waited for Ayar Kachi to attack. However, after a long moment nothing had happened.

The tense silence was more than Tyler's nerves could bear. "Why isn't he–"

With a deafening roar, Ayar Kachi lunged from the dust cloud with supernatural speed, closing the distance between him and Tyler in milliseconds. Tyler lost his breath, too shocked to move. *Oh fuck!*

Ayar Kachi lifted a gnarled claw-like hand to attack, but as he brought it down a sudden torrent of wind blasted Tyler, forcing him outside of range and knocking him on his bottom.

"Now!" Rafaela cried.

Tyler watched in awe as the witches surrounded Ayar Kachi. They raised their hands in unison, and a shimmering wave of kaleidoscopic color burst into existence, clearing away the haze of the room and trapping the evil spirit in a globular sphere of energy.

Ayar Kachi howled in fury and struck at the vibrant colorful mass, but it held firm. The witches continued to chant, and the globe brightened until it was nearly blinding to look at.

"Keep it up!" Rafaela encouraged. "We've almost got it at the right intensity to contain him."

Carmen cried out, and icy fingers shot down Tyler's spine at the sight of the dark river of blood that flowed from her nose.

"I can't hold it!" she moaned. "I, ah!"

Carmen staggered, nearly crumpling to the ground. The orb of prismatic light fractured, no longer restraining Ayar Kachi. Before the others could act, Ayar Kachi spun around like a tempest on a rampage. With a brutal howl of rage, he swiped at Carmen. She fell back with widened eyes, clutching her hands to her neck as a sickening gurgling sound came from her throat and blood seeped through her fingers. Her eyes rolled into the back of her head and she collapsed upon the ground with a loud thump.

Ayar Kachi turned to face the other women with a cruel smile on his lips.

"Carmen, no!" Rafaela shouted.

In one swift motion she pushed her palms towards the evil spirit, her fingers splayed as a cry of agony erupted from her lips. A fierce torrent of wind manifested at her command, bulldozing into Ayar Kachi with a hiss and pelting his form against the nearest wall. She held him there as her irises glowed with amber fury.

Taking advantage of the brief halt in action, Tyler darted

beside Carmen and inspected her wound. Her neck had been shredded savagely, and her breaths were increasingly faint. Tyler shook his head. "I'm sorry, I don't think she's going to make it."

Rubi and Doria rushed over and dove by Carmen's side. Doria placed her hands above her gruesome wound. After a moment of frantic chanting with no visible change in Carmen's condition, Doria sobbed and clung to Carmen. "No, no, no, no, no."

Rubi rose to her feet, her irises burning orange like hot coals. She took a step towards Ayar Kachi. "*That* was a huge mistake. Hold him, Raf."

"Gladly," Rafaela said icily.

Orbs of fire burst to life in Rubi's hands, and she hurled one at the evil spirit with a sharp cry. The fiery ball caught in the funnel of wind Rafaela was powering and slammed into Ayar Kachi's chest in a burst of flames. Ayar Kachi bellowed in pain, erupting into a mass of black mist. He rematerialized several feet outside of Rafaela's wind, but Rubi was ready and thrust another fireball at him, hitting him in the shoulder. He spun and fell to the ground, struggling to get up.

Additional fireballs manifested in Rubi's hands, but Rafaela closed the distance between them and grabbed her arm. "*Don't.* You and Doria have to take Tyler and Diego and go."

"You can't be serious!"

"I'll hold him off, then retreat when I can. *Go.*"

Rubi held Rafaela's gaze for a moment then nodded, the fireballs in her hands extinguishing. "You heard her, people. Let's move!"

Diego, Doria, Rubi, and Tyler scrambled together, then sprinted across the room as fast as they could. Ayar Kachi reached out for them as they passed, but was beaten down by a whistling shriek of wind. Free of pursuit, they crossed the covenstead's threshold and were greeted by the humid night-time summer air.

"Now what?" Diego asked. "My truck's broken down."

"We have a jeep. Come on!" Rubi ordered.

The witches led the way to a green jeep nearby and the four of them crammed inside with Rubi in the driver's seat, Doria on the passenger side, and Tyler and Diego in the back. They raced off with a squeal of the jeep's tires, and Tyler gratefully let his pulse slow before thinking on what just happened. Carmen died trying to stop Ayar Kachi. Was Rafaela strong enough to survive him? If anyone was, it was her. She seemed so strong, so in control.

Tyler glanced around the car. The color in Diego's face had paled, and he stared solemnly at the carpeted floor. Doria sobbed quietly, her eyes squinched tight. Rubi clutched the steering wheel with white knuckles, her irises still blazing a furious orange. In them Tyler could see the agony and pain of her loss.

"Rubi, I–" Tyler began.

"*Don't,*" Rubi commanded, refusing to meet his gaze. "We all knew the risks that came with our positions. I just never thought that Carmen … It doesn't matter. There's no going back now. We have to take care of Ayar Kachi for good, no matter the cost. Are you all with me?"

Doria gave a sniffle and lightly nodded her head, and Diego mustered enough strength to mutter a confirmation.

Tyler met Rubi's austere gaze in the rearview mirror. "Let's end this *pendejo.*"

Tyler followed Doria into the motel room, the absence of adrenaline from Ayar Kachi's assault leaving him fatigued. The room was dingy with simple wall art and dual queen-sized mattresses covered in threadbare comforters and pillows.

Diego entered behind him loudly as he lugged the heavy weapon bag Rubi and Doria had been lucky enough to think of loading into the back of their jeep before Ayar Kachi had attacked.

Doria dragged her feet to the bed nearest the bathroom and sat atop it. She brought her knees up to her chest and wrapped her arms around them, rocking gently back and forth with a distant look in her blue eyes.

Tyler was about to approach her when Rubi shut the door behind him.

"Tyler, Diego. Join me in the bathroom," she instructed. "Bring the weapons and holy water with you."

Tyler and Diego shadowed her into the tiny bathroom and shut the door. The three of them barely fit into the cramped space.

"We should soak the weapons in holy water for the battle tomorrow," Rubi said, her voice devoid of emotion. She had bags under her eyes and her hair was frazzled, making her look as tired as Tyler felt.

Diego sat on the edge of the bathtub. He plugged the drain and gently placed the weapons in the bathtub before looking at Tyler.

Tyler withdrew a large cylinder of holy water from the bag and cradled it in his hands. "How long should we soak them?"

"Not long, just a few hours," Rubi said.

Tyler joined Diego on the lip of the tub and doused the weapons, then found himself staring at the crappy tile floor as an awkward silence filled the tiny area. After a long moment, he snuck a glance at Rubi. She'd sat on the covered toilet and stooped over with her elbows on her knees, using her arms to prop herself up.

"Do you think Doria's gonna be okay?"

Rubi shook her head. "I don't know. Our coven had our disagreements, but we were close. Losing a sister witch is never easy, especially in circumstances like these. I'll talk to her when she's calmed down a bit." Rubi pulled out her phone and her brows furrowed. "I have to keep trying to reach Rafaela. I'll be right outside, okay?"

"But–"

"Not now."

Rubi left the room in a hurry, and Tyler stared after her with a heavy heart. "What was that about?"

"I think she's just stressed with everything that's happened," Diego guessed. "She probably needs some time alone."

Tyler nodded along, but couldn't help the sinking feeling in his stomach. They'd been so confident that their plan was going to work, but now everything felt so hopeless. Rubi and Doria had lost Carmen and possibly Rafaela. How were they supposed to move forward from that? Could they still get the job done?

Luckily, Diego's word cut through his dreary thoughts. "I can't wait till all of this is over. "

"Me too. Got any big plans?"

"With everything that's happened to my family, I was thinking of doing something to honor them. My family always loved music, and I was thinking of opening a place in my mother's name. I want musicians to have a place where their music can be heard, just like those music festivals in Austin."

"Wow, that's a great idea. *Eva's*. That has a nice ring to it."

"Thanks, I think so too. What about you?"

Tyler stared down at his feet. "I don't know. Ayar Kachi kind of took everything over. I thought about leaving the paranormal investigations behind and starting over, but when it comes down to it I really love doing it. Maybe there's a different way to do it I haven't thought of before."

"You'll figure it out," Diego said.

"Yeah, I hope so."

"You will. Do you want to get some sleep? I don't see anything else we can do right now."

"Sounds good to me. I could use a few more hours."

Tyler and Diego went back to the bedroom where Doria was already sound asleep and settled in. Sleep took them quickly.

TYLER SAT on the edge of the queen bed he and Diego had shared, drying his wet hair with a thin, frayed towel.

They had all been worried that Ayar Kachi might find them through his bond with Tyler, so they counted their blessings when he never showed up. Whatever Rafaela did must have been enough to seriously slow him down, but she hadn't answered her phone all night or earlier this morning. Still, that didn't stop Rubi from trying.

Tyler glanced over as Rubi paced the length of the motel room with her phone pressed up to her ear.

After a prolonged moment she sighed and ended the call, throwing her phone on the other bed. "Still nothing. *¡Chingada Madre!*" Her irises flared orange with frustration.

Doria placed a gentle hand on her shoulder, showing none of her despair from the night before. "Let's focus on the now, yes? Rafaela isn't answering, but that doesn't mean she's gone. Her phone could be damaged, or maybe she's hurt and needed medical attention. Either way, we still have a job to do."

"I know. I'm just worried about her, okay? We never saw eye to eye, but I respected her. I don't want the last thing I said to her to be that stupid argument …" Rubi's eyes flared an even brighter orange, and she stopped her tirade to close her eyes and take a deep breath. When she opened them, her eyes were back to their normal warm honey brown. "Thanks for grounding me, Doria."

Doria gave her a light squeeze. *"De nada, hermana."*

Diego came out from the bathroom in a cloud of steam, shirtless with a pair of shorts on. He moseyed over to the bed and grabbed a shirt, pulling it over his head and covering his lean waist and abs.

Tyler averted his gaze as heat rose to his cheeks.

"Now that everyone's well rested, let's regroup," Rubi said.

Diego sat next to Tyler, and Doria took a seat on the other bed.

"Soon we will be heading over to the ruins. When we arrive we'll use Tyler's bond with Ayar Kachi to find his resting place, bless his remains, and give his spirit a proper sendoff. After that, we'll finally be done with this nightmare."

Tyler sighed. "You make it sound so easy, but if any of this goes wrong we're screwed. What if he's there waiting for us when we arrive, or what if my connection to him stops working?"

"Tyler, we decided to wait until midday because Ayar Kachi will be as weak as he's going to get. Most likely he'll be hibernating to conserve his strength. That should hopefully keep us off his radar until we can locate his remains. As for your connection, do you still feel the pull in your chest? Has it not gotten stronger since we left Ayabaca?"

"Well yeah, but that doesn't mean it won't fail later."

"No one can blame you for having cold feet," Diego said. "So much has happened to you and those around you, but right now you have to have faith. We'll back you up, just trust in yourself to see this through. You can do this."

Tyler smiled weakly. "Thanks. Sorry for interrupting, Rubi."

Rubi waved off his apology. "Don't worry, I understand. Getting a gauge of my abilities in my early days as a *bruja* were chaotic to say the least. So as we were saying, the time of day plays a crucial role in us getting inside the ruins undetected. From there, Tyler will have to guide us. You said you believe Ayar Kachi's tomb may be on one of the lower levels, right?"

"That's what I'm thinking," Tyler confirmed. "When Gabe and I first visited, the highest floor was some kind of throne room. We didn't find anything of significance there, so we went down a level. That's where Gabe was attacked, which could mean that he was heading in the right direction."

"Alright, but what are we going to do when Ayar Kachi shows up?" Diego asked.

"That's where we come in," Doria said. "You'll need to depend on our powers for protection. That's why it's so important that we make quick progress towards locating Ayar Kachi's remains once we enter the ruins. If last night is any indication of his strength, it will be very difficult to fight him head on.

"Once we find his body either one of us can perform the sending, but Rubi's powers are more suitable for battle so I will focus on the blessing and funeral rites. Everyone else will need to keep Ayar Kachi preoccupied."

Tyler nodded. "Right, and we've got the blessed weapons we soaked last night, so we'll actually stand a chance to do some damage."

Diego agreed with a bob of his head, then a strained silence filled the room.

Tyler glanced around, noting the tension in everyone's demeanor. They had to be thinking about it too. This was it. There was no turning back once they entered the ruins, no plan B to fall back on. It was this or death for all of them; no one would be backing down from the fight.

"Well I'd say this awkward silence has lasted long enough," Rubi said, breaking the quiet. "Let's get ready to head out. Is five minutes okay?"

Everyone muttered in agreement and went their separate ways to ready themselves.

Tyler grabbed his knapsack and sat on the side of his bed. He emptied the contents onto the worn comforter: a bottle of holy water, a flashlight, and a blessed hunting knife lay before him. He resisted a delirious chuckle that threatened to burst from his lips.

He couldn't believe how quickly spirit hunting had taken over his life, how everything he always thought he knew had just faded into the background. He still had his doubts about what he would do when all of this was over, but he knew whatever it was, it would be something that would make Gabe proud.

Tyler closed his eyes. *Wherever you are out there, I hope you found peace, Gabe. Take good care of your mom and dad.*

Packing his items back in his knapsack and finishing his preparations, Tyler joined the others to depart. It was time to face Ayar Kachi one last time.

CHAPTER NINETEEN

The jeep rolled to a stop before an immense expanse of rainforest, the towering trees like sentinels camouflaging the great evil within their depths.

"We're here, or as close as we're going to get by car," Rubi announced. "Tyler, can you still feel the tightness in your chest?"

Tyler grimaced as he rubbed at the ache in his chest. "Yep, as uncomfortable as ever."

"Alright, let's get going."

The four of them exited the vehicle. Diego took his backpack and bag of weapons they'd soaked from the back of the jeep, and Tyler donned his knapsack.

Rubi led the way from the car to a nondescript gap in the tightly packed tree line. Diego, Doria, and Tyler shadowed her, and as they entered the forest the whoops, hollers, and cries of wildlife went eerily quiet. Tyler frowned as he assessed their surroundings. This was just like when they'd first escaped the ruins. The forest had gone strangely silent then too.

"Hey, what gives with the silent act around us?" Tyler asked. "The same thing happened when I escaped with Gabe after he was marked."

"When you were marked, your aura was imbued with Supay's essence of death," Rubi said. "As a side effect, it repels most animals and people that are sensitive to auras and their energy."

"So I've got rain clouds of doom hanging over me?"

"If that's how you want to put it, yes. But don't worry, this should make our journey to the ruins easier."

They continued their trek unmolested, and very soon Tyler remembered just how awful the rainforest was. The unforgiving humidity made him sweat through his clothes profusely, and with time each step became more and more labored until his body was throbbing from the exertion.

After passing through an especially dense copse of trees, a sudden snap of foliage from behind alerted Tyler. He stopped and spun around, scanning the neverending emerald forest. For a split second he thought he saw a figure among the trees, but as the moments dragged on with no further sighting he chalked it up to paranoia. He was a walking repellant for crying out loud.

Tyler caught up with the others, feeling a pang of guilt when he noticed the scowls on their faces. It wasn't until Rubi announced the ruins wouldn't be much farther ahead that a flicker of joy bloomed warmly in Tyler's chest, combating the strengthening pull of Ayar Kachi's connection.

They proceeded through the rainforest, finding their destination as they broke through another tight line of trees. As Tyler took in the full view of the ruins his breath hitched in his throat. The entrance to the ruins at the top of the moldering stone steps had caved in.

"Oh my god, no!" he shouted, breaking into a sprint. The others followed him, and together they rushed through a field of moss-covered stone boulders and up the steps until the mountain of rubble created an impasse. "Fuck! What happened here?"

"What do you think?" Diego said. "It's got to be Ayar Kachi. *¡Hijo de puta!*" He kicked at one of the nearby stones.

Tyler turned to Rubi and Doria, who were examining the rubble thoughtfully. "Do you think you can clear this?"

Doria shook her head. "This is too much for me to handle. Rubi?"

Rubi stared at the rubble with brightening orange eyes. After a moment she broke her gaze and sat on a step, running her hands through her curly auburn hair. "*¡Mierda, mierda, mierda!*"

Doria sat next to her. "It's okay, *hermana.*"

Rubi batted her hand away. "No, it's not! Carmen would've had no problem dealing with this, but she's … damn it!"

"Come on, don't give up so easily. There's got to be another way inside. We just have to find it."

Rubi wiped at her eyes. "Sorry, I'm just so mad at everything right now."

"It's okay, we all grieve in our own ways. But let's use that as fuel to push us forward, yes?"

Rubi nodded. "Yeah, you're right. Thanks *chica.*"

"*De nada.* Alright everyone, how do we want to handle the search?" Doria asked openly.

"This courtyard is pretty big," Diego reasoned. "Let's split up into pairs of two and look around. That'll minimize the time it will take to get in, and we can call each other if we find anything."

They all agreed to the plan and descended the crumbling stone steps. Doria and Rubi edged along the outer perimeter of the main structure while Tyler and Diego headed the opposite way alongside the lichen-covered walls towering above them.

A short distance away, a small structure caught Tyler's eye. Its walls were much lower than the ones next to them and it seemed separate from the main structure. "Hey, let's check out that building over there."

Diego agreed, and as they got up close Tyler wasn't sure what to think of it. The building was squat and square, covered in overgrown moss. It appeared there was once some kind of mass built atop the structure, but the centuries had whittled it down to a misshapen mess like a pile of sad deflated balloons. The building's entrance was partially blocked by a boulder that had fallen diagonally.

Tyler approached the entry.

"What are you doing?" Diego asked. "The structure doesn't look stable. It could probably collapse at any time."

Tyler turned around, cocking an eyebrow. "How else are we going to find another way in unless we take some risks? I'll be as careful as I can, okay?"

Diego sighed. "Fine."

Tyler gauged the boulder blocking the entry, deciding it was safer to try the gap above than risking being crushed underneath. As he climbed onto the giant stone and squeezed himself through, it gave no sign of collapsing under his added weight.

Observing the structure's interior, he called for Diego to join him. The building had just one chamber about the size of a small garage. There were numerous rows of small stone benches, very few of which were still intact. In the center of the far end of the room was a badly damaged statue. Based on its form and vague features he had no doubt it was a depiction of Ayar Kachi.

Diego scraped his way through the entry and dusted

himself off with a small cloud of debris. His eyes lit up when he viewed the room. "Whoa."

"I know, right? What do you think this place was?"

"I don't know, maybe some kind of altar room or temple? It would explain the statue."

"Man, Ayar Kachi sure was full of himself." Tyler stepped forward and touched the ancient statue. It was soft and smooth, probably weathered down by humidity and erosion over the years. He took a step back, and a strange rumbling under his feet made him freeze on the spot.

"Tyler, get away from the statue," Diego said, concern in his tone.

Tyler remained still as he weighed his options. If he was slow about his steps he'd probably fall through the floor. He'd have to make a quick break for it. Tyler launched himself toward Diego as the floor cracked and fell beneath him. He reached out for Diego's outstretched hands, but fell just inches short of them and the outer rim of ground that was still intact. Tyler screamed as he fell into the darkness until he hit something soft and wet that knocked the air out of his lungs.

The force of impact shook Tyler to the core, obliterating his senses. Slowly, they returned to him.

Tyler ... Tyler ...

"Tyler!" Diego cried.

Tyler blinked hard, focusing on Diego's form above him outlined by dim daylight. "Huh?"

"*Dios mio*, are you okay?"

Tyler groaned as he struggled to sit up. He gave himself a slow pat down to check for any injuries. "I'm sore as hell, but I think I'll be alright."

"Oh, thank god. I'm calling Rubi." Diego pulled out his phone, entered some commands, and put it to his ear. "Rubi, it's Diego. We've got a situation. The ground fell beneath me and Tyler, and he fell through–Yeah, we're in a separate building and–Yes, come back around the front of the main structure and I'll lead the way."

Diego ended the call and glanced back down at Tyler. "I'm going to get Rubi and Doria. Just stay right there, okay?"

Tyler opened his mouth to respond when his sense of smell returned to him. The putrid air made him gag. "Hurry," he croaked. "It fucking reeks down here."

Diego scurried off, and Tyler slowly got to his feet. He grabbed his knapsack and rummaged through his things. Luckily nothing seemed to be damaged from the fall. He grabbed his flashlight and turned it on, doing a slow pan around the room. Rotted broken furniture was placed throughout the space, destroyed frames that must've been beds at one point, and–Tyler flinched back. Numerous corpses littered the small area, all of them in various positions and states of decay.

"Well that explains the smell," Tyler muttered to himself.

Who were these people? Given their proximity to whatever the structure was above he guessed they were some of Ayar Kachi's followers. Too shaken to approach the bodies, he observed that some were huddled in the corner, while others had died on the destroyed beds. Another small cluster of them had collapsed against an ancient rusty metal door, almost as if they'd been trapped inside.

Tyler's heart fluttered. Maybe, just maybe this could be their way into the ruins. He was about to approach the door when a loud scuffle made him stop.

"Diego?" He looked up to the hole in the ceiling, but Diego wasn't there. Another rustle of movement sounded, this time clearly from inside the room. "Hello?"

Tyler scanned the farther end of the room with his flashlight, but he couldn't tell any difference from be–Something suddenly grabbed his wrist. Tyler turned and shined his flashlight, coming face to face with a decomposed corpse. Its skull was prominent, with partial layers of mummified muscle underneath. Its eyes were a milky white as it gave a guttural hiss.

Tyler screamed and punched the dead thing in the face, crying out in pain as his knuckles met bone. The thing was surprised enough to have lost its grip and took a step back, but it quickly recovered and settled its gaze back on him. Other sounds of movement echoed around him, and with the briefest of glances he saw the other corpses coming to life with almost robotic movements.

Backing up under the hole he'd dropped from, Tyler looked up. Diego wasn't there, and there was no way he'd be able to pull himself back up, even if he jumped.

"Guys, I need your help!" Tyler shouted, hoping someone would hear him. "There are fucking reanimated corpses down here with me!"

Distantly he thought he could hear his friends approaching above, but as the corpses inched forward he knew he would be picked apart if he just sat here and waited for them. Tyler scrambled through his knapsack and grabbed his blessed hunting knife, brandishing it at the nearest corpse that had initially assaulted him.

It gave an angry gravelly growl before lunging at him. The corpse collided with Tyler and they fell to the soft, wet ground with a squish. The corpse brought a gnarled skeletal hand down on Tyler and he defended with his blessed knife. The bone that made impact with his weapon made a sharp sizzling sound, and the corpse recoiled.

Tyler's heart leaped into his throat. It was weak against the holy water, just like Ayar Kachi! With the corpse still writhing in pain, Tyler buried his hunting knife deep into the corpse's milky eye. It gave a guttural shriek of pain before dropping to the ground, deathly still. As Tyler withdrew his hunting knife from the corpse several other beastly cries emanated yards away. He scrambled to his feet, and a loud ruckus came from above as several shapes descended into the room.

Diego recovered first and was by his side with a machete in hand. "Are you okay?"

"No, but I will be. The corpses are weak against holy water, so we'll have to rip them apart. Let's go!"

Together they charged forward, focusing on the two remaining corpses near the large metal door. Diego dodged a wild thrust by the corpse on the left and thrust his machete into the dry shriveled muscles of its ribcage. The other skeleton moved in on Tyler lethargically and he dashed around it, catching the corpse with its back to him. He sunk his hunting knife deep into its rotting back and gave a lethal twist. Both corpses fell to the ground with a clatter, but before they could celebrate their small victory another pair of corpses assaulted them.

The corpse attacking Tyler pushed him against the wall, giving an animalistic snap of its brittle broken teeth at his face. Tyler yelped and tried to push it away, its decayed jaws clenching hungrily just centimeters from his face. Tyler shoved at the corpse again, but it was too strong.

"Ungh, get *off me!*" he cried.

Sudden fingers clasped the corpse's skull, and the muscles of its face glowed an angry orange with a wicked crackle before it sank in on itself. Pushing the destroyed corpse aside, Rubi smiled at Tyler and offered a hand.

Tyler accepted the help and stabilized his footing. "Thanks."

Together, they returned their focus on the ongoing battle. Most of the corpses had been disposed of. Diego had just destroyed another skeleton with a brutal downward slash, and Doria faced another, her eyes closed in concentration as it lunged for her.

Tyler made to move, but Rubi stopped him with an outstretched arm. "Don't."

Tyler watched the skeleton rush forward. Right before it made contact with Doria a spear of water erupted from the ground, slicing its body cleanly in half. "Jesus fuck," he muttered in astonishment.

"See? Told you," Rubi said with a gleam in her eye. Once the dust settled and the slayed corpses made no further movements, she moved to the center of the room. "Is everyone alright? Any injuries?"

No one seemed to be hurt, but that didn't stop Tyler's wandering mind from seeking answers. "What the hell happened here? I just fell down here and these … *things* started attacking me."

"It seems Ayar Kachi wasn't the only one who was cursed by the gods," Doria rationalized. "My best guess is that those who worshiped him at the time of his demise were doomed to eternity here. We're just the unfortunate ones to find them."

"Okay, but why didn't Ayar Kachi just break them out of here?"

"Ayar Kachi can't break his curse or those of his followers because they are both bound by Supay's power. By the way, thanks for finding a way in."

"No problem. I just wish it wasn't such a literal pain in my butt. Speaking of moving forward, how are we gonna break this door down? Isn't it bound by the curse?"

"We shouldn't have any problem. The curse on these poor souls was meant for them and them alone. It doesn't apply to us."

Rubi and Doria went to the door and felt around its rusted edges.

"I think we can handle this," Rubi said. "If I heat the door up and Doria gives it a blast of water, the reaction from the opposing elements should bust it open. Let's give it a try. Tyler, Diego, you may want to stand back."

Tyler and Diego edged to the far wall of the room.

Rubi approached the door, her hands glowing with a fiery blaze. She focused her efforts on the door's ancient hinges. After several moments they glowed orange, then a bright furious red. "Doria, now."

Rubi moved aside and a jetstream of water burst from Doria's hands, pounding the heated door hinges. A cloud of steam rose from the hinges as they groaned in protest before snapping open, no longer preventing their journey forward.

Satisfied, Rubi looked to Doria. "Can you force it open from the other side? It shouldn't take too much pressure now."

The two of them joined Tyler and Diego a healthy distance from the door.

Doria clasped her hands and closed her eyes in concentration. The door gave a deep groan before it crashed down before them with a thunderous clang.

"Great job everyone," Rubi said. "From here we should be able to find our way to Ayar Kachi. Arm yourselves. His followers may have caught us by surprise but we can't let him do the same.

Tyler put his hunting knife away and grabbed a machete from Diego's big bag, while Diego replaced his machete with a large spear. Rubi and Doria didn't bother taking any weapons. All four of them lit torches to guide their way inside.

"Are you ready?" Rubi prompted.

The tightening of Tyler's core left no doubt in his mind.

"Yep, The connection here is very strong. We must be close. Diego?"

Diego smiled. "Yeah, let's end this. For *mi madre*, for Gabe, for everyone."

With that, the small group ventured into the depths of the ruins.

CHAPTER TWENTY

A strong scent of mildew permeated the air as the light from the group's torches illuminated three paths in the large corridor: one straight ahead, one to the left, and one to the right. Each path looked nearly identical with strange stalks of fungus growing along the walls in clusters.

"Tyler, what do you feel?" Rubi asked. "Do any one of these paths stick out to you?"

Tyler turned in each direction, feeling no change in the tightness of his chest. "I don't know. I'm not feeling any difference yet. Maybe I should walk a bit in each direction and see if that changes."

"Good idea."

Together they traversed the left passage. After a right turn, the hall was seemingly endless. Numerous rooms lined the corridor that were filled with misshapen lumps of rotted furniture, malformed totems and carvings, and other miscellaneous relics in varying states of decay. About a hundred yards down the path, the tightness in chest loosened by an infinitesimal amount. He lifted up a hand. "Wait. The tightness is fading. Let's turn back around."

They reversed course, quickly coming upon the junction of the splitting paths.

"Let's go this way," Tyler said, pointing down the passage that had been straight ahead when they'd first entered the hall.

They crept forward quickly. This passage didn't have nearly as many rooms as the other did, and when they came to the end of the hall Tyler felt the tightness in his chest bunch tighter. The only problem was that there was nowhere else to go.

"I don't get it," he said. "I feel a stronger connection here, but there's no way forward."

The group examined the dead end and neighboring rooms around them but came up with nothing.

"Maybe it's on a different floor," Doria reasoned. "Can you try to gauge whether it's above or below?"

"Sure." Tyler approached the wall and awkwardly tried out a variety of poses and positions at different angles and heights in an effort to get the tightness in his core to react. When he was unable to get a clear answer, he assumed his normal stance and dusted the debris off of himself. "It's hard to say. I think there was a slight increase when I was closer to the ground, but even if we find a way down how do we know it'll truly lead us in the right direction? This place is a labyrinth."

"All we can do is try," Doria said calmly. "Perhaps the path we haven't tried yet has a way down."

To Tyler's surprise, Doria was right. Exploring the remaining path was a brief endeavor that provided withering stairs both up and down. However, when they took the stairs down they found themselves at yet another dead end. Once more they backtracked, this time ascending two floors.

"Does this look familiar?" Diego asked as they reached the landing.

"Not from the last five halls," Tyler retorted. "Let's just hope this isn't another dead end."

They continued the only way down the hall and made a left into a second corridor. Something about it did seem vaguely familiar, but without a concrete answer Tyler kept moving. It wasn't until he passed a room on his right that his bond kicked into high gear. His chest clenched tightly and a rush of vertigo washed over him that nearly made him faint. He fell against the passage wall and clung to it to keep himself upright.

Diego, Doria, and Rubi rushed to his side.

"What's wrong?" Rubi asked.

"I don't know, I … damn, that hurts!" he said, rubbing his chest. "There's something in this room here. Just give me a second to recover."

"Okay. Doria, stay with him while Diego and I check things out."

Rubi and Diego entered the room, and Doria lingered, giving him a sympathetic rub of his shoulders.

After a long moment, the vertigo faded and Tyler turned to face Doria. "Thanks, I think I'm okay now."

Tyler and Doria entered the room that was now lit by torches set into the wall.

As Tyler recognized the room another spell of dizziness hit him, not from his connection to Ayar Kachi but from the awful memory of what had happened there. On the right hand side of the small space was the same ancient mural Gabe had once admired.

"This is where it happened," Tyler said, his voice strained. "Gabe was first attacked by Ayar Kachi here."

"I'm sorry you're having to relive this," Doria said solemnly. "You're not alone."

"Thanks."

Rubi turned from her evaluation of the strange mural, her

brows furrowed. "I don't get it. This room doesn't lead anywhere. Are you feeling anything?"

Tyler walked from one end of the room to the other, feeling a strong downward pull. "The connection is really strong here, more than I've felt anywhere else. It's directly below us."

Rubi looked to Doria. "Do you think there may be some kind of hidden passage down?"

Doria walked along the walls, pressing against them methodically. "I can't be certain, but it's worth looking for one."

Tyler reluctantly joined Rubi and Diego as they studied the mural. Bloody depictions of men killing each other were displayed across the hieroglyphs. In the center a crowned figure sat upon a throne, surrounded by seven blood-soaked corpses. A blood moon hung overhead, crusted in a flaky red substance that could only be dried blood. "Gabe was looking at this when he was attacked. Maybe there's a clue here."

"The drawings here remind me of Ayar Kachi's demise," Rubi observed with a pensive expression. "Obviously he saw himself as a God, and the seven bodies lying at the foot of his throne were the brothers and sisters he so desperately wanted his revenge against."

"Yeah, and all the violent scenes here would come from the army he was building to bring down his siblings' growing empire," Diego said.

"Are you guys seeing anything else?" Tyler asked.

Diego shook his head.

Rubi did the same before Doria stepped forward. "Let me try. With Ayar Kachi's dark history, there may be something I can glimpse."

Doria's fingers hovered above the mural's surface before she grazed it with the lightest of touches. Suddenly she shuddered, giving a sharp inhale as a milky white cloud covered her pupils and irises. Seconds ticked by, and she came out of her trance with a jolt. Her breaths were heavy as she pushed herself away from the mural.

Rubi eyebrows furrowed in concern. "Are you alright? What did you see?"

Doria grimaced. "I saw it all. Ayar Kachi wasn't going to stop with the murder of his siblings. Once he killed them, he wanted to cut out their hearts and use them in a dark ritual to summon the god Viracocha that created them. From there, he planned to use an ancient weapon to kill the god, carve out its heart, and eat it to absorb its power. His godhood would be realized under an approaching blood moon that would serve as a beacon of his dominance over all of mankind."

"Jesus, what a pompous ass," Tyler said.

"A pompous ass, yes, but Doria, did he truly possess a god-killer? You know we can't let an object with that kind of power fall into the wrong hands."

Doria lifted a hand to her forehead. "I don't know. What I saw was his dark vision. It's not a literal interpretation."

"Either way, The Pentacle needs to know about this." Rubi pulled out her phone and typed some commands before a flicker of irritation crossed her features. "No signal. We'll have to hope we get out of here in one piece."

"Speaking of that," Tyler interjected, "can we focus on the present while we're still breathing? Doria, did you see anything in your vision that might get us closer to Ayar Kachi's remains?"

Doria studied the mural for a long moment. "If Ayar Kachi is as pompous and arrogant as he seems, then any hidden passage might reflect that hubris. In his mind, a blood moon signaled his ascent to his ultimate goal of unlimited power, so maybe ..."

Doria lifted herself on her tiptoes so she could reach the

outline of the blood moon on the mural. When her fingers pressed against it a sharp click sounded, followed by the gravelly noise of stone moving.

Tyler gasped as the mural wall fell back, revealing a dark corridor. "Dude, no way."

Rubi shouldered forward. "Yes way. Let's keep moving."

Rubi and Diego led the way into the hidden passage. At first it seemed just like the outer hall they'd come from until it dropped into a steep circular descent of stairs. Tyler used his free arm to steady himself against the stone wall as he followed his companions. After following the stairs for several minutes, they arrived at a landing. The air was frigid and damp, and even with their torchlight they couldn't see much of anything before them.

"What now?" Tyler asked. Despite his whisper, his voice echoed. Wherever they were had to be rather large and cavernous.

"I don't know," Rubi said.

Doria moseyed up to Rubi. "Do you think you could light this place up?"

Rubi scoffed. "Don't tempt me."

"No, seriously. I know you're used to using your powers in combat, but what if you think 'bright' when you use your gift? Think of it like a flare and visualize what you want to happen."

"I've never tried that before, but sure, let me give it a try."

Rubi closed her eyes and summoned her fiery gift. A ball of flame grew within her hand.

"Okay, now brighter," Doria instructed.

Rubi's brows furrowed in concentration, and after a moment of no change, the flame began to lighten in shade until it became hard to look at.

"Come on, you can do this. Brighter, Rubi, brighter. Like the sun."

With a grunt, the flame erupted into a blinding light that illuminated the large space. The group gave communal sounds of surprise at their surroundings. They were in an enormous cavern. Sharp looking stalactites hung from the earthen ceiling, and gargantuan pillars etched with strange symbols supported the area. A crumbling set of stone stairs led downward to the center of the space where a tomb embedded with gold and jewels rested.

"Is that what I think it is?" Tyler said.

"Ayar Kachi's tomb," Diego breathed. "We made it."

"Yes, but let's focus on the task at hand," Doria stressed. "Before we head down, light all the torches you can. Rubi's light won't last forever and we'll need more visibility to carry out the blessing and funeral ritual."

Together they got to work. Tyler, Diego, and Doria lit torches within reach, and Ruby used her fiery powers to light those too far away. In several minutes the ambient light was enough to see without difficulty, just in time for the flare Rubi had summoned to extinguish.

"Do you think this is good enough?" Diego asked.

"It should do," Doria said. "You can put out the torches you've been carrying, but stay on your guard. Ayar Kachi is bound to show up at any moment."

Diego led the descent to the tomb, Tyler and the others following right behind him.

Nearing their final destination Tyler's chest ached something fierce, as if he'd gone on a bender and chain smoked the previous night. But despite his pain and shaky nerves they reached the bottom with no trouble. The sarcophagus sat serenely five yards away on a large square of moldering stone flooring, its sculpted face in Ayar Kachi's likeness.

"Now that we're here I can begin the blessing," Doria announced. "I need to have physical contact with his remains to pull this off. Tyler, Diego, help me get the lid off. I'll manipulate the water within this space to help you remove it."

Tyler and Diego accompanied Doria to the burial site, but as soon as their hands touched the lid, a voice shouted "Stop! Put your hands up, right now!"

Tyler's gut churned as he recognized the soft yet authoritative voice. Reluctantly he followed the order and turned to face Detective Kirby Kilgore like his companions had. She scowled as she aimed a gun at them and moved carefully down the stone steps they'd just descended.

"That was you following us in the forest, wasn't it?" Tyler asked. "How did you find us here?"

"I followed the breadcrumbs you left with Esperanza," Kirby said. "She made quite an argument, but I strong-armed her into showing me where you were headed. It wasn't easy following you, especially once you found the alternate entrance to the ruins. All that backtracking nearly exposed me, but each time I found a dark room or shadowy corner to hide in. But all of that is beside the point.

"I meant what I said about finding Jill and Andrea, and while you may not have had anything to do with that, I let my own emotions blind me to the truth that you had been involved with the recent murders, too much to be just a coincidence. Tyler, I'm placing you under arrest for your involvement in the murders of Gabriel, Jim, and Nancy Price."

"You can't do this."

Kirby's glower intensified. "Watch me. I bet the locals would love to know that you're trespassing and defiling an ancient burial site."

"You don't understand. This is the burial site of Ayar Kachi, the entity I've been trying to warn you about. The only way to stop him from killing more people is to bless his remains to force his spirit to move on."

Doria nodded along. "He speaks the truth."

"And who the hell are you?" Kirby demanded.

"We're *brujas*, and we assert our dominion over these ruins as our territory. Ayar Kachi is real, and he's been plaguing this community for eons. Please, either let us continue with our mission or stay out of our way. It's the only way we can save Tyler and countless others."

Kirby scoffed. "I have to give you credit, Tyler. I underestimated you. Your ability to gaslight Nancy, Jim, Jessica, and these poor people is really impressive. But you're not going to fool me any longer."

"¡*Dios mío, idiota*!" Rubi spat. Flames erupted in her raised hands. "Does *this* look like gaslighting to you?"

Kirby stumbled back, her eyes wide in disbelief. "H-how did you do that? Whatever you're doing, stop it now!" She focused her gun's aim on Rubi.

"Doria, now!" Rubi cried.

A wall of water shot up from Kirby's feet, knocking the gun out of her hands.

The aqueous wall closed in on her, and she yelped as she was forced against the stone steps. "What on earth is this? Let me go!"

"You're not in any danger, but we can't let you interfere any further unless you're going to help us," Doria explained. "Tyler, Diego, help me lift this."

Diego set his bag of weapons down and moved to help her.

As Tyler followed, Kirby called after him. "Stop, please!"

Tyler turned to face her. "I'm sorry. We can't unless you agree to our terms. We have to stop Ayar Kachi, even if you have to sit there and see it for yourself."

"Okay, okay, whatever you want! Just please, make it stop!"

Tyler approached Kirby, brandishing his machete. "Alright, Doria, release her."

"Are you sure?" Doria said. "What's to stop her from attacking us?"

"I don't think Detective Kilgore is stupid enough to try that. She's outmanned and outgunned. Isn't that right?" Tyler shot Kirby an expectant look.

"Yes, I will help you," Kirby grumbled.

With a flick of Doria's wrist the wall of water receded, and Tyler quickly closed the distance between them. "Give me the gun, then help them take this lid off."

Kirby leered at him before handing it over. She got up to her feet and pushed past him, settling opposite Diego at the sarcophagus's lid.

Tyler dropped Kirby's gun into the bag of weapons before joining them.

"Alright, ready?" Doria said. "Lift!"

Giving a communal grunt, the group pried upon the lid. It screeched in protest before opening with a rusty clang.

Kirby took a look inside the sarcophagus. "Oh god!" she cried. She sank to her knees and gagged at the foul smell.

Tyler moved to assist her when the ground beneath his feet began to quake. Judging by everyone else's looks of surprise, they were experiencing the same thing.

"Ungh, what's happening?" Kirby croaked.

"It has to be Ayar Kachi, but he's never shown this kind of power before," Tyler said, turning to Doria and Rubi. "What do you think it means?"

"I don't know, but it can't be good," Rubi said.

The rumbling of the earth increased in intensity and a monstrous roar rose along with it, causing small bits of debris to fall from the earthen ceiling high above.

"He's coming, brace yourselves!" Rubi shouted.

Diego, Kirby, and Tyler scrambled closer to Doria, while Rubi remained outside of the square stone grid.

The quaking roar crescendoed in volume until the sheer

force of it reverberated through Tyler's chest and rattled his teeth. An explosion of earth and stone erupted from the ground nearby, an enormous cloud of black mist filtering through the hole. Sharp shards and debris rained down on them but were deflected by small circular walls of water.

Tyler glanced at Doria. She returned his look with a nod, but the frown on her face showed her internal struggle.

Free of danger for the moment, Tyler's gaze returned to Ayar Kachi as his form finished materializing. An aura of bright golden light surrounded the renegade spirit. His tall frame had grown to nearly ten feet in height, and his red eyes burned with a hateful heat.

Rubi backed away from Ayar Kachi and Doria stared forward in shock.

"No, it can't be …" Doria muttered.

Tyler took a step back as well. "What is it?"

"His power has been elevated more than should be possible. The spirit energy that's coming off of him … It's Rafaela's. Rubi, be careful!"

Rubi clenched her fists, and two pulsating globes of flames burned to life before her. "*¡Bastardo!* I'm going to rip you apart, limb from limb!"

Rubi hurled one fireball at Ayar Kachi then the other, hitting him square in the chest and shoulder. He grunted in pain, then gave a vicious smile as he raised his hands. A cyclone of wind burst from him, hitting all of them with such force that they were flung to the ground. The wind ceased several seconds later, but no attack ensued from Ayar Kachi.

Based on the irritated look on his face and hunched posture, Tyler guessed that he had been winded by the enormous exertion of power.

Rubi groaned as she got back on her feet, covered in dust. "*¡Mierda!* Raf's life force has made him too strong."

"It doesn't matter, just keep him busy!" Doria shouted.

She placed her hands over Ayar Kachi's corpse and began to chant.

Tyler edged away from Doria, surveying the battlefield. Ayar Kachi was no longer stooped over and had refocused his devilish gaze on the group. He took several steps towards them before orbs of fire collided with his leg and face. He turned towards Rubi and gave a beastly cry of rage.

As he was preoccupied, Diego clutched his spear tightly and ran towards him.

Tyler darted to the big weapons bag. He quickly removed another machete like his and presented it to Kirby, who stood watching the chaotic scene in shock. "Come on, we need your help. We doused this in holy water. If you pierce Ayar Kachi with it, it should hurt him enough to distract him from what Doria needs to do. Are you good?"

Kirby's face lightened several shades, and a terrified whimper escaped from her lips.

Tyler sighed. "Just protect Doria then, okay? Don't let Ayar Kachi hurt her. *I mean it.*"

Kirby slowly took the weapon into her hands, and Tyler left her as Doria continued to chant over Ayar Kachi's corpse.

The assault against Ayar Kachi was frenzied, so much that Tyler wasn't sure where to join in. Rubi had taken the lead and alternated between flinging fireballs at the evil spirit and evading his wild swings at her. After an especially painful looking bombardment of fireballs, Ayar Kachi bared his teeth and charged towards her like a linebacker.

Rubi dodged his attack with a quick sidestep, and while his back was still turned Diego rushed behind the towering spirit and thrusted his spear. It wedged deep into Ayar Kachi's side and he roared in torment. He spun around and raised his hands, sending Diego flying with a shrieking burst of wind. Diego sailed through the air, colliding with a large boulder before falling to the ground, unmoving.

"Diego!" Tyler shouted.

Tyler lunged forward to assist Rubi, who was distracting Ayar Kachi from Diego's vulnerability with another flurry of fireballs. A small trickle of blood ran down her nose. Tyler wasn't sure what that meant, but it couldn't be good.

With Ayar Kachi preoccupied, he darted behind the spirit and slashed at him, slicing his enormous calf with a sizzle. Ayar Kachi retaliated with a whirling backhand, but Tyler ducked. He took advantage of the spirit's disorientation and ran past Ayar Kachi's towering form, taking another stab at him as he went. His machete caught the spirit's opposite upper arm. Ayar Kachi bellowed in pain again, and as Tyler forced himself into a desperate side roll he could feel the wind on the hairs of his neck from how close Ayar Kachi's counterattack had been.

Luckily, Tyler felt the heat from a nearby fireball as he turned back around. Rubi relentlessly hurled fiery orbs at Ayar Kachi to keep him distracted, but her posture was slumped and it seemed the flames from her fireballs were losing their intensity. Rubi was clearly running out of steam, and that meant they needed to hurry this whole thing up.

"How much longer?" Tyler shouted to Doria.

Doria ignored his request and continued to chant over Ayar Kachi's physical body, her hands glowing blindingly bright. She clapped her hands together. *"¡Así sea!"*

A deafening howl of torment came from Ayar Kachi as a white light enveloped him before fading away.

Ayar Kachi's threatening features had diminished to the sickly mottled gray skin, stringy long black hair, and tarnished Incan headdress and ratty loincloth. His skin began to flake and fade away from his body, and his golden aura had disappeared. He whipped around, his fiery eyes focusing on Doria as she grabbed a large canister of holy water.

"Doria, watch out!" Tyler cried.

Ayar Kachi barrelled straight towards her. Tyler chased after him to intercept, but the enraged spirit was easily outpacing him. Rubi launched more low-energy fireballs at him, but it didn't slow his charge. Just yards away from Doria, Diego leaped at Ayar Kachi from the side and impaled him through the chest with his spear. The evil spirit screeched in pain, but before Diego could retreat he grabbed him by the arm. With a sickening crunch, he bent Diego's arm at an unnatural angle before flinging him to the ground.

Fuck, fuck, fuck! Tyler pushed himself forward as fast as he could, coming up upon Ayar Kachi, but as he raised his weapon to attack Detective Kilgore lunged forward with a hoarse cry, plunging her machete into Ayar Kachi's core with quick stabbing motions.

"Get away from us, you fucking freak!" she shrieked.

Before Tyler could intervene Ayar Kachi swung wildly. Kirby took the hit full on and went flying through the air, a sickening crack sounding as she made impact with a nearby pillar.

"No!" Tyler growled. He sprung forward until he was just underneath the evil spirit and thrust his machete. The weapon embedded deep into Ayar Kachi's back and through his front. The spirit ceased moving, giving a long low guttural scream of rage as he fell to his knees.

"Doria, now!" Tyler cried.

Doria emptied the entire canister of holy water onto his remains. *"Bendito espíritu, te ordeno que pases al siguiente plano de existencia. ¡Así sea!"*

Ayar Kachi's bellow crescendoed, accompanied by a rising resounding chorus of voices in every pitch and tone imaginable. For just a moment, Tyler heard a familiar voice in the choir, a light male baritone giving a cry of pure joy. *Gabe?*

The earth quaked as holes began to appear and rapidly multiply in Ayar Kachi's form, replaced by pure light. With one final howl of agony, Ayar Kachi exploded in a flash, sending a multitude of blinding tiny dots of light in a thousand directions.

Tyler gasped in relief as the ever tightening pull in his chest vanished. He yanked down his shirt, crying out with unparalleled exhilaration as his mark disappeared before his very eyes. His elation was short-lived as the earth continued to quake in increasing strength and duration. The pillars supporting the large space began to crack and crumble, and the large stalactites from the ceiling shook, threatening to descend upon them.

"Come on, everyone. We have to get out of here!" Rubi shouted.

"Wait!" Tyler commanded. He ran to Kirby's prone form as Doria moved to assist Diego. The back of Kirby's head was a mess of blood and bone, and her eyes were frozen forward in abject terror.

Cold dread spread through Tyler's core. He never meant for her to get involved in this. She'd only wanted to do good, and she had paid for it with her life just like so many others had. A tear rolled down Tyler's cheeks as he closed Kilgore's eyes. "I'm so sorry, for everything."

With a hollow emptiness in his stomach, Tyler forced himself up and rushed to Doria and Rubi, who were helping a dazed Diego to his feet.

"Is he okay?" Tyler asked.

"His arm is broken pretty badly, but he'll survive," Rubi said. "What about that woman?"

Tyler shook his head. "She didn't make it."

"I'm sorry Tyler, but we have to get out of here before this whole place caves in on us. Hurry!"

Tyler gave one last glance at Kirby Kilgore's body as he took Rubi's place in lifting Diego. *Please forgive me.*

Together they staggered up the steps to the entrance of the tomb as the cavern behind them buckled and splintered with loud snaps and churnings. As they reached the stairs' zenith and exited the space, huge chunks of earth and stone began to fall from the ceiling with enormous crashes.

Rubi snatched a nearby torch from the wall and took the lead. "Move, move, move!" she demanded.

Stumbling up the stairs at an uneven pace, they reached the room with the mural and headed back the alternate way they'd arrived. The ground was still shaking from the cataclysm below, but it hadn't yet affected the dark passages they rushed through.

Tyler desperately hoped that meant they had enough time to get out of here alive.

Taking the stairs and corridors at an increasingly frantic pace, they reached the decrepit room they'd arrived in. Doria summoned a small set of watery steps, and Rubi and Tyler helped guide Diego upwards as carefully as they could. Doria scrambled up the steps after them, and they scrambled through the partially blocked entry as the ground beneath them started to shift and sway.

Together they emerged from the structure and rushed a safe distance away. They stopped and watched as the ruins continued to quake and slowly cave in on itself. In mere minutes, the ruins had crumbled to little more than a minefield of rock.

When the dust finally settled Tyler fell to his knees, immense joy spreading through him as warm tears rolled down his cheeks. "It's over, it's finally over."

EPILOGUE

yler walked down the tree-lined cemetery path, a fresh bouquet of red roses in his hands. The sun shone through the canopy of trees in a lattice of light, and nearby birds chirped happily. Locating the row of graves he was looking for, he walked from the path across the grass and knelt at the headstone that read:

Gabriel Price
August 22, 1998- July 17, 2024
Always loved, never forgotten

Being here again brought everything rushing back to the forefront of his mind: their days of unbridled happiness, their supernatural hunts together, Altalona and the chaos that followed. Warm tears rolled down his face as he replaced the old flowers in a ceramic vase with the ones he'd bought.

"Damn it, I told myself I wasn't gonna cry again." Tyler sniffled and wiped at his wet eyes. "I miss you so much, Gabe. Things haven't been the same without you, but I'm going to do right by you. I want to do good things for people without greed in my heart. I know that's what you would've wanted, and I'm gonna make you so proud." Tyler caressed the headstone with his fingertips. "I'm never gonna stop loving you, baby."

Tyler closed his eyes, letting the rivers of tears run their course. Once the wave of emotion ebbed, he got up to his feet, put the old flowers in a nearby receptacle, and went back the way he came. Jessica walked toward him along the cemetery path wearing a simple sundress with a wide-brimmed hat upon her head, her ebony locks cascading underneath.

Tyler smiled, glad that she was feeling well enough to leave the car. Her first couple weeks of healing were a little scary, but the doctors insisted she'd be fine with more recovery time. Until then, he was her chauffeur. He didn't mind driving her around, especially with all the heads constantly turning at her beauty and warm demeanor. Despite all Jessica had been through, not even Ayar Kachi could dull her spirit.

Tyler neared Jessica, and she beamed at him. "Everything okay, Ty?"

"Yep, all good. Let's head back."

They started the long walk back to Jessica's car at a leisurely pace.

"I'm glad you're feeling well enough to meet me out here," Tyler said.

"Yeah, I'm starting to feel a bit more back to normal. Oh, you missed a spot." Jessica wiped at a wet patch that he'd missed on his face. "Sure you're alright?"

"Actually, yeah. I think I might be ready to move on with my life. I haven't told anyone about this, but when we destroyed Ayar Kachi I heard the voices of his victims. Gabe was there. He sounded so happy, and I knew then that I didn't have to worry about him anymore. He's free now, just like all the other victims."

Jessica took Ty's hand in hers and gave it a squeeze. "I'm

so proud of you, hun, and I know Gabe is too. You fought so hard for him, for me, for everybody. You're a hero."

Tyler chuckled as warmth rushed to his cheeks. "I don't think I'll ever get used to that title."

"How's everyone in Peru doing?" Jessica asked.

"They're doing really well, given what happened. Rubi and Doria buried Rafaela and Carmen, and since then they've increased and filled the empty spots in their coven. They've started investigating old supernatural cases to make sure previous threats have been truly exterminated. They're worried about more aberrations from the gods that they've encountered in the past, but they said they'd keep me posted if there was anything to worry about. By the way, they said they appreciate your discretion with all that happened."

"Of course. I doubt anyone would believe me if I told them what happened. What about that Diego guy that helped you?"

"He's good. He'll be out of his cast for his arm in about a month. Until then he'll be staying in Altalona with his cousin Maya and grandma Esperanza. I'm glad he's making a quick recovery, but I still feel really guilty for what happened to Kirby. Without her I'm not sure we would have been able to pull this off."

"You did all you could to protect her. I'm sure she realizes and appreciates that now."

"Yeah, I hope so, but I'm still worried about the authorities. The coven from Peru talked to their US counterparts and they helped throw off the scent with some hocus pocus to suggest Kirby never left the states. I don't know exactly what they did to convince them, but if it ever falls through I'll have to be prepared for it."

Jessica frowned. "Should I be concerned?"

"For now I think we'll be okay. Even if they found out the truth of what happened, there's no way they'd be willing to accept that magic and monsters exist. And if they can't accept that, then they can't explain what truly went down."

"A catch twenty-two."

"Exactly."

"Well, keep me posted on how things progress. You've fought so hard to get some sense of normalcy back in your life, and I'll be damned if anyone is going to ruin that for you."

"Thanks, boo. I will."

"What about your mom?"

"We've been having some nice chats back and forth. I told her I went on a road trip to clear my head, and she seems to understand that I just needed to be alone for a while. I figured the less she knows the better. If I told her what really happened I don't think she'd ever go outside again."

Jessica chuckled. "I get it. I might be a little jumpy for the next decade or two, but I'm glad it all worked out. It's finally over."

Tyler smiled as a gentle warmth spread through his chest. "Yes, it is."

They reached Jessica's car, and Tyler helped Jessica into the passenger side seat before starting the car and driving off. As the cemetery faded into the distance, Tyler felt a large weight lift from his shoulders. Maybe, just maybe, everything would be okay from now on.

JESSICA'S CAR rolled to a stop in her driveway. Tyler helped Jessica out, then unlocked the front door as she checked the mail. Jessica went inside with her bundle of mail, and Tyler moved to follow when a strange chill shot through his spine, followed by a tightness in his chest.

Tyler turned around but didn't see anything. The sensation dissipated as quickly as it had come and he hesitated for a moment, scrutinizing his surroundings.

"Hey, what's taking so long?" Jessica called, bringing Tyler back to the present.

"Coming!" he called.

Inside, he joined Jessica in the living room. Mellow music was playing, and Jessica had a strange expression on her face as he sat beside her on the couch.

"What's up? Is something wrong?" he asked.

Jessica smiled and shook her head. "I've been thinking it over, and I'd like for you to move in with me permanently. This whole ordeal brought us closer together, and the house feels so much cozier with you in it. What do you think?"

"Oh my god, seriously? Yes, yes, yes!" He hugged Jessica tightly and was met with a groan of pain. He backed up instantly, profusely apologizing.

"Oh, that's going on your first month's rent," Jessica laughed.

"I'll gladly pay it. Once I get back on my feet I promise I'll pay my full half of everything."

"Don't worry about it," Jessica said flippantly. "I'm not hurting for money, and you've been through the ringer. I just want you to make the choice that's right for you. Speaking of which, there was something in the mail for you."

Jessica handed over a letter, and Tyler's stomach bunched up in knots as he read who it was from. "Oh my god, it's from Prism!"

"Oh, that new LGBT TV network? All of those networks you applied to these past few weeks started to blur into one after a while. Well go on, open it!"

Tyler ripped through the envelope and read through its contents. He read it a second time in disbelief before he cried out, unsuccessfully holding back tears of joy. "They've reviewed all the footage that Gabe and I released, and they want to speak with me about the possibility of hosting a paranormal TV show on the network!"

Jessica squealed in excitement. "What are you going to do?"

"I don't know. I thought my days of paranormal investigation were over when I didn't hear anything back from the other networks, but maybe this is a chance to do things the right way. I think I'm gonna go for it."

Jessica shrieked her approval. "I can't believe this is happening! I know someone from TV!"

Tyler giggled. "I'm not on TV yet."

"Technicalities love, technicalities. Is there anything you'd like to do to celebrate?"

"Netflix and chill?"

Jessica grinned from ear to ear. "I thought you'd never ask."

AFTERWORD

Thanks so much for taking the time to read The Ruins (Soul Cursed #1). If you enjoyed reading it, why not take a moment to rate or review on Amazon or GoodReads?

I appreciate you taking the time to voice your opinion and hope you enjoy my other stories too.

Thanks for showing your support!

ABOUT THE AUTHOR

Jonathan Pongratz is a writer and author of action-packed horror, scifi, and other speculative fiction stories. His bold characters are resilient against the sinister and mysterious forces confronting them, but in real life Jonathan is afraid of bees, attics, and large bodies of water. Let's face it. Jonathan wouldn't last five minutes in one of his dark tales.

You can learn more about Jonathan at JonathanPongratz.com or at the social media links below.

Reaper: A Horror Novella

How do you fight a monster?

Halloween night, 1992. Promised the allowance he's always dreamed of, Gregory has to babysit his little sister Imogen and hand out candy.

That was before the basement door opened on its own. Before the strange door appeared in the basement. Before Imogen was taken from him by that terrifying monster.

Now, Gregory has to scramble to put the pieces together before it's too late. Where did the door come from? What was that creature? Can he save his sister, or is she already gone forever?

~

Reaper: Aftermath

Gregory ended the world. Can he save it?

It's been five years since the Reapers ripped Gregory's family apart and invaded Earth, leaving behind a wake of decimation. Gregory and a small group of survivors now scavenge the wastelands, living in constant fear of discovery.

Weighed down by relentless blame for the planet's destruction, Gregory seeks to make up for his past mistakes. He gets that chance when a surprise attack forces him through a Reaper door. Gregory finds himself in a bizarre place with no way back, a place that may provide answers to the Reapers' past and where they came from.

Can Gregory find a way to destroy the Reapers and restore order to his broken world, or is the human race doomed to lose the war against these ruthless monsters?

~

Conscience

Utopia comes with a price.

Rory Bennels lives in a world ruled by a business entity known as the Corporation. For years he's executed cerebral uploads for the recently deceased, but when the famed anarchist Epher Lore ends up in his lab, a series of events occur that shakes Rory's world to the core.

The BEK Curse

"Just let us in. This won't take long."

Early retirees Maria and Richard Wilcox adore their new home out in the country. The past six months have been sheer bliss as they settled in and prepared for their golden years.

Until the night they answer a knock on their door.

The unexpected visitors are a pair of children. Richard tries to be cordial, but something about the kids is off. Something sinister, something menacing, something inhuman.

And then the children demand to be let in.

What do they want? Is this all a prank? Can Maria and Richard get them to go away, or will their dreams of a peaceful retirement together go up in flames?

www.ingramcontent.com/pod-product-compliance
Lightning Source LLC
Chambersburg PA
CBHW022130310726
48972CB00007B/2281